"A passionate and intelligent premiere sure to secure Ms. Taylor's place in contemporary romance. Bravo!"

—Helen R. Myers, bestselling author of MORE THAN YOU KNOW

"You're right. We can't trust your people or mine," Jason finally said.

"Then we'll trust each other," Lane replied, meeting his gaze.

What was he going to do now? He couldn't solve this case fifty miles from nowhere, holed up in a twelve-by-twelve cabin with an alluring partner. Every man had his limits, and he feared he was fast approaching his.

Even now, he was on fire. Mesmerized.

But he couldn't leave Lane alone. Not while her life was in danger from a pack of truck hijackers that had suddenly turned as aggressive as a wolverine with its hackles up. The hunters had become the hunted.

Still, could he live with the consequences of keeping her with him?

Dear Reader,

We've got a special lineup of books for you this month, starting with two from favorite authors Sharon Sala and Laurey Bright. Sharon's *Royal's Child* finishes up her trilogy, THE JUSTICE WAY, about the three Justice brothers. This is a wonderful, suspenseful, *romantic* finale, and you won't want to miss it. *The Mother of His Child,* Laurey's newest, bears our CONVENIENTLY WED flash. There are layers of secrets and emotion in this one, so get ready to lose yourself in these compelling pages.

And then…MARCH MADNESS is back! Once again, we're presenting four fabulous new authors for your reading pleasure. Rachel Lee, Justine Davis and many more of your favorite writers first appeared as MARCH MADNESS authors, and I think the four new writers this month are destined to become favorites, too. Fiona Brand is a New Zealand sensation, and *Cullen's Bride* combines suspense with a marriage-of-convenience plot that had me turning pages at a frantic pace. In *A True-Blue Texas Twosome,* Kim McKade brings an extra dollop of emotion to a reunion story to stay in your heart—and that Western setting doesn't hurt! *The Man Behind the Badge* is the hero of Vickie Taylor's debut novel, which gives new meaning to the phrase "fast-paced." These two are on the run and heading straight for love. Finally, check out *Dangerous Curves,* by Kristina Wright, about a cop who finds himself breaking all the rules for one very special woman. Could he be guilty of love in the first degree?

Enjoy them all! And then come back next month, when the romantic excitement will continue right here in Silhouette Intimate Moments.

Yours,

Leslie Wainger
Executive Senior Editor

Please address questions and book requests to:
Silhouette Reader Service
U.S.: 3010 Walden Ave., P.O. Box 1325, Buffalo, NY 14269
Canadian: P.O. Box 609, Fort Erie, Ont. L2A 5X3

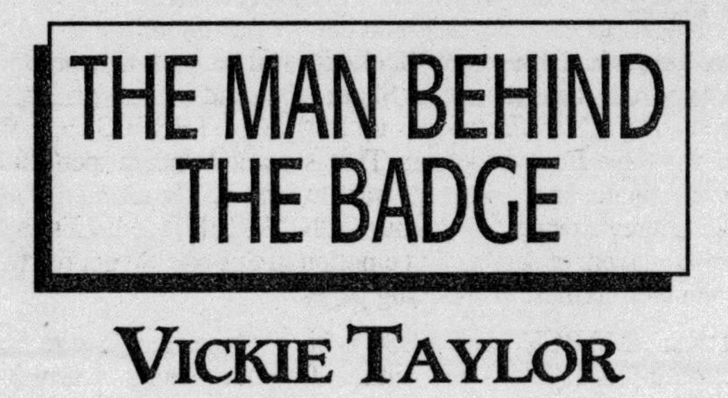

THE MAN BEHIND THE BADGE

VICKIE TAYLOR

Published by Silhouette Books
America's Publisher of Contemporary Romance

SILHOUETTE BOOKS

ISBN 0-373-07916-8

THE MAN BEHIND THE BADGE

This edition published by arrangement with Harlequin Books S.A.

Printed in U.S.A.

Dear Reader,

I love stories that reflect both the frailty and the strength of the human spirit. It's no wonder, then, that when I sat down to write *The Man Behind the Badge,* the characters that took shape on paper brought not only their honor and courage to the story, but their doubts, fears and regrets, as well. The roads they traveled were not always gentle.

I have to admit, I had great fun torturing Special Agent Jason Stateler and Detective Sergeant Lane McCullough. But then, I knew all along that in the end their love for each other would provide all the fortitude they needed to persevere through their struggles. It just took a while for *them* to figure it out!

Although our lives may not be as adventurous as Lane's and Jason's, we all travel difficult roads from time to time. I hope you'll find, as I did, that seeing them overcome their trials and find lasting love makes it easier to believe the rest of us can, too.

The Man Behind the Badge is my first novel. I'm overwhelmed at the response it has gotten from the writing community, winning several writers' contests and being named as a finalist in the Romance Writers of America's Golden Heart competition. Now I can't wait to see what kind of response it will get from the community that really matters—the readers' community! I hope you'll enjoy reading it as much as I enjoyed writing it. Whatever your reaction, I'd love to hear from you. Please send your comments to:

Vickie Taylor
P.O. Box 633
Aubrey, TX 76227

Sincerely,

Vickie Taylor

To Freddie and Sarah, for *all* the things you do, but especially for not letting the horses go hungry when I'm so engrossed in writing that I don't notice it's past feeding time.

To Deb and Sheri, two of the nicest people I know, and who always believed. ("Well, *of course* you sold your book!")

And to Bear, who I sometimes think is smarter than I am.

Chapter 1

"She was snooping. Just waste her and get back to work."

A chill crawled down Jason Stateler's spine as he stepped through the doorway. Whether it was from the cold-blooded death sentence he'd overheard, or because he'd stepped from the hot, steamy, Georgia night into the cavernous cool of the warehouse, he wasn't sure.

Concealed in the shadows of the upper level, Jason gazed down at the warehouse below him. The large concrete-and-steel structure was almost empty, for now. The truck just pulling in held tonight's load of stolen electronics. He used the rumble of its diesel engine to mute the sound as he closed the door behind him.

His eyes swept along the concrete floor to the ring of fluorescent light near the loading dock, and he scowled.

Damn. He didn't need any complications tonight. This purchase would establish him as a serious buyer. And hopefully earn him a meet with the head of the truck-hijacking ring acquiring the goods.

He should have known it wouldn't be that easy.

Even as he'd handed the briefcase stuffed with cash a few minutes ago to Alejandro, the middleman, he'd felt again the premonition of doom that had plagued him all week. It made the hairs on the back of his neck stand up. Someone stepping on his grave, his grandmother used to say about that feeling. He only hoped the pending catastrophe would hold off long enough for him to finish this job.

The truck at the dock shut off its engine, plunging the warehouse into silence with a last acrid gasp of exhaust.

His gaze was drawn again to the floor below him. In the center of a circle of harsh light sat a woman, hunched miserably in a metal chair. Grumman, Alejandro's beer-bellied lackey, circled her like a buzzard. His shuffling footsteps echoed in the rafters like flapping wings.

Morales, the slick that ran the day-to-day business, leaned against an open packing crate a few feet away. Swathed in indifference, the slim Hispanic smoothed his pleated pants, casually crossed his loafers and rolled a toothpick between his teeth. Only the tick in his eye, a spasmodic blink that tugged his cheek up and his brow down, gave him away. He was excited.

The thugs had caught themselves a fish and were enjoying watching it wriggle on the end of their line.

"Don't be in such an all-fired hurry, Morales." Grumman trailed a black-nailed finger down the nape of the woman's neck. "We got all night. And missy here and me have some business of our own to get down to, after she tells us what she's been up to." He laughed when she shrugged off his touch.

Bile burned the back of Jason's throat. God, he hated scum that preyed on whatever helpless creature fell into their path.

The woman's shoulders curled inward around her bowed head. Tangled waves of dark hair, black or nearly so, tumbled en masse over her face.

She lifted her head long enough to capture a few of the more outrageous strands behind one ear, baring a cheek marked by the back of someone's hand. Jason couldn't tell from that distance if her mouth was naturally full and pouty, or swollen from another blow. The severe lighting washed out her complexion—that and her fright making her look bloodless, almost porcelain.

The woman seemed somehow familiar to him, but he couldn't be sure where he'd seen her before. Was she the presence he'd sensed all week? The eyes on him?

Grumman's grubby hand tickled the woman's jawbone then clenched her chin, yanking her head toward his. "Now, darlin', you're gonna tell us one more time what you was doin' nosing around out there."

To her credit the woman didn't cringe, but Jason swore he could see the frantic pounding of her heart. The faded blue work shirt she wore unbuttoned over a thin white tank top left little to the imagination. Especially when her chest heaved with every panicked breath. Grumman was practically drooling in her lap.

Like a mouse looking for a crack in the floorboards, her eyes darted around the room. "I—I told you. I was looking for someone." Her voice squeaked and she licked her lips. Her eyes flicked up to Jason, widened, then bounced away. "My boyfriend," she added.

Morales sneered and threw up his hands. "*Dios.* We do not have time for this. Lose her so we can get back to work."

Twisting his fingers in the woman's hair, Grumman jerked her up and dragged her across the cement floor.

"Wait! M-my boyfriend—"

"Must'a stood you up," Grumman cut her off, "'cause there ain't nobody here but us. Too bad, too. I expect he's gonna be real hard put to find another looker like you."

"No! He said to meet him here...."

"Quit stalling and get rid of her," Morales ordered.

Jason's breath caught in his chest. She was in real trouble. Grumman was mostly bluster, all brawn and no brain, but Morales was as smart as he was vicious. He fancied himself the

Al Capone of Atlanta and wouldn't hesitate to kill to protect his operation.

Jason swallowed a curse, unclenched his cramped fists and forced his lungs to function. He was no Elliott Ness, not by a long shot. Helping this woman could cost Jason months of work, if not his life. But that didn't matter now; he had no choice.

Twisting the knob behind him, he pulled the door open a few inches. With a deep breath he slammed it shut and clomped down the stairs as if he had just arrived.

Whoever she was, he hoped she was quick on her feet.

Up close she was taller than she had looked from above. Two, maybe three inches short of his six foot one. Her cutoff shorts exposed mile-long thighs and smooth calves, slim but toned. Definitely not mousy.

Pulling Grumman's hand from her hair, Jason backed the man ten feet off with a lethal glare, then turned his attention to the woman. Forcing himself to sound gentle, he crooned, "Baby, you're early."

It wasn't until then, when she tipped her head up, that he got his first good look at her. Full, soft lashes blinked over startled green eyes. Unguarded. Vulnerable.

And the mouth was definitely naturally pouty.

He must be mistaken about knowing her. If he'd seen her before, he would remember it. One look at her sucked the breath right out of him.

He shook himself mentally. Get a grip. Pulling her to him, he willed her to relax, to go along, and she didn't resist.

His arms circled her waist and tightened, molding her against his chest and hips. At her height, she fit perfectly against him. Her cheek cradled naturally in the crook of his neck. She set her hands lightly, uncertainly, on his waist, not exactly holding him, but not pushing him away, either.

Smells he thought he had forgotten assaulted him: musky perfume, tangy shampoo and an underlying sweetness he knew he should be able to name but couldn't.

His senses reeled, tilting his world off balance. It had been so long since he'd held a woman. Too long. He'd forgotten how right it felt. How comfortable. How he could lean in and make words next to her ear, knowing they would be felt as much as heard.

Honeysuckle, he thought, the sweet scent was honeysuckle.

Just loud enough for the two henchmen to hear, he murmured, "I'm sorry, babe. I didn't expect you here." Then in a whisper meant only for her, "Call me Jason and play along." Telling himself he needed to make sure Grumman and Morales were convinced, he teased her with a gentle kiss.

She stiffened, her mouth rigid and unforgiving. Slowly he ran his hands up her arms, over her shoulders and down her back. Soothing. Taming.

Holding his mouth so close to hers that he felt his own breath reflected from her lips, he reassured her. "It's all right. No one's going to hurt you." Hoping she would realize he meant himself, he took her mouth again, probing, taunting, beseeching her cooperation.

When she still refused to yield to his gentle urgings, he groaned—out of frustration or need, he didn't know. His pulse leaped, adrenaline and something else driving him on.

Somehow he had to get past her fear. If she didn't respond to him like a lover, the game would be up. The two thugs behind him would kill them both.

His palm glided down her back to the rounded flesh at the end of his reach. Growling into the kiss, he pinched her there. Hard.

Her startled gasp gave him all the access he needed. His tongue dove into her opened mouth.

He tightened his grip on her, anticipating her struggle. To his surprise, it never came. After only the slightest hesitation, she responded fervently. Apparently she had gotten his message and decided to hold up her end of the bargain.

Her tongue sparred with his. Her hands found their way under his jacket, and her fingernails grazed his back through his black, knit shirt. He slanted his mouth, searching for deeper contact, and she moved in perfect counterpoint.

The longer this went on, the more trouble his mind had convincing his body that this was just an act. It wanted more. His jeans chafed, his skin suddenly sensitive.

The sparring escalated to a duel. A contest to be won at all costs. His pulse clashed with hers, both runaway.

He didn't even know this woman; she shouldn't be able to do this to him. But even as his brain screamed to get her out of there and get the hell away from her, his hunger told him to stay. Just a little longer. Just a little more.

Behind him, Grumman cleared his throat in an exaggerated gag, obviously enjoying the show. "Now, now, Mr. Bigshot Buyer, you ain't layin' claim to our little foundling, are you?"

Jason turned on him like a bull on a matador, itching to charge. "I ought to kill you for touching her, Grumman."

Grumman scratched his paw over two days' worth of stubble and shuffled backward, but kept grinning. "Aw, Jason. You didn't tell us you was expecting no broad. How was we to know?"

Jason's anger was much too real, fueled by his unexpected and unwanted reaction to the woman. He couldn't afford to let this get personal. He wanted to deck Grumman and choke the grin off the degenerate's face, but common sense told him he needed to get the woman out. Now.

Grumman snickered once more, eyeballing the length of the woman's bare legs.

What the hell. Jason had never been one to let common sense get in the way of what he wanted.

Just as he swayed toward the confrontation, soft fingertips feathered across his shoulder. Her cool voice dampened his rage.

"Jason, honey," she drawled softly, "shouldn't we go now?"

Her fingers trailed through the curls at the base of his neck. She had definitely caught on to the act.

"Mr. Grumman, I'm sure this was just a misunderstanding," she continued, a tremor in her voice. "I only arrived in town today. I got in a little early, and thought I'd surprise Jason." She turned Jason's head toward hers with her fingertips under his chin. "Now I'd really like to go to your place and take a long soak."

Still, he wavered. Long fingers twisted the hair at the back of his neck and pulled. Hard.

Ouch. He got the message. She was right. The last thing he needed now was a fight. Jason let out a long-suffering sigh and tried to look mollified. Normally he would stay and watch his goods being unloaded and make sure he got what he paid for.

Tonight, however, other needs took precedence. "Sure, baby. Let's go."

Morales shoved himself off the crate he'd been leaning on, tossing the toothpick from his mouth to the floor. "Aren't you going to introduce us to the señorita, Jason?"

Morales smiled, but his eyes were deadly serious. He wasn't buying it.

Jason tightened his grip on the woman. Before his mind could process the options for introducing someone he'd never met, she took the matter out of his hands. Stepping forward, graceful as a minister's daughter at a Sunday social, she offered Morales her fingers, palm down, for a delicate shake.

"Lane McCullough." She dragged out the *a* and softened the vowels of her last name in a refined Southern drawl. "From down Macon way. Pleased to meet you Mr.…Morales, is it?"

Jason watched nervously, his palm itching for the gun tucked in the small of his back. Who was this woman? He'd assumed she was an innocent bystander somehow reeled into Grumman and Morales's game. Now he was beginning to wonder. Either she was as cool under pressure as anyone he'd ever seen, or she was too stupid to know how much danger she was in. And he didn't think she was stupid.

She smiled demurely at Morales.

He drilled her with his stare.

The cosmos narrowed to a fine point in time and space for Jason: Morales's black eyes. He felt the air around them thicken as the seconds ticked by.

Finally Morales accepted her hand, kissing the back. "*Sí*, Enrico to my friends." Blinking through another facial spasm, he continued. "I apologize for any...inconvenience...we have caused."

Morales released her hand.

Jason released his breath.

"How long will you be staying in Atlanta, señorita?" Morales asked.

"I don't know, I—"

"Probably just a short visit," Jason cut in. He didn't want to have to explain her absence the next time he saw these guys.

"Well then, señorita, we will not keep you." Morales's gaze flicked from Lane to Jason, wry amusement lingering in the look. "I'm sure you have much...*catching up* to do."

In a show of acceptance, Lane bowed her head and stepped back.

Jason caught her around the waist when she reached his side. "Get the trucks unloaded tonight, Morales. I'll have my own rigs here in the morning to pick the stuff up."

Without waiting for an answer, he propelled the woman toward the door, counting the steps while their backs were exposed.

The air outside felt as cloying to Jason as the heavy tension in the warehouse. He could see, by the one dim mercury light, how the blacktop shimmered, slowly releasing the heat that five days of Georgia's worst heat wave in thirty years had baked in.

Checking over his shoulder as they made their way across the parking area toward his Corvette, Jason willed his muscles to release the knots that had formed. He was relieved that only their own shadows followed them to his car.

Now that he had rescued her from Grumman's interrogation, he had a few questions of his own. Like who she really was and what she was doing at the warehouse. The goons inside weren't the only ones with an operation to protect.

He looked sideways at Lane.

Her stride was surprisingly fluid and agile for such a long-limbed woman. He might even call her elegant, Jason thought. She swung along beside him looking completely at ease and innocently seductive. A woman who had just narrowly escaped death had no business looking that way. Her composure made him nervous.

About twenty strides from his car, her gait suddenly slowed. She had her lip between her teeth and her right arm curved behind her, fidgeting with her blouse at the small of her back. The 'Vette was the only vehicle around and she was staring at it like it was a snake. He supposed she would have reservations about getting in a car with him; after what she'd been through tonight, who wouldn't.

Nearing the car, he glanced over his shoulder to be sure they wouldn't be overheard. "Get in. I'll give you a lift home...or somewhere."

"I have a car down the street a few blocks."

He wasn't ready to let her go just yet. Because he still wanted to ask her a few questions, he told himself. "Then I'll give you a lift to your car. It's late and you shouldn't be alone out here. You've had enough trouble for one day, I'd say. Besides, the goons might still be watching."

He unlocked the passenger door for her and to his relief she slid in without argument, although he felt her tense subtly when he placed his hand on her shoulder to guide her down. Then she curled her long legs into the car after her and reached out a slender arm to pull the door closed behind her.

Refusing to let himself think about what those willowy limbs could do wrapped around the solid trunk of a man, he turned his mind back to the problem at hand. He had to find out why she had been at the warehouse tonight, and if she was a threat to his work there.

He walked around to the driver's side, his mind reeling with indecision. Maybe he should insist on taking her home himself; it would give him more time to find out what she knew.

Even before the complete thought registered in his consciousness he knew that was a bad idea. His body still hummed with possibilities sung to him by that kiss. It had been a long time since this particular song had gotten stuck in his head. He wasn't sure he wanted to hear it. If he took her home tonight, he wouldn't settle for dropping her at her door. Not with the hunger she'd aroused in him gnawing at his gut. And she'd had a bad scare tonight. Taking advantage of her now would be...well, taking advantage of her.

He filled his lungs with the humid night air and forced his mind and body into obedience. He'd ask his questions quickly and drop her at her car. Tomorrow he'd tell Grumman and Morales that she'd been called back to Macon, a sick aunt or something. Anything else would be too dangerous, for both of them.

So why did he feel like he'd just held the bat while the best pitch of the season sailed past his belt buckle? *Face it, you're afraid to swing.*

His fist clenched until he felt the key's jagged edge bite into his palm. With a final glance at the warehouse to make sure they were alone, he lowered himself into the driver's seat.

And came nose to nose with the barrel of a gun.

"Christ, those morons didn't even bother to search you?" Forget the morons inside, what about himself? How had he missed a gun when he'd had his hands all over her? *By getting too caught up in the feel of warm flesh to worry about checking for cold steel, that's how.*

She held the snub-nosed Smith & Wesson like a pro. Two-handed and rock steady. Her soft green eyes had hardened to cold jade.

It occurred to Jason that he had significantly underestimated Lane McCullough.

That she was able to keep her gun trained on her prisoner with any steadiness at all amazed Lane, considering her insides were quivering so hard that she was sure the whole car must be vibrating. The kiss in the warehouse had left her unsettled. In a matter of seconds he'd possessed her so thoroughly that she feared there might be nothing left of herself when it was over. She had fought back for survival's sake—asserting herself, not giving in, making sure she took as much as she gave—but it had used every ounce of reserve she'd had.

No man had ever affected her so deeply, so quickly.

"Who the hell are you?" she asked.

The glow from the lone streetlamp gave his face a sallow, cadaverous look. Shadows made his expression look hard. It didn't matter. In the ten days she'd been watching him, she had memorized every plane of his face, seen its true nature.

He finally spoke up. "Don't you already know? I'm surprised you haven't already checked me out. You have been watching me, haven't you?"

How did he know that? She was sure she hadn't given herself away. He couldn't have caught more than a snatch of her as she turned a corner or a glimpse of her through the car windshield as she passed him on the street. She had been careful. Until tonight, that is. "I checked you out—enough to know that Jason Turnbull doesn't exist."

His eyes seemed to hold a glint of satisfaction at that. "But I'm here, aren't I? So why don't you just think of me as the guy who just saved your life."

She wished he hadn't reminded her of that. She owed him, but until she knew who he was and why he had helped her, she had to be cautious. Maybe his motivations weren't any more honorable than Grumman's. Maybe he just wanted her to himself.

That thought sent shivers up her spine. Resisting the urge to squirm, she flexed her hands on the grip of her weapon. They both tensed as a pair of headlights suddenly dispelled the shadows between them.

Once the car had passed them by, Jason turned back to her.

"Now, who the hell are you?"

"I'm the public servant who's going to do the citizens of Atlanta a favor and bust your little operation here."

Jason's hooded eyes snapped open to a wide stare. "You're a cop?" Slowly his forehead fell to the steering wheel to rest across his knuckles. He didn't even twitch when she slid her hand under his jacket and relieved him of his pistol.

She hadn't expected to take him so easily. Now that she had him, what was she going to do with him?

She should have busted him days ago, when she'd first seen him standing on the warehouse dock, supervising a crew unloading computer components from an unmarked semi. Intuitively she'd known there was more to him than a few pilfered electronics.

When she'd seen him then, he'd been little more than a silhouette against the sun. Her eyes had skimmed upward from his wide, sure-footed stance to powerful thighs, slim hips and broad shoulders. He stood unmoving, arms crossed, back straight and head high. His mirrored glasses reflected the cloudless sky. If the breeze hadn't ruffled the longish, brown hair over his forehead, he might have been a statue.

It was the illusion of strength that had first seduced her; she could see no weakness in him. Early in life she had learned that every man has his foibles. Her ability to pick them out and exploit them was part of what made her a good cop. Pinpoint a criminal's weakness and he was vulnerable. Vulnerable was catchable.

As she'd watched this man, though, she'd found no cracks in the surface. No flaws in the mold. He was solid—an impenetrable representation of his inner reality. Granite hard and just as cold.

The dock workers had given him a wide berth.

Still bent over the wheel, Jason's shoulders shook, interrupting her reverie. She tossed her head to clear her thoughts. Impenetrable or not, he was now her prisoner.

He shuddered again, a little harder.

She inched away, wary. What was he up to?

When he leaned back and opened his eyes, she saw clearly what he was up to. She felt the heat of a flush on her cheeks.

He was laughing at her. He had one eyebrow arched and a sardonic twinkle in his eye as he asked, "What now, copper?" He talked out of one side of his mouth, like a character in a B movie.

Copper? No one says that. "Now you go to jail, and later I come back for your little *friends,*" she said.

He frowned. "I don't think so."

He pulled himself forward in the seat and leaned close to her. For an insane moment, Lane thought he was going to kiss her again. Her breath caught in her chest. Then his hand slid off the steering wheel and reached down, near her knee.

"Hold it." She thrust the gun at him automatically. "Don't move." Her heart lurched in a delayed reaction.

Both his hands came up, palms forward. "Take it easy. I just want to show you something." With his left hand still in the air, he reached down with his right, more slowly this time.

She divided her attention between his hands, glancing up and down rapidly as he probed along the seam of the upholstery, pushing, then pulling, at the leather seam.

"I hope you don't have a weapon down there," she warned, "because I'd hate to have to shoot the guy who just saved my life."

His eyes held hers as his mouth twisted wryly. Finally he pulled his hand back, holding a small leather wallet. Her stomach sank. She recognized it instantly, and from his self-satisfied look, he knew it.

As he flicked open the wallet, he watched her face and asked, "What now, copper?"

Even in the dim light she could make out the large, block letters on the identification: FBI.

Chapter 2

Lane left Mr. FBI cooling his heels in an interrogation room while she waited for his identity to be confirmed. Now, as she watched her catch through the observation window, she smiled. No doubt about it, she wanted to know more about this man. Normally she didn't get involved with fellow cops, and agents with the Federal Bureau of Investigation were nothing but cops in better suits, but this one tempted her. Sorely tempted her.

He sat with the sole of his work boot propped against the edge of a scarred table, balancing his wooden chair precariously on its two back legs. His face had assumed a half-scowling, half-bored look that suited him.

Seeing him up close for the first time tonight had been a shock. The hair she had listed simply as ''brown'' in her case reports was actually rich pecan, sun-streaked with honey. And now that she'd seen him without the mirrored shades, she had no color word to describe his eyes. They were golden, with bits of red and burnt orange and brown like a maple tree in the fall.

Even his mouth looked like it would be beautiful, if it only had a reason to smile.

Somehow the close-up view seemed incongruent with the aloof criminal image he tried to project. She suspected he knew it, too. That's why he distanced himself from the other goons and hid behind reflective sunglasses.

Her wandering thoughts came back to point as Lane's captain, Roland Bowling, walked into the observation room and stood beside her. She sighed. From the look on his face, she guessed the news. "He's legit?"

"I just got off the phone with his supervisor at the Bureau. He's on his way down. Said he wanted to handle this situation personally." Roland handed her a fax of Jason's picture and FBI personnel identification signed by Atlanta Supervisory Special Agent in charge of the Organized Crime division, Jim Sturman.

"Two weeks on this case, and it looks like all you've managed to catch is a Fed with an attitude." His words were harsh, but she knew her boss well enough to hear the teasing in his voice. He'd been talking to her that way since she was small enough to bounce on his knee.

She grinned. "Yeah, but it's a big attitude."

"You can hardly blame him, Lane. Being marched into a police station at gunpoint is bound to be tough on a guy's ego."

"If he hadn't been such a pain in the car, I wouldn't have had to do that. He yelled at me the whole way here, calling me crazy and demanding his gun back. He actually thought I could just let him go and forget the whole night ever happened."

She looked to Roland for support. "You know I had to check his story before I could let my guard down."

Even FBI IDs could be bought if you knew where to shop and could afford the price. But, with his identity confirmed by the FBI's local office, she felt foolish for dragging Jason in like pond scum. At least she'd spared him the handcuffs.

She appreciated Roland's squeeze on her shoulder more than

she let on. The quiet, black bear of a man was more to her than a captain. Twenty years ago, when his hair wasn't quite so gray and the lines around his eyes weren't quite so deep, he'd been her father's partner. Roland had stayed her father's partner, even through the tough times, right up until the senior McCullough died. After that, he'd been her family's closest friend.

"What were you doing out there tonight?" This time his voice held no teasing tone. "It's your day off, for heaven's sake."

She knew she'd had no business at that warehouse. By-the-book McCullough was way out of line. "I just wanted to stop by to see if there was any activity. I didn't want to miss my chance at that bunch."

He sighed. "So you went out there alone? Where the hell was Dan?"

"He's been tied up in court all week. You know that." She didn't tell him that she couldn't have dragged her partner to that warehouse even if he hadn't been testifying all day. To her constant irritation, Dan North was more concerned about expending as little effort as possible before his retirement—still some twenty years down the road—than in making arrests. But he was still her partner, and as long as he didn't actually cross the line into something crooked, she wouldn't rat on him.

"You could have pulled one of the other detectives. There's not a man out there you haven't helped at one time or another. Any one of them would have gladly returned the favor."

Lane shrugged. "I didn't plan on getting that close."

"My momma didn't plan on having a fifth child at forty-four years of age, either. Goes to show things don't always work out the way we plan. I thought I taught you better than to set up surveillance without backup."

"You did." She tried to accept his gentle reprimand gracefully. After all, she did deserve it, and it was better than an official write-up.

Roland turned back toward the window to the interrogation

room. ''What's so special about this case that you'd take that kind of chance?''

From the direction of his gaze, she suspected he already knew. ''Nothing. My curiosity just got the better of me.''

''Your curiosity nearly got you killed. You're damn lucky to have gotten out of that warehouse alive.''

Lane let her gaze slide along the same path as Roland's, settling on the figure in the interrogation room. Luck had nothing to do with it; the man on the other side of the window did.

A uniformed officer rapped on the door, then stuck his head in. ''I sent Millano and Peters out to get your car, Detective McCullough. They'll bring it back here for you.''

Lane recognized the man as the new night-shift desk sergeant, but had to check the tag on his shirt to remember his name. ''Thanks, Stevens.''

''You're welcome.'' He addressed Roland then. ''There's an FBI guy here to see you.''

Roland turned to Lane. ''That would be Supervisory Agent Sturman. I'll straighten things out with him. But that one,'' Roland pointed at Jason, ''is your problem.''

Lane gulped. After the way she had humiliated him tonight, she didn't think Special Agent Jason Stateler was going to be an easy man to straighten out.

Balancing two cups of slimy coffee from the pot in the detectives' bullpen, she kicked open the door to the interrogation room.

Jason dropped his chair back onto all four legs. ''Well?''

Lane's heart lurched under the intensity of his stare. ''Your supervisor confirmed your identity.''

He only visibly gloated at his victory a second before his shoulders slumped back to indifference. She handed him one of the paper cups.

He sipped, then grimaced. ''Mmm, stationhouse coffee. There's nothing like it.''

''It's definitely an acquired taste.''

He frowned and dropped his gaze into the swirling brew.

Wondering where he got the energy at this time of night to maintain that angry front, Lane studied him. The birth date on the personnel sheet the Bureau faxed over put him in his mid-thirties, but the fatigue in his face tonight made him look older. Even sitting down, his height was evident. He must be a good two inches taller than her, which put him at six one, and he filled out that height very nicely.

Her fingers remembered the bulk and density of the muscles over his back and shoulders. Now, with his jacket off, her eyes could see the contours already imprinted on her mind. Those weren't the muscles of a lazy man. She wondered what he did to cultivate them.

The thought of looking down on a bare-backed Jason Stateler straining to lever his sweaty body off the floor for one last push-up was enough to leave her mouth dry. Lord knows what it would do to her to picture the exercise from another angle. Looking up from underneath, perhaps.

She wriggled in her seat, yanking herself back to reality. She must be more tired than she thought, for her mind to slip into the gutter so easily. "You should have notified us you were working in this area."

Jason snorted and looked up from his coffee. Traces of blue under his eyes proved it had been a long day for him, too. "That would kind of defeat the purpose of being undercover, wouldn't it?"

"Interdepartmental protocol calls for notification of a local authority of all investigations within its jurisdiction—"

"Yeah, yeah, I know, so you can plaster a bulletin on every corkboard in the hallway until some dirty cop sells my ass to the highest bidder. In case you didn't notice, Ms. McCullough—"

"*Detective* McCullough."

"Fine. Whatever. In case you didn't notice, you were the one who put us both in jeopardy tonight, nosing around in a situation you didn't know anything about. So don't talk to me about protocol. And stay away from my case."

"*Your* case? I've been watching stolen electronics move in and out of that warehouse for two weeks!"

"Two weeks?" Jason's head snapped up, yellow flames flickering in his eyes and shoots of angry red lighting his cheeks. "I've spent four months living with those bastards, working my way up to the man who's running the show. I'm this close to getting a meet with the main man." He held up his thumb and forefinger, pinched close. "It's a lot bigger than stolen electronics. That warehouse is just one of the sales sites for an outfit hijacking trucks and networking the goods across a four-state area." He downed another swig of coffee.

"I didn't know the goods were crossing state lines," she said.

"Well, now you know. I have jurisdiction in this case. If my cover isn't blown because of this, that is. Otherwise I'll be nowhere. Starting over."

"That's not my fault. And your cover—"

"Well, well," Captain Bowling's deep voice interrupted. "I'm glad to see you two are getting along so well."

Lane and Jason turned in unison toward the captain. A blush crept into her cheeks. She hadn't heard the door open behind her. From the glower on Jason's face, neither had he.

Jason scraped his chair back on the linoleum floor, stood, and hooked his jacket with a finger. "Great, now if someone will just tell me where I can pick up my gun, I'll be on my way."

From behind the captain, a blond man shuffled into the room, leaning on an elegantly carved mahogany cane with a duck's head handle. Lane squelched her surprise and her pity almost before it registered. She knew all too well that pity was the last thing someone with a physical disability wanted or needed.

"Not so fast, Agent Stateler," the blond man said, tugging at the knot in the navy tie that already hung loose under the open collar of his shirt. His gray, pin-striped suit was so rumpled that Lane wondered if Roland had caught him working late at the office, or if the supervisor had been called at home, and picked the suit he had worn that day off the floor and put it back on.

Roland dispensed with what Lane suspected would be the last of the pleasantries, his head swiveling from the blond man to Lane and back. ''Special Agent Sturman, Detective Lane McCullough. Lane, this is Supervisory Special Agent Sturman, of the Organized Crime Unit.''

Sturman nodded and offered his hand while his eyes raked down her body and then up again. Some men had that habit of feeling a woman up with their eyes. It always turned Lane off. Coming from him, it made her shiver. His eyes looked like they wanted to be blue, but someone had washed away all the color, leaving behind only the silver-gray base.

He let go of her hand and gestured both her and Jason toward chairs. ''Please, have a seat. We need to talk.''

Jason bristled. ''We just finished talking, Jim. Now I'm going back to work and *Detective* McCullough is going to keep herself far, far away from my case.''

''Detective McCullough has information and contacts in this area which might be useful to you,'' Roland pointed out.

''I'll give her my card. She can call me,'' Jason responded drily.

''Agent Stateler,'' Sturman said to Jason, ''Captain Bowling and I have spoken about this, and we agree that you and Detective McCullough should work together on this case.''

''No way. I work alone.'' Jason shoved his way toward the door.

''Stateler.'' Roland stopped him with a tone of voice Lane recognized as the one usually reserved for wayward rookies and cold-blooded killers. ''Unless I misunderstand your supervisor, you don't have any choice.''

Sturman leaned forward, propping his elbows on the table. ''Thanks to your little role play tonight, she now has a firm cover story as your lover. Her sudden departure might make our targets suspicious.'' A smile curled across Sturman's face, then fell away quickly, as if he had consciously suppressed it.

He couldn't quite kill the gleam in his eyes, though. Lane wondered what he found so humorous, especially when Stateler was clearly *not* amused.

Jason turned a pleading gaze her way. "You don't want to do this."

Across the table Lane noticed Sturman's interest in the interplay between her and Jason. She didn't understand all the dynamics here, but something was definitely not right. She almost felt sorry for Jason. "I work the cases I'm assigned," she finally answered.

Jason swallowed hard and turned to his boss. "Jim..."

The FBI supervisor leveled a gaze at him that brooked no argument. "For the duration of this case, consider yourselves joined at the hip. You are partners. Make it work."

Most people wouldn't have noticed anything unusual in Jason's reaction. In fact he covered his emotions so well that most people would probably swear he hadn't reacted at all. Lane supposed that was what made him such a good undercover agent. But she watched his physical responses with the trained eye of an investigator and a student of human nature. Every muscle tightened. Each breath came faster and shallower than the last. Jason Stateler was more than angry. He was afraid.

When Sturman left, Jason sat alone in the interrogation room with his head bowed. He had no idea what time it was, but by the weight of his limbs and the amount of grit in his eyes, he would guess it must be late and knew it was past midnight. He felt like he'd been trapped in the tiny room for days. It seemed even smaller than when he came in, as if the walls were closing in on him.

He scrubbed his face with his hands. A partner. God. The last thing he needed was some local yokel screwing up his investigation. Especially one with huge, green eyes, raven hair and legs a mile long.

He'd argued long and hard with Sturman after Lane and

Bowling had left. Harder than he had any right. With another supervisor, the things he said might have cost Jason his badge. Or at least a formal reprimand. But Sturman always gave him a little extra leeway. The man owed him that much, at least. But even Jason's leeway wouldn't make Sturman change his mind tonight.

The door creaked open and Lane's head poked through the crack. "Is the war over?"

"No, just the first battle."

She pushed the door open farther, walked in and closed it behind her. She'd changed clothes, exchanging jeans for the shorts she'd had on earlier. That should have been some comfort for Jason, but the way the worn denim molded itself to her curves, the jeans concealed little more than the cutoffs.

Pulling out the chair next to him with her foot, she set a cup of coffee on the table in front of her, pushed another toward him and unslung a drawstring purse from her shoulder, hanging it on the back of her chair.

"Who won?" she asked.

Grudgingly he took the brew she offered. "I'm still here, aren't I? Who do you think?"

He took a sip from his cup, then a deeper drink. The sooner he got to the unpleasant task at hand, the sooner this hellish night would be over. But first he needed information. Somewhere in his operation was a leak that needed to be plugged. "How did you find the warehouse?"

"I trailed Grumman and Morales from a local fence. They had just palmed off a load of camcorders."

Jason almost dropped his coffee. "Damn. None of those goods were supposed to be traded locally. They're skimming."

"I thought so. They took great care to make their moves when you weren't around."

"Moves, plural?" He rolled his eyes and slumped back in his chair when she nodded. "Those idiots led you right to me."

"Well, not quite. The first two times I lost them. The third time I had to follow them through three sleazy bars, a cheap hotel frequented by hookers and a very unauthorized off-track-betting establishment before they quit for the night and went back to the warehouse.''

Jason had to admire her determination, but he wasn't about to let her know it. He raised the cup to his mouth and drained it. ''So why didn't you bust me then?''

Her gaze fell quickly to the table. Her chest rose and fell in a soft sigh as a rosy flush tinged her cheeks.

In a flash of insight, he knew that was how she must look when she—whoa, don't go there. Too late. His blood rushed south so suddenly he almost couldn't hear her answer.

''I wasn't sure I had enough on you.''

She shouldn't try to lie, he thought as he struggled to control his rebelling body; her eyes were a dead giveaway. ''With a warehouse full of stolen goods and a briefcase full of money? You had plenty.''

Her flush deepened, but she raised her head and met his eyes. ''I thought you might lead me to something even bigger.''

Still not the truth, and he knew it. She twisted her half-full coffee cup around and around in her hands.

Lord, he needed more coffee, but he'd be damned if he would ask her for it. ''So what happened?''

She looked up at him, the flush slowly fading from her cheeks. ''What happened when?''

''You were investigating me, and then you were caught. What happened?''

''I guess I got too close. I saw you carrying a briefcase, and Alejandro came in. I figured it was a payoff, and I wanted to hear what was happening. I sneaked down to the loading dock, but you finished your business and walked away before I got within earshot. Then Grumman jumped me.''

He had the information he needed. It was time to unleash the beast within him and send her running for the hills. But it was hard to do with her looking at him like that, all wide-eyed like he was a puzzle she could piece together if she just worked it long enough.

He dragged a hand through his hair. ''Do you know what you're getting into?''

''I think so.''

''Do you? Do you know what Sturman meant when he said we'd have to be 'joined at the hip'? You told those goons you were *visiting* me. That means you're going to have to stay with me. You're going to have to live with me, eat with me—'' He stopped short of ''sleep with me.'' He didn't have to say it. By the look on her face, he knew she got the idea.

Her chin angled up a fraction. ''Whatever it takes, I can handle it. I've worked undercover before.''

''Is that right?'' He grabbed her purse off the back of her chair. ''Let's just see.''

Yanking the drawstring top open, he upended the bag, spilling the contents over the tabletop.

Lane managed to corral a lipstick before it rolled over the edge, but she missed the ballpoint pen. She didn't bother to retrieve it. ''What do you think you're doing?''

He went for the wallet first, flipping through its contents while she watched, looking stunned. At first he found nothing unusual—credit cards, vehicle insurance card, all in the name Lane McCullough. Then he looked more closely at her driver's license. It had a Macon address. He frowned. ''You really are from Macon?''

She snatched the wallet and cards from his hands. ''Of course not. I told you I'd worked undercover before. I already had the Macon cover set up. I switched out the identification when I changed my clothes.''

''But all this is in your real name. A cover in your real name isn't going to do much good if they run a check on you in Atlanta.''

She looked at him like he was daft. Maybe he was too tired to deal with this tonight. Things weren't making sense.

''If they run a check on me in Atlanta, they won't find anything. McCullough is my real name. Lane isn't. It's...sort of a nickname.''

Sort of a nickname? What the hell did that mean? In his experience, a woman who went by a nickname usually did so for a reason. Like her real name was Eugenia or something. He started to ask her if that was why, then bit the question back. He didn't want to know; too much personal knowledge did not fit into his plan. Still, he couldn't help but wonder.

''Eleanor,'' she said.

''What?''

''Before you even ask, my real name is Eleanor.'' She looked embarrassed. ''And don't say a word about it. Eleanor was my grandmother's name, and I'm proud to have it.''

He bit the side of his cheek when he realized he was grinning. ''Umm-hmm. That's why you go by Lane.''

Her cheeks turned an even deeper shade of red.

He grabbed another handful of women's junk from the table. The compact he tossed aside. The plastic business card holder, he opened and studied more carefully. ''The Nail Station. Is this your Macon cover?''

''A friend of Captain Bowling owns the salon where I supposedly do manicures and the house where I supposedly rent a room. Everyone there will vouch for me if anyone comes around asking questions.''

He tossed the business cards next to the compact and unfolded a couple of crumpled papers. They were charge slips and an ATM receipt from Macon area locations. Dated a couple of months ago, but still a nice touch. He had to hand it to her, she was good.

She couldn't be that good. He grabbed the bag itself and fished through it, searching out the secret little pockets all women's purses had. He smiled in victory when he found his prize. She froze when he held it up: a dry-cleaning ticket, dated last week from an *Atlanta* cleaner.

''This would be hard to explain, since you only got into town yesterday.''

Her eyes flashed, anger and embarrassment storming through them. ''You're really reaching.''

"Am I? A simple mistake like a laundry ticket could get us both killed out there." He could vouch for that from personal experience. Sometimes it didn't take any mistakes at all.

"I'll get rid of the ticket," she said, holding out her hand for it.

He ripped up the paper and threw the scraps on the floor. "Don't worry about it."

Her fist clenched on the table in front of her. "And just what makes you think *your* cover is so brilliant? I ran the plates on your car and got your alias from DMV. It took about ten minutes for me to figure out that Jason *Turnbull* doesn't exist."

He grinned a Cheshire cat grin. "Yeah, but I'm supposed to be one of the bad guys. The other bad guys don't expect me to use my real name. If all it took was a few computer queries to get my whole life history, they'd know I was lying."

"What kind of convoluted logic is that? Your cover is to not have a solid cover?"

"It's the kind of convoluted logic that keeps me alive. And the fact that you don't understand that tells me you're not ready for this assignment."

"I can hold my own on any assignment," she said, unflustered.

Didn't anything get to this woman? What would it take to make her understand? He couldn't work this case with her like they were real partners.

Jason pounded his palm flat on the wooden table, sending the paraphernalia from her purse jumping and spikes of pain jolting up to his elbow. Like a lightning strike his hand shot out and latched across her throat, his thumb and index finger probing each side in the hollows behind her jaw. "Damn it, don't you get it?"

His chair scraped back, nearly tumbling over as he stood and towered over her, his hand still at her throat, not tightening, just holding, touching. "Don't you know what they would have done to you tonight if I hadn't been there?"

His hand trailed down to the scoop of her T-shirt. Her heartbeat vibrated through his fingertips, setting off a sympathetic vibration deep in his gut.

Her eyes turned watery but never wavered, never blinked. ''If I recall, I wasn't the one who had my weapon taken away from me tonight,'' she said calmly.

Damn her. He jerked his hand back as if it had brushed hot coals. She was right. He'd let his guard down tonight, falling as hard for the helpless-woman act as Grumman and Morales had.

He wouldn't make that mistake again. ''You're going to regret this.''

''I think I already do.''

Good. If he couldn't scare her off, at least he could make her hate him. It would make it easier to get rid of her when the time came. Until then, he didn't want a spark of pleasant feelings between them.

Without warning, his mind flashed back to their kiss in the warehouse and his body felt the heat. The crush of her against him. When it came to feelings of any sort between the two of them, maybe *spark* wasn't such a good choice of words.

Chapter 3

Unfolding herself from Jason's low-slung car, Lane blinked back her sleepiness and followed him into a squat building that was slowly sloughing stucco from its gray facade. He navigated a maze of identically bland hallways into a stairwell, never checking to make sure she was still behind him.

If she hadn't been so tired, his cold-shoulder treatment would have made her mad. Instead, she took perverse pleasure in the spectacular view of his backside that the brush-off afforded her. While he propelled himself up the stairs at a jog, she followed at a slower gait, unabashedly admiring the scenery.

On the second landing he turned into the hallway. Lane smiled wickedly. Too bad, she could have suffered one more flight.

Outside Apartment 316, Lane waited in the shadow of her new partner's silence while he opened the door. Not that she expected him to say anything. He hadn't opened his mouth since he'd stormed out of the interrogation room, slamming the door behind him hard enough to rattle the frost off the frosted glass. That was at 1:00 a.m., over an hour ago.

Since then, he'd pulled back someplace inside himself where she wasn't welcome. In the space of a few hours he'd gone from kissing her with the heat of a star going nova, to blasting her with a cold front that would freeze the ears off an Eskimo.

Now if she just knew why.

The tiny apartment didn't provide many clues. No personal touches like photos, knickknacks, magazines flipped open to half-read articles. Nothing to tell her what kind of man he was. Just stark, white walls and mass-produced furnishings: a black vinyl couch and lacquer coffee table, chrome and glass end tables that didn't match, a floor lamp with a bulb harsh enough to scorch the eyeballs out of a desert lizard.

The only splash of color in the place came from a full-size punching bag, one of the really heavy kinds you'd expect to find at a gym. It hung where she supposed the dining table was supposed to go.

At least that solved the mystery of the bulging muscles. It wasn't hard to imagine him burying his bare fists in the cracked leather over and over, grunting with each stroke, until his chest sheened with sweat and his body ached with the impact. It was a natural outlet for whatever was eating at him, and she had no doubt something was eating at him. She just didn't know what.

She hated to think that it was her, but that was how he was acting. She'd never felt so immediately and intensely disliked as when he'd stared up at her after being ordered to partner with her. Okay, she was a little too tall for most men, and she hadn't had time to do much with her hair that morning—it was flying wild after a day in the heat and humidity—but was she really that unappealing? In the warehouse it hadn't felt like that had been the case.

Jason threw the bolt on the door behind her. He rolled his shoulders, and she could almost feel the tension in his neck and back.

She would never find out what was bothering him if he kept

up this silent treatment. And working together was going to be next to impossible if they couldn't speak to each other.

She pasted on a weary smile, the best she could manage at 2:00 a.m., and tried to lighten the mood. "So, I thought the FBI set you guys up in luxury suites while you infiltrated notorious crime syndicates."

"You've been watching too much TV." He pointed around the economy-size dwelling. "Kitchen is in there. Bathroom is that door, and the bedroom is down the hall."

Bedroom, as in singular? Unsure which way to go, she opted to stand still, taking in his homecoming ritual. He hung his keys on a hook outside the kitchen, tossed his jacket over the back of the couch and methodically rolled the straps of his shoulder holster around the butt of his gun before dropping it on the coffee table. Arching his linked fingers over his head, he stretched and plopped onto the couch with a weary sigh.

He didn't seem to notice she was still there until she cleared her throat.

His head swiveled. She'd caught him off guard. He looked tired. And worried.

For the first time since they'd left the precinct, he really looked at her, and, without his usual mask of indifference, it was like she could see right inside him.

His golden eyes might be as brilliant as a summer sunset, but the secrets locked behind them were dark and dangerous, like a panther trapped in a cage.

A connection flared between them. The live wire touched her insides, its filament pulsing with tiny electrical shocks that started her heart thumping uncomfortably against her ribs.

No, he didn't dislike her. Nor did he find her unappealing.

She gritted her teeth as her cheeks turned hot under his stare. Her face had to be flaming red. She hated that about herself—her inability to control that one simple reflex.

"Um, where…?" She waved her hand from the couch toward the bedroom.

"I'll take the couch," he said. He lowered his eyes, and the heat around her quickly dissipated, like he'd snuffed a candle she'd been holding too close.

"You don't have to do that. It's your apartment."

"It's the Bureau's apartment. You take the bed."

"You're taller, and that couch is small. You should take the bed."

"Damn it, Lane, would you stop arguing with me and go to bed."

Well, it was progress. At least he was talking to her again. Besides, she didn't really want to sleep on the couch. It looked lumpy.

The bed, on the other hand, she thought as she walked into the room at the end of the hall, looked perfectly cozy. Unlike the chrome and plastic furnishings in the other room, it was good, solid wood. A bit of an antique.

She tucked herself into it, liking the way the mattress sagged just enough to roll her to the middle, holding her safe, like a lover's embrace.

Burrowing her cheek into the pillow, she inhaled deeply, picking up traces of the same scents she had smelled when he held her at the warehouse. An oddly comforting contrast of fabric softener and virile male.

Virile, at least, in her dreams. She awoke with a vague recollection of him calling her, her name hoarse on his lips. Unsure how long she'd slept, she rolled to face the window, meeting only darkness. The world outside lay trapped in that time between night and morning when neither sun nor moon saw fit to give it shape.

Murmured words, soft but urgent, wafted in from the living room. Sitting up, she strained to hear more. Something clattered as if it had fallen.

Her pulse danced. Silently she took her gun from the night table and slipped out of bed. Arms stretched in front of her, piercing the blackness, she slid her feet along the carpet, her trepidation growing with each step. By the time she reached the door, the blood pounding in her ears threatened to drown out the sounds from the other room.

She peered around the corner, seeing nothing. The silence was as thick as the darkness. A shadow, barely identifiable as an arm, flung itself out from the couch. Knuckles rapped on the coffee table. Breathing, fast and heavy, cut the stillness.

"No, no, no." The anguish in his voice tore at her heart. She lowered her gun and tiptoed to the end of the couch. Continuing his litany of denial, his chest arched off the cushions and his fists clenched in tangled sheets at his waist.

She watched, fascinated and at the same time discomfited to be privy to such a private struggle. Who'd have thought the big, bad FBI agent had nightmares?

She'd almost convinced herself to leave, when his face contorted in such pain and rage that it hurt to watch. She never could stand by and let a living creature suffer. Pushing his weapon away from where he must have knocked it to the floor, she knelt beside him and brushed her hand over his forehead. Her fingers righted an errant lock of hair, but it immediately sprang back to its boyish disarray.

There was nothing boyish about the rest of him, however. The lowered sheet revealed a smooth, almost hairless chest. In her somewhat limited experience with unclothed men, she'd never seen anyone built like him. His body flowed together, muscle, bone and sinew, one tied seamlessly together with the next.

He tensed, arching up again, and she longed to reach out and touch him, stroke him.

To channel the energy of his dream into something more productive.

Her fingertips wavered over him. She couldn't do it.

But he could. Quicker than a rattler, Jason grabbed her hand and flattened it against his chest. His pulse played a powerful rhythm on her palm.

Pushing himself halfway up, his eyes flickered open. Thinking she'd woken him, she held her breath, but he didn't seem to know she was there.

"Karen?" he called. "No, no, Karen." His voice was thick as he collapsed back onto the sofa, still clasping her hand to his chest. His skin was damp and searing hot. He shook with the intensity of whatever scene his mind unreeled for him.

This was no ordinary nightmare. Realizing that waking someone from a night terror could be more traumatic than riding it out, she cooed and stroked his forehead with her free hand until his eyes closed and the tremors gradually died.

Amidst his struggles, the sheet had slipped down until it rode the ridge of his hip. As Jason gradually softened his grip on her hand, she reached down to pull it up before his clammy body chilled. Grasping the hem of the bedding, her fingers brushed his abdomen, and she paused at what she felt.

His soft skin gave way to a band of ridged flesh just below where the waistband of his jeans would fit. Checking to make sure he was still asleep, she carefully ran her fingers over the puckered scar.

He hissed like she'd burned him, and the muscles around his stomach clenched.

She jerked her hand back. It was hard to see in the dark, but the wound felt old, healed. Surely she couldn't have hurt him with that light touch. Nevertheless she stayed by his side until she was sure he wasn't in pain. After a time he filled his lungs in great gulping breaths and sank slowly back into a dreamless sleep.

Wondering at the complexity of the human mind and its defense mechanisms, Lane crept back to bed. The image of the panther pacing its cage leaped to her mind again as she left him in the darkness.

The man had his secrets, all right. And apparently they wanted out.

Jason woke to a pounding headache and a body that felt like it had spent the night on the wrong end of a battering ram. He knew the symptoms; he'd had enough nightmares in the past four years to be an expert. After yesterday, he should have expected a rough night.

At least he hadn't woken Lane. Or had he? He vaguely remembered her face floating above him, her green eyes cool like seawater on his heated skin. Hopefully he had just transposed her into his dream. He wasn't ready to deal with her questions, if it had been more than that.

He stood and, remembering his houseguest, slid his jeans over his knit boxers before stumbling to the bathroom for aspirin. Shielding his eyes from the morning light, he rounded the corner without looking and ran straight into her.

Stumbling, he nearly tumbled them both to the floor. On instinct, he grabbed her elbows and righted them both.

Damn. Her breasts were flush against his bare chest and her abdomen grazed the unbuttoned waistband of his jeans. Every touch of her skin to his pricked like tiny pinpoints.

''Uh, sorry,'' was the most intelligible thing he could say. Seeing her here in his hallway, fresh-faced and damp from a shower, wearing one of his white T-shirts and nothing else, as far as he could see, robbed him of the ability to form complex thoughts.

She swallowed hard and took a step back, pulling herself from his grasp and shaking her head. ''My fault.'' Chewing her lush lower lip, she seemed as affected as he was. Her nipples peaked behind the thin layer of cotton covering them.

If they weren't careful, this thing between them could get out of hand very fast.

Thoughts of what it would do to him if that happened stilled his body as effectively as a dip in a cold mountain spring.

She fidgeted at the carpet with her toes. ''My things were filthy,'' she said. ''I hope you don't mind...I borrowed a T-shirt until I could get them washed.''

''No problem. There's some sweatpants in there, too, if you want them.'' Glancing down at her bare thighs, he hoped she would take him up on the offer. It would help his peace of mind. "We'll go by your place later and get some of your clothes and things."

Preferably long-sleeved, baggy things, he thought.

She nodded, and he stepped around her, into the bathroom. After downing the aspirin and half a glass of water, he stepped underneath the shower. With his head tilted back, he let the spray hit him full in the face, as if he could wash away the visions that haunted him, that had haunted him for four years, since the last time he'd worked with a partner.

He could still feel the blood flowing through his fingers.

Clenching his eyes shut, he fought the compulsive need to scrub his hands. To scour himself until all traces of his guilt had been cleansed away.

Under the pounding of the shower, he built his resolve like a wall, brick by brick. History would not repeat itself. He wouldn't let it.

If he couldn't run her out of this investigation entirely, he would simply keep Lane McCullough safely stashed in his apartment. He would have her make an occasional public appearance on the doorstep in case he was being watched, and tuck her away in his bedroom, alone, each night.

As for acting like lovers, that was not going to happen. No more touching, accidental or otherwise. He'd be cool but polite. Keep his distance. Work his ass off and finish this case before anything else could go wrong.

He stayed in the shower until he'd used up the last of the hot water, and he shivered in cold. When he emerged, feeling less like a dinghy adrift at sea and more like a cutter, tacking against the wind but still on course, he smelled eggs. Hurrying into his jeans, he headed for the kitchen.

Lane stood there with her back to him, concentrating over the stove. She had opted for yesterday's jeans instead of his sweatpants, but still wore his T-shirt. It bloused out just above her belt, accentuating her small waist and the gentle curve of her backside.

He must have regained some sense of balance within himself, since he was able to look at her appreciatively without going weak-kneed for the first time. The counter in front of her was cluttered with cheese, vegetable remains and bits of chopped-up ham. It looked like she'd added a little bit of everything in his refrigerator to the omelet in the frying pan.

She turned and smiled at him, a good-morning smile that could melt a pound of butter. His stomach sank.

Cool but polite was getting harder by the second. Despite the way he had treated her last night, she'd set the table for two.

Jason cranked up the air conditioner in his Corvette while Lane gave him directions to her house. The heat wave that had settled over central Georgia showed no signs of retreat. At 10:00 a.m., an uncomfortably strong sun already blazed through the windshield as he parked the car.

Her home surprised him. He didn't know what he had been expecting, but this wasn't it.

The sweet scent of honeysuckle drifted across the yard from a huge, tangled vine draped across the side fence. He smiled at the familiarity of the smell. It reminded him of her.

Lowering his sunglasses, he surveyed the place as they walked to the door. A ring of greenery girdled the one-story frame house. Evenly spaced shrubs lined the edges of the walkway. The grassy yard had been sheared. But it wasn't the neatly landscaped lawn that caught his eye, it was the river of wildflowers that snaked through it, undoing the air of manicured hoitiness with blooming torrents of color, like a child's crayon scribbled across a master painting.

Despite his attempts at disinterest, he was impressed.

"Most cops don't have time for this." He gestured toward the yard in a sweeping motion.

She looked at him quizzically for a moment, then lifted her brows. "Ah, neither do I."

Jason frowned. Then who did? He hadn't asked if she had a significant other. He hadn't asked a lot of things.

She slid the key into the front door while he eyed her from the bottom of the stoop.

"Your husband?" he asked before he could stop himself.

"No." She laughed and walked in, leaving the door open behind her.

Well then, who? Jason strode in after her, intent on getting an answer, but met only an empty living room.

The house's interior radiated the same vitality as the yard. Light flooded the room from panoramic windows on the east and south walls. Clinging ivy grew up the sides of a primitive stone fireplace. A modernistic painting, mostly blue with red splotches and yellow slashes, crowned the mantel. Clay pots of assorted sizes sprouted tender-looking seedlings on the hearth below.

"Lane?" he called.

"Back here."

He followed her voice down a long hall to a small bedroom, studying the pictures strung along the wall as he went. For the first few steps, a happy young couple smiled out at him in black-and-white. About a third of the way down the hall, they beamed over two infants swaddled so tightly in receiving blankets that only the tips of their tiny noses peeked out. Jason took a few more steps and smiled at a candid shot: two identical girls hung upside down from a tree limb, their dark ponytails swinging toward the ground and their emerald eyes shining below tomboy smiles.

The last picture in the group made Jason pause. Before the bleachers of a high school stadium, the same girls, older now, wore graduation gowns. Both clutched ribbon-tied scrolls in their hands. But in this shot, one girl stood while the other sat in a wheelchair. The woman from the early photographs, looking frail, leaned heavily on the back of the chair. In this one photograph, no one was smiling.

Jason moved on, and found Lane in a bedroom that hinted at a softer side to the hard-edged detective. Pale roses dotted the bedspread. The curtains were lace, and the bureau she was pulling clothes out of was Victorian.

A second woman sat straight-backed, almost prudishly, on the edge of the bed. Lane's companion was smaller, frailer, with cheeks slightly more hollow and bird-boned hands that looked like they could be crushed with an overzealous handshake, but the two women shared the same raven hair and luminous green eyes. Even their expressions were identical, caught mid-giggle.

''Kell, this is my new partner, at least temporarily, Special Agent Jason Stateler. Jason, meet my sister, Kelly, the green thumb around here.''

Kelly turned a bright face up at him. Despite her carriage, he couldn't call her prudish. Impish might be more accurate.

Picking up a bamboo cane that had been hidden alongside her thigh and propping it on the floor in front of her, Kelly leveraged herself off the bed. When she stood, he could just make out the spines of a torturous-looking back brace beneath her loose blouse. That explained her posture. He should have guessed its source was physical affliction, not attitude.

Jason walked farther into the room and extended his hand. Lane smiled up at him, but a warning howled from her eyes. The look clearly read, ''Be nice, or else.''

As if he would be anything else. Then again, she had no way to know that. He hadn't exactly been overexerting his social graces since he'd met her.

He shot her back a ''Chill out'' look with narrowed eyes and knew she got the message when one corner of her mouth quirked up. He stifled a groan. They'd been together less than a day, and already they were carrying on conversations with nothing more than expressions. This was not a good sign.

Pasting on his most charming smile—some women had even called it sexy, he recalled, but that had been a lifetime ago—he extended his hand toward Lane's sister. ''Nice to meet you, Kelly.''

She studied him openly, her fragile fingers ensconced in his palm. "The pleasure is mine."

Apparently satisfied with his manners, Lane pulled more clothes out of the bureau and piled them in an open suitcase on the bed.

Kelly winked at Jason conspiratorially while Lane's back was turned. "Actually, I'm quite relieved to meet you."

"Relieved?" He raised his eyebrows. The twinkle in Kelly's eyes looked more like mischief than relief.

"I was getting worried about my sister, spending all her time, including her days off, doing surveillance on some grungy warehouse." Kelly's tongue rolled in the side of her cheek as her gaze slid to Lane's back. "Now I see what she found so interesting."

"Kelly!" Lane spun around, her face instantly as crimson as the blouse in her hands.

Jason propped his shoulder and hip against the door frame as Kelly laughed, a high, tinkling sound, like crystal bells from a body fragile as glass. He liked the sound. It had been a long time since there'd been cause for laughter in his life.

Watching the color slowly fade from Lane's cheeks, though, he couldn't find the same humor. She blushed a lot. And every time the heat suffused her cheeks, he felt the burn deep inside his body.

It only got worse when she swayed back toward the dresser and turned around with something lavender and lacy in her hands. His body tightened another notch as she folded it into the suitcase.

Unbidden, the image of her wearing the scrappy gown leaped into his mind. He knew just how it would fall over her curves. He could feel the cool silk sliding under his fingers, the heat of her skin underneath.

It only seemed natural for his imagination to take him to the next logical scene, his hands pushing the gown over her head bit by bit, his tongue exploring each new inch of creamy, white territory he exposed.

What was it about women's lingerie? All a man had to do was glance at the flimsy thing, and he couldn't wait to see it on his woman. Then as soon as he did see her in it, he couldn't wait to get it off.

Ah, hell. When had Lane become "his woman"? For that matter, what made him think he would ever be able to call any woman "his" again? He no longer had that right. Pulling his eyes away from the lingerie, he found himself snared by Kelly's devilish grin. Apparently his interest in her sister's undergarments hadn't gone unnoticed.

Suddenly his own cheeks felt a little warm. "Um, Lane, I'll wait for you in the other room," he said, retreating.

He fidgeted with the fern in the center of the dining room table until he heard shuffling steps on the tile behind him.

"Can I get you something while you wait?" Kelly asked. "I just made a fresh pot of tea."

Jason winced inside. From the aroma floating in from the kitchen, he'd bet the tea was herbal, her own blend. Not all the plants growing around here looked ornamental.

"Sure. Sounds good." What he really needed was a shot of good strong coffee. Black. But the smile on Kelly's face when he accepted made it worth downing a few ounces of soaked dead leaves. He sat down at a chair facing the kitchen.

She winced as she reached into the cupboard for mugs.

"Here, let me get that." He jumped up so quickly he banged his knee on the corner of the oak table.

Kelly tipped her head back and laughed, the pain gone from her face as she set the mugs on the counter and watched him rub his shin. "You stay put. I'm perfectly capable of getting us both a cup of tea."

She poured two mugs from the ceramic pot on the stove, set them on a tray, which she picked up with one hand while she leaned on her cane with the other. "It's my own concoction," she commented when he picked up his mug and sniffed tentatively. "I find the herbs help when my back is giving me trouble."

He sipped. Not bad. But not coffee, either. The spearmint flavor tingled his tongue.

She settled herself into the chair across from him. "So, you're with the FBI? Sounds exciting."

"Most of the time it's pretty boring. Lots of legwork, very little action."

"Ah, but the action there is must be mind-blowing."

His hand clenched on the mug, the heat of the tea burning his fingers, even through the ceramic. *Yeah, mind-blowing,* he thought. *When a fraction of a second turns your perfect life into a living hell, that's how to describe it—mind-blowing.*

"Sometimes," he said quietly, getting up to pace the length of the dining room. A Chopin strain drifted out the door of an attached office. Inside, shelves overflowed with novels, nonfiction, magazines and reference books from the floor to the ceiling. The desk in front of the window had a computer. Stacks of loose paper teetered on the desktop and littered the tile floor.

He guessed this was Kelly's workspace, not Lane's. The same spearmint flavor he'd smelled, and tasted, in the dining room permeated the office, and the chair by the desk was fitted with an orthopedic backrest.

Kelly ambled up behind him.

"You're a writer?" Jason asked.

"Very good, Sherlock. I freelance mostly, for women's magazines. But I've published a couple of romance and science fiction novels, as well."

Jason had run out of small talk. He shuffled his feet uneasily and a ragged puff of orange and white fur stirred behind a porcelain planter. The cat stretched languorously, then sauntered over to Kelly, limping noticeably.

"Something wrong with your cat?" he asked.

Limp or not, the animal leaped agilely onto the windowsill next to Kelly and pricked the hem of her shorts with its claws.

"Nothing new." Gingerly she stooped and pulled the cat into her arms by the scruff of its neck. "He's just an old alley cat who fought one too many turf wars. Lane found him holed up under the back porch after a particularly nasty scrape. It took a lot of coaxing, but she finally got him to give up and accept her help." She ruffled the cat's fur behind its ears. "Right, J.D.?"

"J.D.?"

Kelly grinned. "James Dean. He's our rebel without a cause."

He nodded absently, reaching for a cluster of potted daisies on the windowsill and brushing his fingers over their tender petals. The vibrancy of this house pulled at him the way the sun pulled the faces of the flowers toward the window.

Everything was so…alive.

"You really do have a green thumb." He wondered if Kelly heard the longing in his voice.

She hobbled over to him, the rubber tip of her cane squeaking occasionally on the tile floor. "I'm a nurturer by nature, I guess."

He dropped a corner of his mouth in a wry frown. "I can't seem to keep anything alive more than a week."

"In that case," Kelly said, laughing, "I'm not so sure I want my sister moving in with you."

Jason's vision darkened. He set his cup down for fear he might drop it.

Kelly reached for his hand. "Hey, I'm sorry…"

Forcing himself to breathe, he gently extricated his fingers from hers. He read the confusion in her eyes and knew he owed her an explanation. A reassurance. Something. But his mind tripped over the words. He couldn't sit here and sip tea and chat like an old hen.

He had one foot out the front door when Lane emerged from the hallway, a suitcase in one hand and a sagging canvas bag in the other.

"All set," she said cheerfully, handing him the bags when he reached for them.

As he stepped across the threshold the slamming door punctuated his exit. He didn't deserve to be welcomed here. Not when this house was more alive than he'd been in years.

Chapter 4

Lane watched from the porch with Kelly, who still cradled the cat in one arm, as Jason squeezed her suitcase and book bag into his tiny Corvette. The pain that had been etched on his face when he walked out slowly dissolved, leaving behind a scowl.

She quizzed her sister. "What was that all about?"

"I'm not sure," Kelly replied, sounding distressed.

Lane looked after her mysterious partner. "Well, don't worry about it. He's a hard one to figure out."

Kelly's expression brightened. "Yeah, but think of the rewards if you ever did." She glanced Jason's way, then winked at Lane. "He's a hunk."

"Kelly!"

"Well, he is!"

"He's my partner, Kelly. We're just working together. And he's not even very happy about that."

"He didn't look too miserable when he was watching you pack."

Lane put her hands on her hips and tried to look stern, but she could never stay angry with her sister, and Kelly knew it.

Kelly wiggled her eyebrows. ''He's quite a departure from the stiff-necked geeks you usually bring home.''

Lane felt a blush creep up her neck. She knew who Kelly meant. ''Carl was not a geek.''

''I think he used my PC once to get on the Internet and check out some of those cyber-sex sites.''

Lane had dated Carl Yermin, the department's computer specialist, for almost a year. She finally gave up on him on New Year's Eve when the party he had invited her to turned out to be an all-night on-line chat session about the social, moral and technological significance of the approaching new millennium.

''Okay, he was a geek,'' Lane admitted. Not unlike the CPA she had dated before him, or the insurance adjuster before that.

In the driveway, Jason bent his long body into his sports car.

''Now that man,'' Kelly said, ''is the epitome of nongeekdom.''

''Just because a man has a great body doesn't mean he has the personality to match. He has a nasty attitude and a nastier temper.''

Kelly tapped her cane stubbornly. ''At least that's better than a Milquetoast, like Carl.''

What was wrong with a Milquetoast? Men like Carl had a lot to offer—they were safe, predictable, stable. That's exactly what she needed, wasn't it?

''Besides,'' Kelly continued. ''Remember how J.D. scratched and hissed when you first found him? But he grew to love you...eventually.''

Lane smiled at the memory, and at the comparison. ''Yeah, but how many bottles of antiseptic did we go through in the meantime, treating my wounds? Thanks, but I don't care to see Jason Stateler's claws.''

They both giggled. They hadn't had a conversation like this since they were in high school, before the accident.

Lane kissed her sister on the cheek before she went down

the walkway. Jason was already in the car with the engine running.

She climbed in beside him and waved one last time to Kelly. Her "little" sister could take care of herself, but Lane always hated to leave her. They were all each other had.

"You didn't tell me you had a twin," Jason commented, backing the 'Vette out of the drive.

"You didn't ask," Lane replied. Didn't he wonder about her the way she did about him? "Where to now?" she asked.

"Back to the apartment."

Trying to coax out more cool air, she fiddled with the knob on the air vent. "What for?"

"So you can settle in, get some rest, while I check a few things out."

Her hand froze on the vent control. She stared at him in astonishment. His eyes never veered from the road. *He was serious.*

Frustration crowded out patience in the part of Lane's mind that warned her to go slow, to give him time to adjust to having a partner. Her indignation rang clear as the cloudless sky. "Thanks, but I outgrew *naps* a number of years ago. We can check things out together."

He turned a quelling look on her.

She mirrored the stubborn expression right back at him, then stared out the windshield when his flawless features began to melt her resolve. God, even when he was being obnoxious he was handsome.

She crossed her arms over her chest and kept her eyes locked onto the road ahead. "Fine. Drop me off, so I can call a cab. I'm planning on staking out the distribution center today. I thought you might want to join me, but if you have other plans—"

Squealing brakes cut short her words. Maneuvering the car to the side of the road, he turned a withering glare on her.

Never one to wither, she glared back.

"What distribution center?" he asked.

"The one where the trucks that bring the stolen goods to your warehouse come from." She kept her tone nonchalant and examined her fingernails casually.

"And how did you find that?"

She groaned and dropped her hand to her lap. "Look, from a local fence, I followed Grumman and Morales to your warehouse. There I saw you. I tried to follow you a couple of times, but you kept losing me. The day before yesterday, I managed to keep up with you long enough to see you meet with a short man with dark hair—the same one you gave the cash to last night."

"Alejandro?"

"Whoever. I figured he was the middleman between you and the boss of the operation, so I followed him. He led me to a place where truckloads of goods come in, get rearranged onto trucks with other stuff and go out. Some sort of distribution center. I've just been waiting for a chance to go back and stake it out."

"Where is it?"

She pounded her voice into an edge sharp enough to cut to the bone. "If you want to treat me like a partner, I'll show you. If you want to treat me like your concubine and lock me in your apartment, you'll have to find it yourself."

He considered her in silence for a few moments, his face cast in carefully constructed impassivity. But the look didn't fool her. The man had a lot on his mind. She just wished she knew what it was.

With a heavy sigh, he put the car in gear and stared out the windshield. "I have to go by the warehouse first. I have drivers coming in to pick up the load I bought last night."

She smiled in satisfaction and settled herself deeper into the leather seat. "Fine."

"Stay in the car," Jason told her as they pulled into the alley beside the warehouse.

''Maybe I should go with you, so the agents posing as drivers know who I am, in case there's trouble.''

He shut off the car and turned toward her. ''They aren't agents.''

''Then who...''

''Local thugs I hired.''

''Your boss lets you get away with that?'' Inviting the enemy into your own camp didn't seem like a smart idea.

''My *boss* doesn't much care what I do as long as I bring somebody in wearing handcuffs when it's over. Until that point, the Bureau pretty much leaves me alone, and that's how I like it.''

Lane couldn't imagine working a case like this without the support of her friends and colleagues in the department. ''What? You mean you don't check in, file reports? You don't call for backup? Besides being dangerous, isn't that...lonely?''

He stretched his legs out the car door, stood up and then leaned down to peer back in the car at her. ''Now you're catching on.''

The man was full of surprises. She'd wanted to know more about him since the minute she'd seen him, but there was a limit to what she'd put up with. Did he really think he could bring down this operation without any help from anyone? Why would any cop—or agent—want to work that way? Her curiosity about him was rapidly turning into annoyance. Mysterious was one thing; incomprehensible was another.

She rolled down windows as he walked away, ignoring the way rivulets of sweat trickled down the crevice between her shoulder blades and the way the leather seats stuck to her thighs when she squirmed. All in all, she thought she made a pretty good bimbo, filing her nails and smacking her wintergreen gum as she waited.

From the car window she could see Jason as he leaned on the railing on the office level above the loading dock. He probably wasn't any more comfortable than she was. The leather jacket he'd donned over his jeans and T-shirt looked odd, as hot as it was, but it was necessary to conceal his shoulder-holstered weapon. Grumman and Morales, directing workers on the dock below him, wore similar jackets. For a similar purpose, she was sure.

The workers lifted the last of the boxes into Jason's two waiting trucks. While her partner talked to the drivers, Alejandro walked out of the building and toward the car. Great, she thought, glancing up and seeing that Jason hadn't noticed her visitor. Setting her handbag on the driver's seat, she rested her hand on top, reassured by the bulge the handle of her service revolver made under her palm.

"Good morning. You must be Señorita McCullough." Alejandro's voice dripped sweetness without sincerity. "It is warm again this morning, no?"

Lane mustered a cool smile despite the fear clutching her heart. It must be this place, reminding her of what could have happened yesterday. Oddly, it wasn't Morales's or Grumman's threats from last night that replayed in her mind. It was the feel of Jason's hand on her throat, and his words, "Don't you know what they would have done to you," that scared her.

She forced herself to inhale slowly. "Yes, it is unbearable, isn't it? You must be Alejandro."

She lifted her hand out the window in greeting. Where was Jason?

Alejandro, instead of shaking the hand she offered, opened the car door and took her hand to guide her out of the car.

"I am sorry your time with your...companion...is interrupted by something so mundane as work, but business is business, no?" he said when she stood in front of him.

She didn't know how Jason could stand to work undercover day after day. It made her feel dirty.

Unable to come up with a smooth response, she simply nodded, her heart pounding.

"Perhaps you would come inside awhile and join me in a cool drink while you wait," Alejandro said.

Lane's heart doubled its rate. No way did she want to go

anywhere with this creep. But she couldn't blow this assignment. She had something to prove. "How nice of you. Let me just get my bag." *And my gun,* she thought.

Leaning into the vehicle, she stretched farther across the seat than was necessary. As she backed out with her bag, she pushed off the steering wheel, pressing her palm to the center. The horn blared a plaintive note, a call for help that she hoped Jason would hear, but it wasn't necessary.

A large hand clamped on Alejandro's shoulder and turned him around, none too gently. Jason's voice was low and gravelly and oh, so welcome. "What do you think you're doing, Alejandro?"

"Ah, Jason, my friend. There you are." Jason let Alejandro go with an almost unnoticeable shove.

"I asked what you were doing. Grumman said you wanted to talk to me—*inside,*" Jason said.

Alejandro raised his hands to shoulder height. "Yes, yes. I was merely inviting your lady to join us, where it is more comfortable. It is a hot day to sit in a black car while the men conduct business. "

Jason's eyes flashed daggers at Lane, then landed back on Alejandro in a dead calm. "That won't be necessary. Why did you want to talk to me?"

"I wished to speak with both of you, actually. I wish to extend an invitation. Do you like boxing, Jason?"

"Not particularly," Jason answered. Lane couldn't help but think of the big, red bag hanging in his dining room. For a man who didn't like boxing, he did have all the accouterments.

"Pity," Alejandro said. "Tonight is a spectacular event. My countryman, Montoya, fights for the heavyweight crown. But perhaps, if you don't enjoy the sport itself, you will at least join me afterward for the victory celebration."

Jason took Lane's elbow and turned her toward the car. "I don't think so."

"That is a shame," she heard Alejandro say over her shoulder. "I had hoped to discuss this special order you wish to make. Or have you forgotten you asked?"

Jason dropped her elbow and spun toward Alejandro. "I haven't forgotten. You've been putting me off for days."

"And now I wish to listen."

Jason hesitated before he replied. "Maybe I could stop by for a while."

"Ah, but it is a party, Jason. You must bring the beautiful señorita, or you will be out of place. Besides, I feel bad, taking her away from you so much when she has traveled all the way from Macon to visit you."

Jason's nostrils flared. For the first time since this confrontation began, his mask slipped, and Lane could see the indecision roiling within him. She couldn't believe he would consider passing up this opportunity just because he didn't want to take her to a party. But it looked like he would.

"I don't th—" Jason started.

Lane cut him off. "Sure, we'd love to come, wouldn't we, sugar. How thoughtful of you to ask."

Alejandro turned a gloating glare on Jason, who returned it with a murderous glint.

"I am honored to have you as my guests. Tonight then, at the Presto Club after the bout," Alejandro said, wiping his forehead with the back of his hand. He let his gaze linger over Lane. "And next time you are left alone to broil in this heat, fair lady, please, join me inside for that drink."

Jason looked like he could kill the man on the spot as Alejandro walked away.

As soon as Alejandro was out of earshot, Jason took her by the arm. "What the hell do you think you're doing?"

"Taking advantage of a chance to get a step closer to bringing down this operation. A chance you were about to pass up, by the way, for no good reason."

"I had plenty of good reasons."

"Such as?"

"Such as Alejandro has no intention of talking business tonight. He's playing mind games with me, trying to rattle me—and he's using you do to it."

His grip on her arms had become painful. "It looks like his strategy is working." She looked pointedly at the spot where his fingers dug into her flesh.

He released her, swearing. "He just wants to pump you for information tonight. Just like he wanted to when he tried to lure you inside the warehouse just now." He shook his head like he'd just remembered why he'd come back to the car a little while ago. "Damn, Lane. You weren't really going to go in there with him?"

He didn't wait for her to answer. He grabbed her again, but this time, his grip was light. "Listen to me. Don't you ever leave your position without telling me. Don't ever get out of my line of sight, do you hear me?"

He turned her loose and dragged a hand through his hair.

His reprimand should have made her angry, but the tone underneath made her pause. It wasn't the fury she'd expected. She'd have to call it anguish, carrying almost the same resonance as the words he'd uttered in his dream, "No, Karen, no." She almost felt sorry for him, for what she was putting him through, whatever that was. "I hear you."

He wheeled on her. "Then hear this. You had no right jumping in like you did. I am in charge. I make the decisions where we go and who we meet with on this case. You—you are just window dressing."

She was struck dumb, absorbing what he'd said. Then her mind exploded in a red haze. "Window dressing!"

"Yes. You hang on my arm and look pretty when the bad guys are around and stay out of the way when they're not."

Cold with fury, she marched up to him until her chin almost touched his. "Why you conceited, overbearing, cantankerous...argh! I happen to be a very capable investigator. Just because you, in your pious righteousness, have decided you don't want a partner does not mean you can tell me what—"

Before she could finish, he pulled her body flush against his. ''What—''

His cheek brushed across hers, his whiskers scouring her lightly.

''What—'' she tried again ''—are you doing?'' she finished breathlessly, her earlier thought lost.

''We're being watched.'' And then his mouth closed over hers, his lips as soft as his earlier words had been harsh. Over Jason's shoulder, she saw Alejandro leaning on the rail of the loading dock, taking in their performance. Closing her eyes, she leaned into the kiss.

Time passed, whether seconds or minutes she couldn't say. When she opened her eyes, Alejandro was gone. The loading dock was quiet. Jason broke away from her.

His chest heaved as he drew in three deep breaths before he spoke. ''Get in the car,'' he said quietly.

When she didn't move, he dragged his hand through his hair in a gesture that was becoming achingly familiar to her. ''Please,'' he added.

Twenty minutes of silence, punctuated only by her one-word directions, stretched between them as they wound through downtown Atlanta toward the distribution center on Burl Street. Lane used the time to try to fit together the pieces of what she knew about Jason into some identifiable pattern.

The form eluded her.

''Stop behind that building over there,'' she said when they reached the periphery of an industrial complex. She pointed toward an abandoned tenement.

Jason stopped the car in the alley she suggested but before she got out, he stopped her with a hand on her arm. Suspecting another battle approaching, she narrowed her eyes. ''You aren't going to try to get rid of me again, are you?''

The corner of his mouth tweaked up. ''No. I'm beginning to think I'm better off keeping you close by, where I can keep an eye on you. You get into too much trouble when you're left on your own.''

He said it so gently. Not like before, when those same words would have cut deep. Was this a peace offering?

''Does that mean you trust me enough to include me in your investigation?'' She held her breath waiting for his answer.

''No.''

Damn the man. He set her up for that fall. She unlatched the door and stepped out, tugging her book bag behind her, and then marched away from the car. He was really getting to her.

He had reeled around the hood of the car and stood in front of her before she got three steps. Lowering her head, she let her hair fall over her face. She'd be damned if she'd let him see the tears pooled in her eyes.

She tried to slide around him, but he caught her elbow.

''Lane, wait.'' He scuffed his boot on the pavement. Slowly, she raised her head and knew he saw her tears.

''Ah, hell,'' he said, his eyes drifting closed a second before opening to bore into hers. ''I don't trust anyone, and neither should you. That's Rule Number One for staying alive undercover. But that isn't why I don't want to work with you.''

She dipped around him, this time avoiding his grasp. ''Then I guess it's just because you don't like me.''

He flinched. ''Is that what you think?''

Lane shrugged and kept walking, her back to him. The weeds around the building scratched at her ankles. Without stopping or turning around, she asked, ''Why else would you be trying so hard to get rid of me?''

His footsteps crunched solidly behind hers. ''Did you ever stop to think that I might be concerned for your safety?''

''Ha! Because of the criminals, or because I'll be alone with you?''

Jason ignored her jibe, following her through the broken window she'd crawled through.

He stopped her at the foot of a decrepit staircase, holding her in place by the strap of her book bag.

"Would you be reasonable? I already had to bail you out once—no, twice."

Bail me out? She yanked the strap out his hand. "I wasn't quite dead and buried the other night, remember? I still had my gun. Your pals would have been in for quite a surprise if they'd tried anything. And I wasn't going into the building with Alejandro. Why do you think I *accidentally* leaned on the horn? I was trying to attract your attention. So forgive me if I don't bow and scrape when I thank you for saving me, Sir Galahad."

With a huff she whirled around and started up the staircase. She missed a rotten spot on the second step in her hurry to put some distance between them. The old plank cracked, startling her, and she lurched backward in surprise. Just as she thought she was about to land in a heap on her seat, a strong forearm clamped around her middle.

He arched his back and lifted her, steadying her backside against his chest as he spun her down to the foot of the stairs. Even after she had slid through his arms and her feet had landed safely on the floor, he steadied her.

Neither of them moved, frozen in the moment. With his in-drawn breath, his chest pushed harder against her back, sending shivers rippling through her. She'd never reacted so primitively to a man's touch. He had to have felt it.

Twisting slowly around in the circle of his arms, she smiled up at him tentatively, the fight gone out of her. "Thanks, uh, Galahad."

With a muttered oath, he set her aside and eased up the rickety stairs, testing each step carefully before committing his full weight. The old boards creaked in complaint, but held.

She handed him the binoculars after they reached the top. "It's the third one down from the cross street," she told him. "There are two loading docks leading into a gray, cinder-block building."

The line of sight was clear, she knew. She'd checked it out when she first found the place. The tenement's disrepair made it the perfect lookout spot. A chunk of the wall was missing, like a giant termite had taken out a bite, opening the street below to their view. The only disadvantage was that the ceiling was also missing. In a heat wave like they'd been having, the afternoon sun would show them no mercy.

''Did you check out the ownership of that building?'' he asked, raising the binoculars to his face.

''Of course.'' She made a rude noise to show her disgust. What did he think she was, a rookie?

''And?''

She sighed. *And nothing.* ''And, I got lost in a maze of partnerships, corporations and holding companies. My partner promised he would follow up on it when he's through in court.''

She wasn't holding her breath, though. Dan North's idea of following up was usually to prop his feet on the desk and stare at the information she'd already gathered, as if the answer would magically appear.

Jason pulled a cell phone from his pocket and made a call. In seconds he had relayed all the pertinent information about the location of the distribution center and listed the things he wanted to know, including whether or not any of the companies who might own the location were related to the ones who'd had goods stolen.

''You just made some poor Bureau research clerk's life miserable,'' she said as he closed the phone and put it in his jacket pocket.

''No I didn't.''

''I'm telling you, the paperwork on that place is a mess.''

''Won't matter,'' he said.

She raised her eyebrows and knew by his expression that she didn't have to ask the question.

''My researcher isn't at the Bureau, and he doesn't push paper. You'd be surprised what anyone with a computer, a modem and too much time on his hands can find out these days.''

She couldn't believe it. ''You're using a hacker?''

He shrugged. ''Sometimes unofficial channels are more efficient than hassling with the bureaucracy.''

Settling herself in a small nook of shade behind the tallest part of the crumbling wall, Lane mulled over what Jason had said. Using local thugs as drivers, and hackers to do research. It seemed she wasn't the only one Jason didn't trust. If she didn't know better, she'd think he didn't trust his own Bureau.

She might have offered to take a turn watching the distribution center, but instead she pulled out a notepad, pen and textbook from her bag. Since he was so anxious to work alone, she'd leave the surveillance to him.

Besides, these days, stakeouts provided her only quality study time.

Mid-morning became afternoon and, as Lane had predicted, the sun beat down on them relentlessly. She'd sell her soul for a cold diet soda.

The heat didn't seem to affect Jason: he hadn't moved from his watch for the last two hours.

''Still nothing?'' she asked, looking up from her books. The sweat trickling into her eyes made it hard to focus on her work.

He shook his head, then rolled it around his shoulders. As she turned the pages of her book, she felt him watching her. Finally he turned away, pacing the room. She smiled at the way his hair stood on end when he dragged his hand through it.

Afraid he would turn around and catch her staring at him, she looked back down to her notes. ''You might want to stay over on this side of the room. The floor in the middle is pretty rotten.''

In fact, there wasn't a floor at all on the far side of the room, just a gaping hole open to the ground level.

Jason stepped gingerly back onto the solid boards. ''Damn death trap. Hell of a place to pick for surveillance.'' Venting a restless-sounding sigh, he sat down beside her.

She ignored him. Let him taste his own medicine.

He peered sideways at the book on her lap. Following his

eyes to the text, she noticed she'd been on the same page for an hour.

"What are you doing?" he asked.

"Studying."

"For what, the captain's exam?"

She snorted. "Hardly."

He leaned closer, reading over her shoulder, and she tilted the text away from him. His fingers latched on to a page, pulling it back his way.

"C'mon, let me see."

"No, give it back."

"What's the big secret." He pulled harder. When that didn't work, his free hand tucked itself into her side and tickled, distracting her.

She slapped his hand away, laughing, until she looked up at him. Her laugh stopped halfway to her lungs.

His eyes twinkled at their game and his mouth twitched. Then the man actually smiled. A land-o'-mercy, honest-pleasure smile.

Little crow's feet crinkled beside his eyes. His lips curled back from even white teeth, and his left cheek dimpled, mesmerizing her.

He took advantage of her lapse to slide the notebook from her boneless hands.

"Applied Psychology and Social Dissociative Disorders?" Jason whistled. "I'm impressed."

"I told you, I'm studying." She tried to snatch the book back, but missed.

"And I asked why."

"Why this particular book? Maybe I'm hoping for some insight into your character," she teased.

"Very funny," he said. But he wasn't laughing. And he didn't look ready to give up.

She really didn't want to get into this with him. Men tended to be intimidated by women with brains. Especially women with brains and a psychology degree.

"I'm working on my doctorate," she mumbled.

"What?"

"I'm getting my doctorate," she enunciated clearly, "in psychology."

He sat back, looking stunned. "Wow. Beauty, brains and a badge."

She'd expected a wisecrack, but not one delivered with such an undercurrent of genuine respect. The turnaround in his attitude toward her made her vaguely uncomfortable. So did his nearness, but in a different way.

"And here I thought you only appreciated my body." She risked a look up at him and caught him assessing her.

"Wrong. I'm trying very hard *not* to appreciate your body." For a joke, his eyes were far too serious.

What was she doing flirting with this man? She was way over her head with him. Jason wasn't a civilian. He wouldn't have second thoughts when he put his arms around her and found a loaded gun tucked into the small of her back. In fact, she thought, he just might find it exciting.

A Milquetoast was much safer.

Besides, he had made it perfectly clear he did not want her around. Just because he got bored and tried to make a little conversation did not mean he had changed his mind.

Was it her imagination, or did he just lean a little closer?

"So what's the degree for, getting tired of playing cops and robbers?" he asked.

"No. I'm specializing in criminal psychology—thought maybe if I understood the bad guys better, I could catch them faster. Who knows, maybe someday I'll join the FBI."

The smile faded from his face. "Profiler, huh? It's a tough life, from what I hear."

She wished that smile would come back. "Or...I don't know...maybe I'd like to do something different someday."

"Maybe I'd like for you to do something different someday, too," he said.

How had she ever thought this man cold? His expression

was still hard as stone, but the heat radiating from him eclipsed that of the sun shining over his shoulder.

His hand reached out, hesitating an inch from the strand of curls that had fallen over her eyes. He squinted at his fingers like he couldn't quite believe what they were doing. Like they were possessed with a mind of their own.

While they hovered, a horn blared twice from the street below.

Jason's hand fell and he jumped up, grabbing the binoculars as he ran to his lookout spot.

Lane followed him, rising more slowly. It was about time they got a break in this case, but somehow she couldn't muster nearly as much interest for what was happening outside as she had for what might have happened inside, if they hadn't been interrupted.

"Who is it?" she asked, standing behind him.

He peered through the high-powered lenses. "I don't know. But Alejandro just walked out to meet them."

Handing her the binoculars, he covered the ten feet to the staircase in two strides. Even as she called for him to wait, he clattered down the steps two at a time. In his rush, he was pushing his luck that the old staircase would hold together.

"Where are you going?" While she descended more carefully, he was getting away from her.

Climbing through the window, he looked back at her as she reached the bottom of the stairs. "Stay here. I'm going to see who Alejandro is meeting."

Not waiting for her answer, he had started toward the alley already. She ducked out the window behind him.

"Lane, please." His eyes implored her, the laugh lines at their corners gone now, as if they had never existed. "Keep watch from upstairs."

She hesitated. Taking her indecision as consent, he jogged off toward the complex.

From their lookout, she watched him steal toward his target.

With each step he took, her dread grew. He was much too close, treading the edge of insane.

And cops on the edge scared her.

The car idled in front of the distribution center. Alejandro leaned down to talk to the driver as Jason crept up behind him.

Her heart thundered in her chest.

If they see him, he's dead.

Chapter 5

Lane's heart thrashed against her breastbone as Jason edged along the building flanking the alley where the mystery car—a black Lexus—had stopped.

What did he hope to accomplish, getting so close? The car's windows were tinted; he wouldn't be able to ID the driver. Still, he slunk deeper into the alley, taking cover behind a Dumpster a mere ten feet behind the Lexus.

The man is a lunatic. He's almost on top of them.

The sky darkened as quickly as her mood. Until then she hadn't noticed the clouds that had blown in overhead, bringing the smell of rain.

Alejandro's back was to Jason. The truck-hijacking ring's money man hunched over the passenger-side window to talk to the sedan's driver.

A breeze swirled paper scraps around the base of the trash bin. Alejandro laughed and straightened up, digging a cigarette from his pocket. Lane's heart clogged her throat as he twisted in Jason's direction, cupping his hands to shield the lighter from the breeze as he lit the smoke. He puffed twice, then turned back to the car.

She saw Jason draw himself flush against the trash bin so he could overhear the nearby conversation.

Minutes dragged by. Thunder rumbled across the Georgia hills and gooseflesh rose on her arms, as if raised by the static electricity of the storm moving in. If he lived long enough, she was going to kill Jason for putting her through this.

Finally Alejandro stepped back and slapped the roof of the Lexus twice. It pulled away, but Lane's breathing didn't return to normal until the car was out of sight and the warehouse door had closed behind Alejandro.

Her hands trembled while she waited for Jason. He had gone too far, she thought as she headed downstairs. ''What the hell did you think you were doing?'' She blocked his way as he rounded the corner in front of her.

He stopped short, and what might have been a smile faded from his face. ''Trying to get a license plate on the car. I couldn't get an angle to see it, though, but I got—'' A raindrop splattered on his cheek, and he wiped it off with the back of his hand, only to have it quickly replaced by another.

''Got what?'' she asked. ''What was so important you had to risk your life for it?'' She moved forward, intentionally encroaching on his personal space. The rain streamed down in a steady shower.

''Nothing,'' he said. ''I don't suppose you got the license plate?''

She hadn't even thought to look. She'd been so scared, she had forgotten her responsibilities. Shaking her head, she spun around, kicking at the growing puddles on the ground as she stalked away. It wasn't like her to neglect her duty, no matter what the circumstance.

He was suddenly in front of her. For a big man he was quick. ''What is wrong with you?'' he asked harshly.

''What is wrong with *me?* You got so close to Alejandro that he could have smelled your cologne if the breeze had been blowing the other way. You took too big a risk. You put yourself on the line.'' She leaned a millimeter closer. ''And you put me on the line, too.''

The rain shower increased to a downpour.

Jason jerked his head to the side in one violent shake of denial, whipping water off the ends of his hair. ''No—''

''Yes. If you had gotten caught, I would have had to come after you. Like it or not, I am your partner. What happens to you happens to me. And just so you know, I'm not taking any more orders from you, Mr. FBI, so next time you think about running off without me, don't, because I'll be right behind you.''

Jason stared at her during her tirade, then tipped his head up to the angry sky, letting the rain run unabated down his cheeks. Turbulent clouds roiled overhead as the storm blew quickly by.

Slowly he lowered his eyes back to hers, then studied her. The corners of his mouth crinkled up. ''Are you done?'' His chuckle sounded dangerously close to breaking into a laugh.

His mood swings were definitely starting to irritate her. She found nothing remotely funny in this situation.

''Not quite,'' she said, stalling, trying to figure out what was going on in his demented mind.

He cocked an eyebrow at her and grinned suggestively. ''Are you sure?''

She hadn't seen a look so mischievous since her nine-year-old cousin painted red dots on Kelly's cat and claimed the poor animal had contracted chicken pox. Of course, her nine-year-old cousin hadn't packed such a wallop of raw sensuality.

''Why?'' she ventured.

''Because I wouldn't want to give you an order or anything, but I think we should go up and get your books. I think your dissertation is getting very soggy while you stand here yelling at me.''

Jason's shoes squished as he walked down the hallway to his apartment. He hated soggy shoes. Cramming his hand into his pocket, he fished for his keys, carefully keeping his eyes straight ahead as Lane waited behind him.

He should have told her where she could get off, giving him a hard time for doing his job. He about lost his cool when she accused him of putting her in danger. But she looked so darn cute standing there in the rain, dressing him down.

He was sure she hadn't noticed how her wet tank top clung to her curves, outlining the soft mounds of her breasts and the lacy texture of her bra.

He'd wanted to touch her, to shelter her from the rain. But he held back; touching was forbidden.

The strap of her book bag bit into his shoulder until he got the door open and swung it to the floor inside. The books must weigh sixty pounds when they were dry. Wet, they'd bog down an elephant.

Lane headed to the bedroom to change into dry clothes while Jason went into the bathroom. When he emerged in sweats and a cotton T-shirt, he saw Lane curled up on the couch. Jason headed for the kitchen.

The apartment was stuffy. The short-lived rain hadn't cooled things off. If anything, the air hung even hotter and heavier than before. The least he could do was pour her a cold drink while she mourned her drowned work.

He'd been acting like a jerk, trying so hard to keep her at a distance. Worse, he'd made her think he didn't trust her. Didn't even *like* her. No matter how hard she tried to cover it up, he could see the hurt he'd caused in her eyes.

Pulling two tumblers down from the cupboard, he decided to call a truce. It wasn't her fault she misunderstood his intentions. She couldn't know that it wasn't her he didn't trust. It was himself.

In some distant recess of his mind, he knew he was giving in. That this was the first step down a dangerous road. But he cut that thought brutally short.

So what if he felt the need for a little companionship? After what he'd heard Alejandro say this afternoon, this case would be over within a few days, anyway. He could enjoy her company for a few days without things getting out of hand. Couldn't he?

A twinge of guilt pricked at his conscience for not telling her about the payoff he'd heard Alejandro confirm with the man in the car—the man Jason assumed was the head of the operation. But his conscience was easily soothed. Just because he wanted to talk to her didn't mean he was crazy enough to actually involve her any further in this case than he had to.

Carrying two tall glasses of iced tea, he walked back to the living room. With books and papers dripping from every tabletop, the room looked like it had been turned upside down.

Like his life.

Just when he thought he'd dug a hole deep enough that the light of day would never again shine in, Lane McCullough came along with a halogen lamp.

She sat at the end of the couch, her chin propped on her fist and her damp locks curling wildly around her face, staring morosely at her books.

"They'll dry, won't they?" he asked, handing her a glass of tea.

"Probably. With curly covers and the pages all stuck together." She took a long drink from her glass.

When she finished, her tongue darted around the edges of her mouth to pick up the excess moisture. He wished he'd thought to turn away before she lowered the glass. She really did have a great mouth.

"Thanks," she said, lifting the tea in salute.

"You're welcome."

Obviously neither of them knew what to say next. They sat in an uncomfortable silence until Lane sighed and set her glass down on the end table, reaching for the phone. "I need to check in with the precinct," she said, lifting the receiver off of the telephone as she pulled it into her lap. "They'll be expecting a report."

He slid down the couch toward her and pressed his finger over the button that cut off the line. ''Not on my phone.''

''What? Why not?''

He took the receiver from her hand and placed it back into the cradle, then lifted the phone from her lap. ''It's too easily traced. A call from here to the police station could blow our cover.''

She was quiet a moment, then raised her eyebrows at him. ''Isn't that just a little bit paranoid? The kind of tapping you're talking about takes specialized equipment and access. We're after a two-bit truck-hijacking ring here, not the Russian Mafia.''

Jason surged to his feet, leaving the phone propped on the back of the couch, out of her reach. ''Don't underestimate these people. They are not two-bit, and it's not as hard as you think to get phone records.''

''Oh, I forgot. I'd be surprised what any fool with a computer and a modem can find out, right?'' she asked, more than a touch of sarcasm tainting her words. ''Do you really think Morales and Grumman know a CD-Rom drive from a four-wheel drive?

''No. But if I can hire a hacker, so can they.''

She tapped her finger on her jaw. ''All right, I'll give you that. But that doesn't mean that they're actually smart enough to do it.''

Jason didn't want to fight with her over this. Not now that he'd finally decided to make peace with her. He had actually started to feel human again.

He eyed her seriously, swallowed hard and set the phone back in her lap. ''Fine. You make the choice. You decide if it's worth the risk.'' Then he walked away, into the kitchen.

As he poured himself another glass of tea, he heard her pad into the room behind him. Turning around, he found himself staring straight into serious green eyes.

''Maybe we could stop somewhere at a pay phone while we're out tonight,'' she offered.

He felt his smile growing from the inside out. She held her tea glass out, and he refilled it from the pitcher in his hand.

"Sounds like a plan," he said.

She returned his smile nervously. "Well, I'd better get moving if I'm going to make myself presentable for Alejandro's party."

He'd forgotten about the damn party. He wished there was some way out of it. At least some way to keep Lane out of it. He eyed her sweats and T-shirt. "Did you pack anything appropriate for this little soiree?"

He stood, dumbfounded at what was wrong, as her cheeks turned bright red. She fought back the blush, and her eyes narrowed. "I'm sure I can find something that won't embarrass you too much. After all, we wouldn't want your *window dressing* to be inappropriately dressed." With that, she stormed out of the kitchen.

Ouch, he guessed he deserved that. What on earth had he been thinking when he'd called her that, anyway? Just because he'd been scared out of his wits when he saw her at the car talking to Alejandro didn't give him the right to insult her.

He'd give her a while to calm down, and then go and talk to her. Through the doorway he heard the bathroom door slam and the shower come on, then shut off a few minutes later. Suddenly he wished he had something stronger to drink than iced tea.

When the doors and drawers and whatever else stopped slamming, he eased down the hallway. "Lane?" he called.

"What?" she answered sharply. Apparently she hadn't vented quite all of her anger yet. Her head and bare shoulders curved around the bedroom doorway. Swept back from her face, her hair was held in by a comb jeweled with stones the same color as her eyes. A few tendrils escaped to fall in soft spirals beside her face, touched up with a bit of makeup, but not overdone. The effect was both elegant and elemental. A heady combination.

He schooled his features into impassivity. It was going to be a long night.

"What?" she asked again, softer this time.

"Um, I just wanted to tell you... About what I said about you being window dressing." Taking a deep breath, he met her gaze head-on. Her eyes never wavered. The woman never backed down from anything. He should know that by now. "I was out of line. I'm sorry."

She gave him a caustic look, but it was somehow softer than it had been. "Does that mean I'm promoted all the way to faithful-but-inept sidekick?"

How could she make him laugh even when he was groveling? It took him a moment to regain enough composure to continue. "I know you're a capable investigator. If you weren't, you would never have found that warehouse, or the distribution center."

"Or you."

"Yeah, or me."

Lane grinned. "Hmm. I'm glad you've come to your senses, but it does present a bit of a problem."

"What problem."

Her eyes sparkled like the devil's scepter as she stepped out from behind the doorway. "The dress I picked is more suited toward window dressing than capable investigator garb." She turned around slowly in front of him. "Should I change it?"

"After," he said, his voice quavering more than he would have liked.

The emerald gown clung to her body like an erotic embrace, dipping just low enough in front to be tantalizing but tasteful. In back it dipped somewhat lower.

"After what?" she asked.

He grinned. "After you're done giving me CPR."

It was going to be a very, very long night.

Lane watched Jason surreptitiously as he held the door for her on the way out of the apartment. His attitude had changed.

Not that she was complaining, it was definitely for the better. She just wasn't sure she understood it.

She slipped her hand through the wristband of the tiny satin purse that matched her dress.

He frowned at it. "Where is your gun?"

She put her tongue firmly in her cheek and smiled up at him. "You don't want to know."

He blinked, then looked like someone punched him in the solar plexus. She couldn't help but laugh.

He steered her down the hallway in the opposite direction from the way they normally went and stopped in front of an elevator. Since he always took the stairs, she hadn't known the building had an elevator. At any rate she was grateful. The narrow skirt on this dress didn't allow her much maneuverability. She probably would have had to go down the steps sideways.

The bell dinged and the doors slid open to the first floor. Jason guided her into the hallway and out the front doors of the building with his palm on the small of her back, the brush of his fingers tingling her bare skin.

"Now that we're on speaking terms again," she said as he settled himself behind the wheel of the Corvette, "shouldn't we get our stories straight?"

"What stories? You're a hairstylist from Macon and I'm...I'm from Michigan."

"I'm a nail technician. And you're from Michigan, that's it?" She shook her head and rolled her eyes. "I forgot. Your cover is not to have a cover, right?"

He turned his head her way when they stopped at a red light, but in the dark interior of the car, she couldn't be quite sure if the glint in his eye was exasperation or amusement. "What else do you want to know?"

She thought a minute, and Jason accelerated through the intersection when the light turned green. "How did we meet?"

"How do you usually meet men?"

Definitely amusement. And maybe a little curiosity?

"At work."

"You usually date cops?"

She wrinkled her nose. "No. Never."

Even in the dark she could see his eyebrows shoot up. "You usually date criminals?"

"You're the first."

"Who else do you meet at a police station besides cops and criminals?"

"Lots of people."

"Like?"

Boy, when he decided to get curious, he went all out. She did not want to talk about Carl tonight. "None of your business. We were talking about how you and I met, remember? You're the one who told me not to underestimate these guys. We don't want them to cross us up."

His expression sobered. "All right, all right. I've never been to Macon, so we'd better make it here."

"Good. We can say we met at a club or something. What clubs do you know in Atlanta?"

He shrugged, obviously thinking. "The Blue Note, Rhapsody."

"You like Jazz clubs?"

"Yeah."

"That's great. Me, too. There was a festival in Piedmont Park last April. How about we met there?"

"Fine."

Lane sighed. "Yeah. Fine. No." Would she ever get a complete sentence out of him? "Tell me about this special order you're trying to make with these guys."

"It's a new chip, supposed to revolutionize cellular telephone technology. Supply is limited and demand is high, so they're worth a fortune right now. And there's only one company in the Southeast that makes them, right here in Atlanta. They only make one shipment a week. If I can convince Alejandro that the deal is big enough, he'll let me place my order directly with the main man. Then if they hit the shipment, and I make payment, I've got him."

"But you're setting up those drivers to be hijacked."

"None of the drivers who've had their trucks taken have been hurt. Well, except that one ex-Marine in Alabama who pulled a gun on them and got pistol-whipped for his trouble. But I'll have the Bureau replace the regular drivers with agents, just to be sure."

"Oh, you're actually going to let the Bureau in on what you're doing?" she asked sarcastically. "How by-the-book of you."

He made a face at her before he checked the rearview mirror for the umpteenth time. He took the time to study each car as traffic wove around them on their circuitous route to the Presto Club. As the crow flies, they could have been there fifteen minutes ago. But Jason never went anywhere, she was learning, as the crow flies.

At a quarter past nine they pulled up to the club. Jason tipped the valet, but insisted on parking the 'Vette himself. "I want to check the lot for that Lexus," he explained as they pulled away from the valet stand.

He circled the lot twice before he gave up and admitted the mystery car was not there.

The club was even more obnoxious and noisy than she'd expected. Blue lights flashed, instantly making her wish she'd taken an aspirin before she'd left the apartment. The dry, smoke-filled air was worse than the heat and humidity outside.

Taking her hand, Jason made a slow circle around the place, checking it out and probably looking for Alejandro, she realized. They both took drinks from a scantily clad waitress, carrying a tray of assorted beverages. Jason reached for his wallet, but the waitress stopped him, her fingers lingering on his forearm. She leaned close. Much closer than necessary, Lane thought, to be heard over the music.

''Drinks are on the house tonight,'' the waitress said. She didn't back away from Jason.

''Who should I thank?'' he asked.

She pointed to a table in a dark corner nook. Lane could just make out Alejandro's profile.

Another customer waved for the waitress's attention. Before she walked away, she leaned back toward Jason. ''Y'all have a good time now. And you let me know if I can do anything else for you.'' Her gaze roamed up and down Jason's long form suggestively. ''Anything at all.''

The nerve of some women. The waitress didn't even try to cover her come-on. Or her...assets, Lane thought as the woman sauntered away, her short-shorts weaving side to side with the sway of her hips.

At least Jason hadn't returned her attention, his concentration focused on Alejandro's table. Their suspect sat at a table with three other Latino men, shadowboxing the smoky haze around him in an animated display of uppercuts and left-handed jabs. When he noticed Lane and Jason, he waved them over.

Alejandro crushed out a cigarette and stood up as Lane approached. Lane didn't take his gesture as gentlemanly. Not when she knew the true nature of his character.

''Jason, Señorita McCullough, I am happy you decided to join us,'' Alejandro said, sitting after Lane had taken a seat.

Jason tucked himself into the last remaining chair. ''I take it Montoya won the fight.''

''Yes, it was a beautiful bout. You should have seen him, he fought like a mad bull.'' Alejandro regaled them with a blow-by-blow account of the boxing match. Midway through his account of round three, the other men at the table excused themselves. They apparently had heard this before.

Others came and went, and Alejandro interrupted his tale long enough to greet each partygoer. Much to Lane's dismay, several times he repeated key parts of the fight for the benefit of the newcomers. One and all paid homage to the great Montoya.

Lane whiled away the time by memorizing each face, creating a mental catalog of suspects. Her catalog entries soon overran her mental capacity to store them, and one set of features blurred into another.

The night dragged on, ever tediously. By 11:00 p.m., Jason's eyes looked as watery and glazed as hers felt, and yet they were no closer to the leader of the truck-hijacking operation than they had been that afternoon.

The latest minglers left the table, and Jason jumped at his chance, cutting Alejandro off before the man got in another word about the fight.

''It's getting late. Are we going to talk business or not?'' Jason asked.

Alejandro looked amused and lit another cigarette. Lane resisted the urge to swipe at the cloud of smoke in her face.

''Ah, yes,'' Alejandro said. ''You wish to make a special order. Tell me what it is you want so badly.''

Jason shook his head. ''Not here. And not to you. I want to talk to the boss. I'm not tipping you off to this until I have some guarantees.''

Alejandro no longer looked amused. A man with an ego the size of his probably didn't like being relegated to the role of underling. He shrugged. ''We already have more business than we can handle.''

Jason slid his chair back abruptly, stood up and tugged Lane up with him by the hand. ''Fine. If you don't want my money, I'll go elsewhere,'' he said, turning to leave.

Alejandro blocked their way around the table. The two men locked eyes, measuring each other. Alejandro took a drag from his cigarette and exhaled the smoke slowly. ''How much money are we talking about?''

''Two hundred fifty thousand, more or less.''

Alejandro's eyes narrowed a fraction. ''A quarter of a million. That kind of payoff is difficult to pass up.''

''So do we talk to the boss, or not?'' Jason asked.

The noise of the club, the beat of the bass drum, the clink

of glassware, faded behind Alejandro's pause. Lane's heart beat triple-time.

"I'll think about it," Alejandro finally said. He stepped quickly to Lane's side, ignoring Jason, his eyes only on her. "I think better with a beautiful woman in my arms. May I have the honor of this dance, *señorita?*"

Before she could decline, he led her toward the dance floor.

She glanced once over her shoulder at Jason. With his fists clenched and his jaw rigid, he looked like he was trying to decide whether to rush Alejandro, or just pull his gun and shoot him.

Jason felt his blood pound all the way down to his fingertips as Alejandro led Lane to the dance floor. She looked over her shoulder at him as she walked away. But instead of the fear he expected to see there, he saw a warning. She told him not to blow this. They needed this chance.

But they didn't. He had another way to corner these goons; she didn't have to put herself through this. Only she didn't know that. Because he hadn't been honest with her. So now she had to let a slug touch her. Dance with him. And Jason had to stand by and watch. Fitting punishment for himself, he thought, but what had she done to deserve this?

Some days he hated this job. More days he hated himself.

He took his seat at the table as Lane and Alejandro stepped into a light rock tempo. She was a natural, finding the rhythm easily and gliding along with Alejandro's steps. Grinding his teeth, Jason tracked their movement across the floor. The urge to run after her hit him so hard he had to hold on to the seat of the chair to stop himself when he lost sight of her for a moment.

The waitress wearing the skimpy shorts stopped in front of him, her rear prominently displayed in his face, then turned around and offered him a drink. He didn't even know what he said to her, just that she stormed off with a bitter curse.

Lane's dark curly head bobbed into view amidst the throng of dancers, and he blew out a pent-up breath.

The upbeat song ended. Jason sat back, expecting Alejandro to steer Lane back to the table. He knew the guy was trying to get the upper hand in this battle of wills. It was working.

A new strain of music floated off the bandstand, and Jason looked up in time to see Alejandro back away from the bandstand, with Lane's hand captured in his. Unlike the upbeat tune before it, this song was slow and seductive. And Alejandro had requested it. Damn him.

He pulled Lane close and swayed with the music. She looked stiffer than before, but went along. Jason closed his eyes against the sight of her in Alejandro's arms until he realized that he couldn't look away, not when she might need him.

Alejandro tightened his grip on her. Lane struggled subtly, pressing her palms against his chest, but Alejandro only held her tighter.

That was it. Jason jumped up, almost tipping over the chair behind him. He reached the dance floor in four strides and had pulled Alejandro around to face him before he'd decided whether to give the man a warning or just bury his fist in the SOB's face right away. If the man liked boxing so much, he was about to get a hands-on demonstration—up close and personal.

"Cutting in?" Alejandro asked while Jason was still thinking.

Lane stepped between them. "Jason and I haven't had a chance to dance in a long time," she said. She rested one hand on his shoulder and the other at his hip, as if ready to step into his embrace. "I'm sure you understand, Alejandro."

Alejandro bowed his head and stepped away, smiling. Even giving up his dance, the man obviously knew he'd won this round.

Jason stood still a moment before he found Lane's eyes looking up at him.

"Aren't we going to dance?" she asked.

He tried. Really tried. He reached around her, tried resting his hand higher, then lower, but found only the bare skin of her back. Abruptly he tugged her toward the door. ‘‘No.’’

Maybe someday he’d be able to touch a woman like that again and enjoy it. Maybe he could hold her and feel her move against him without guilt and horror rushing in and stealing his breath, driving him to his knees like a sudden wind shear.

Maybe. But he doubted it would be in this lifetime.

Chapter 6

Alejandro stood by the door with his arm around a waitress's waist and his hand resting on the backside of her short-shorts. "Leaving so soon, my friends? We haven't finished discussing your special order."

Jason didn't look at the man as they brushed by. "You have my number. Call me," Jason's look swept over the waitress sidled up against Alejandro, "when you've finished thinking."

The air outside the club, cloying as it was in this heat, cleared Jason's head enough that he remembered to scan the parking lot once more for the black Lexus he'd seen at the distribution center. That car was the key, he knew. When he found its owner, he would find the leader of this ring of thieves.

Telling himself he was checking for tails, he wound his Corvette around the side streets of Atlanta. The truth was, he was avoiding going back to the apartment. He couldn't take Lane home yet. Not when the place was so small, so quiet and so...private. The less time he spent alone with her, the better.

"How about some dinner?" he asked her. It was already

late. They could eat, and then he could send her off to bed. Alone.

Lane chose a tiny Italian place just outside the city limits. As he opened the door, the soft whine of a violin straining toward a higher note drifted out. Inside, candlelight flickered off red-and-white-checked tablecloths.

No problem, he thought, *just a romantic little dinner for two.*

Lane nodded toward a pay phone down a narrow hallway. "Why don't you get us a table. I'll make my phone calls."

He shuffled restlessly. From the dining area, he wouldn't be able to see her at the phone. "I'll wait," he told her.

Lane shrugged, obviously not missing the fact that he wasn't letting her out of his sight. "Whatever."

He gave her a few seconds of privacy, then strolled down the hall after her. "I'll call again as soon as I can," he heard her say before she hung up.

"Happy now? You've done your duty and let your captain know you're still in one piece."

Lane wrinkled her brow. "Captain Bowling wasn't there. That was my real partner, Dan."

He knew she hadn't meant anything by it, but the way she said, "real partner," bothered Jason. What did that make him? He didn't know this Dan, but he already intensely disliked the man. Lane, still frowning, didn't look too happy with him, either.

"So what's wrong with Dan?" *Besides the fact that he's your "real" partner.*

"I'm just surprised he's there at this hour. Dan considers working from five o'clock to 5:05 excessive overtime."

"Maybe he's got a new case."

She shook her head. "He's in court all week."

Jason's mistrustful instincts stirred. Cops didn't usually bust their butts after a full day in court, not unless something big was at stake. He made a mental note to check the guy out. Quietly, of course.

He looked at Lane, schooling the suspicion from his face.

Undoubtedly she wouldn't like what he was thinking. "Ready to sit down?" he asked.

"One more," she said, digging in her purse for coins. Jason pulled out a quarter and handed it to her. Watching as she dropped the coin in the slot and dialed, he pushed his hands into his pockets and propped his back against the wall. She smiled as she greeted her sister.

Kelly. He should have figured; he knew they were close. While Lane chatted with her sister, Jason strolled to the end of the hall and back.

"Are you sure, Kelly?" he heard Lane ask, looking up at him as he reached her side again. "This case could take a while. I hate to think about you staying there alone so long. You know Aunt Sarah wouldn't mind staying with you."

Lane winced and rolled her eyes at the ceiling. Kelly obviously did not want Aunt Sarah for a housemate.

"Okay, okay, Kelly. I know you can take care of yourself," Lane continued. "You just be careful, and don't overdo. I'll check in with you as often as I can. Take of yourself."

She listened a moment. "I will, Kelly." Then, looking up at Jason she added, "Yes, I'll take care of him, too."

Jason smiled.

"Me, too, Kelly. 'Bye." Lane settled the handpiece into its cradle.

"How is your sister?"

Lane rolled her eyes again as they walked into the restaurant's main dining area. "Happy to be rid of me for a while. She says I cramp her style."

Jason was fascinated by the way a tiny furrow formed above the bridge of her nose when she frowned. Sometimes the smallest things about her intrigued him.

"Kelly's pretty independent, but I still worry about her being alone," she said.

Jason held a chair for her at a corner table. "She seemed self-reliant to me."

"Yeah, but she'll always be my little sister. Even if she won't ever take my advice."

"I thought you were twins."

She grinned at him as she spread a linen napkin in her lap. "I was born at 11:55 p.m. Kelly was born at 12:09 a.m. Even though we were only fourteen minutes apart, I'm a day older. She should show me more respect."

He chuckled with her, the first real moments of pleasure he could remember in...it seemed like a lifetime.

A dark-haired waiter stopped at the table and handed them menus. A few minutes later he brought back the two glasses of wine they'd ordered and took their dinner order.

When they were alone again, Jason asked Lane, "So is Kelly okay? You seem worried about her."

The furrow of worry reappeared on her face. "Her back has been really bad lately. She won't go to the doctor, says he'll just say the same thing he always says, 'Get some rest.' But I think it has been so bad she hasn't been sleeping. And she still insists on sitting at that darn computer all day, working."

"What happened to her back?"

"This time?" she asked. "She declared war on the weeds in her garden, and the weeds won."

"I meant originally."

Jason stared, mesmerized, as the pad of her finger circled the lip of her glass before she answered.

"Drunk driver." She drew a deep breath. "We were in high school, and Kelly was trying out for the cheerleading squad. She wouldn't say so, but I knew she wanted my dad to come and see her cheer. So I badgered him until he promised to take her."

She shook her head. "He forgot, as usual. He'd been a good father once, but he'd become so disillusioned in those last few years it was like he forgot he even had children. I was furious. I knew his being there meant a lot to her, so I called around until I found him. We argued and I shamed him into taking her. That was the last time I ever talked to my dad."

Lane took a slow sip of wine. "They were rushing because they were so late. My father was killed instantly. Kelly's seat belt saved her life, but caused a Chance fracture—a break in one of the lumbar vertebrae in the lower back, L4, to be exact."

Jason wished he hadn't asked. He could see old wounds opening in Lane, fresh pain pouring through them.

"She was wheelchair-bound at first. After her back healed, she had to learn to walk all over again—it took years of physical therapy. Even now she has terrible pain and has to wear a brace when she does anything strenuous. She loves her gardening so much, but she pays a price."

"I'm sorry. I hope they got the bastard that did it."

Lane flinched and then set her lips in a thin line. "You misunderstand. My father *was* the drunk driver. I called him at his favorite bar. I should have let him be, but for once, I wanted him to be the father she needed instead of the used-up cop he was."

Jason cursed his stupidity. He'd made her hurt even worse, and the need to make it better ran deep within him. Reaching out, he brushed his hand over hers on the table. "I'm sorry," he repeated, meaning it even more.

"Don't be. Kelly and I have moved on. We're fine." Easing away from his attempt at comfort, she wrapped both hands around the curve of her wineglass as if it took two hands to steady it. "Besides, I don't believe in saying 'I'm sorry.'"

Jason frowned. "Why is that?"

"Because that's what he always used to say. Sorry he missed my swim meet because he was too hungover to get out of bed. Sorry he couldn't come home at night because some bartender wouldn't give him his keys. Sorry my mother grew old too young, worrying about him. By the time someone gets around to saying they're sorry, the damage is already done."

She looked up at him, struggling with a smile about as real as a circus clown's painted-on tears. *"Sorry always comes too late."*

What a sad attitude, he thought. How could she say she'd

accepted her father's death and her sister's disability when the wounds still festered so obviously?

Morbidly he wondered how deep her injuries went. Lane had struck him as such a solid person, the kind who had every aspect of her life totally together.

He should have known no one was that lucky. And Lane wasn't that simple. She had more turns and twists in her than a maze.

Dredging up the past like this was hurting her, and still his fascination wouldn't let him stop. "Your father was a cop?"

"Twenty-two years," she said. "But at the end there wasn't much of him left behind the badge. He said the world had changed. With the gangs and the pushers and the kids on crack he couldn't tell the good guys from the bad ones anymore. I guess he thought booze could help him figure it out."

"And you still became a cop." It was a statement of wonder, not a question, but she answered it, anyway.

"Yeah, well, I've always been kind of competitive. I guess I needed to prove that I was tougher than my old man."

"There's got to be more to it than that."

She sighed. One shoulder lifted, then fell. "I have this need, you know, to know what makes people tick." She lowered her eyes but looked up at him through heavy lashes, thick and damp. "That's really why I didn't bust you at the warehouse, you know. I was curious about you."

Damnation. His heart sunk like a stone in water. As if it wasn't hard enough to keep his distance from her, she had to tell him that. She was *curious* about him?

"Anyway, I needed to know what drove my father away from his home, away from us. I thought that by becoming a cop and going through what he went through every day, I would understand what went on in his mind."

"And do you now?"

She shook her head. "Eleven years on the force, and I'm still trying to figure it out."

"Ah, thus the psychology degree."

She looked surprised. ''I never thought of it that way. Maybe it is my dad I'm trying to understand more than the criminals.''

The more he knew about Lane, the more he found to admire. Her strength, her compassion, her openness—traits he didn't see often in his line of work.

He knew he should stop. This had already gotten far too personal. But he had to know it all. He waited until the waiter had set down her plate of linguini with clams and his lasagna, then asked, ''What about your mom?''

''She hung on a few years, long enough for me to get through college and come home. But Daddy's death killed her, too. It just took her longer to die.''

''And you've been taking care of Kelly ever since?''

''We've been taking care of each other.''

The concept wasn't foreign to Jason, people sharing their lives, balancing each other. It had just been a long time since he'd realized how much he missed it.

She put up a brave front, no less than he would expect from someone with her courage, but he could see in her eyes how painful these memories were.

Without letting himself think about it, he slid his hand across the table and covered hers, turning it over and stroking his thumb in the curve of her palm. She squeezed her eyes shut. Stubborn pride, he imagined, keeping the tears she'd gathered from falling.

At that moment any plan he'd ever made to keep her at arm's length fled. He couldn't remember why he'd ever wanted such a thing, anyway.

If the cell phone in his pocket hadn't trilled right then, breaking the pull he felt toward her, he honestly couldn't say what he would have done next.

With a start he lurched back in his chair, letting go of her hand to pull the phone out and raise the antenna. After listening awhile, he made a curt acknowledgment and hit the End Call button.

A few days ago this would have been good news. He would

have relished the opportunity presented to him. Now it tied his stomach in knots. Lane was watching him, he knew, waiting for an explanation.

''Alejandro arranged for me to meet the main man.'' Returning the phone slowly to his pocket, he sighed. ''Tomorrow.''

Already drying, her eyes looked brighter. A fox back on the hunt. ''That was quick.''

He pushed his plate away, no longer hungry. ''Too quick.'' *And way too easy,* his instincts told him.

''Lucky for us that, whoever he is, he's greedier than he is cautious.''

''Yeah. Lucky us,'' he grumbled.

She either hadn't noticed the foul turn in his mood, or she was ignoring it. Stabbing the last bite of linguini from her plate, she quizzed him. ''So what's the setup?''

Setup. He wished she'd used a different choice of words. ''It is in an alley on the east side.'' *God, they would pick an alley.*

''Ugh,'' she said, wiping clam sauce from her lips with her napkin. ''Alleys are tough. How do you want to work it? Do you want me with you, or off a ways where I can cover your back?''

The knots in his stomach tightened, twisted. ''Neither. I want you to go to the police station and help your partner follow up on the ownership of the distribution center.''

She gaped at him, and he knew he was in trouble. ''I really thought we were past this.''

''Lane, this is just an introduction. It's no big deal.''

''Fine. Then we'll take care of it, and then both of us can go to the police station,'' she said.

Desperation clawed its way into his voice. ''There is no reason for you to go.'' He threw his napkin down on the table in front of him. ''Hell, there's no reason for either one of us to go.''

Damn. He hadn't meant to say that. She was too smart, and too quick, to miss the implications. As if on cue, she tipped her head up to him, the anger in her eyes quickly replaced by questions.

He wanted to lie to her. It should be easy enough. What was working undercover except lying for a living? So why had the ability abandoned him with one leap into her deep, green eyes?

He blew out a resigned breath. "I got close enough this afternoon to hear Alejandro ask the guy in the car about a big payoff they're expecting," he admitted. "It seems they're cashing out on a big deal, and both Alejandro and his boss are going to be there. The money changes hands three days from now, 9:00 a.m."

"Then all we have to do is catch them in the exchange. We'll have the top man with his hands dirty. Do you know where?"

He nodded, a tight knot forming in his stomach. If he'd held his secrets, he might have been able to keep her out of this. No such luck now. She'd insist on being right in the middle of it.

And heaven help him, he'd be there with her. "The place you showed me. Burl Street. The distribution center."

She fidgeted with her fork, absorbed by the reflection of candlelight on the silver. Thinking so deeply like that, she reminded him of himself when his mind was stuck in overdrive.

"We'll need some help." She tapped her index finger on her lip as she brainstormed. "Teams to cover the back entrance to the distribution center. And men at both ends of Burl Street." She snapped her fingers. "The abandoned building we used today will make a good command center. They can monitor us from there when we go in."

The knot in Jason's stomach grew with every word that came out of her mouth. With her last sentence, it became a living thing, kicking and squirming in his belly like it wanted out. "Whoa, slow down. We're talking about a simple bust, not the standoff at Waco. Maybe we should keep it low-key. The fewer people that know about it, the better."

"Jason." She sounded exasperated. "This is a huge break.

We can't afford to miss this chance.'' She pushed the hair away from the nape of her neck, tipping her head back as she thought. ''Why didn't you tell me about this earlier? We have a lot of planning—''

She must have figured out the answer to her own question, because she quit mid-sentence. She let her hair fall and it cascaded over her shoulders. ''You weren't going to tell me about this at all, were you? Or anyone else, for that matter. You were planning to do this alone.''

He watched the energy fizzle out of her like helium from a leaky balloon.

She stared at him in disbelief. ''My God, you really don't trust anyone, do you?''

Jason's frustration at four years of life in self-imposed hell fueled his anger until it nearly reached the boiling point. He wanted to spew out that he had trusted someone once. She'd been his partner in every sense of the word—half of everything he was. She'd been a petite thing, but full of life and energy. Despite her size, Jason had trusted her at his back more than any of the bigger, stronger, male agents in the Bureau.

Where had it gotten him? Worse, where had it gotten her? He'd trusted Karen Bastille so much that he lowered his guard. With that guard down, he'd done the unthinkable, made the unredeemable mistake and Karen had paid for it with her life.

Jason used the pain that remembering always brought on as a tool to regain control of his anger. Fixing his features into the impenetrable mask he'd used so often, he met the compassion in her eyes with a hard gaze.

Didn't he trust anyone? ''I don't really think you want me to answer that,'' he said flatly.

Lane gathered up her purse and rose from her chair with a calm that she hoped belied her inner turmoil. How could anyone live like that, without faith? And why did she care?

She made it outside the restaurant without looking back and

then gave in to the urge. What was she going to do, leave without him? She wouldn't get a block. Not dressed like this.

Jason had stood up and had his wallet out. He dropped several bills on the table and strode toward the door in an unhurried step. She noticed for the first time the way his eyes constantly scanned left and right as he walked. The way he rolled off the balls of his feet. And the way his arms hung loose at his sides, propelling him along, but never far from his body. Most people would think he was completely at ease. That was the illusion he hoped to create. Lane knew, though, that every action had a purpose.

His eyes scanned for dangers lurking in the shadows. His gait prepared him to move quickly in any direction, suddenly. His hands were never far from reaching for the pistol slung under his left shoulder.

His illusion didn't work on her anymore. Cocked like the hammer of a gun, ready to explode in less than the blink of an eye, she saw him as every bit the hard-edged cop that he was.

Her stomach roiled and cramped. Was that why he bothered her so much? Because he was a cop? And a troubled one, at that, like her father?

He passed through the door and nudged her toward the parking lot with his hand at her elbow. With her self-doubt on the rise, she quickened her pace and opened a few feet between them, needing the space to sort out her feelings.

As her feet hit the pavement, tires squealed. A TransAm pulled away from the curb. Two staccato bursts ripped through the quiet night.

Lane felt Jason in motion behind her a fraction of a second before her own reflexes kicked in. Jason's body hurtled into her, slamming her against the eatery's brick exterior.

His body twisted in front of her, his gun out and leveled on the sports car in one smooth motion. His finger was on the trigger. The car veered off as a beer bottle arced out the window and plinked to the pavement. Rock music blared in her ears.

She knocked his arm down before he could pull the trigger. A pimply faced teenager in a ball cap stared slack-jawed at them out the window of the TransAm. The car backfired a third time when the driver gunned it into the street against the light.

Jason's free hand trembled where it curved protectively over her head. His chest heaved as he pulled back enough to cup her face in his hands, the gun he still held chilling her cheek.

"Lane?" His voice shook with the tremors she felt passing through his body. "Are you hurt?"

She gasped to recover the breath he had knocked out of her. She couldn't respond, not yet, for lack of air. When he gathered her to him as if to pick her up and run for help, she put a hand out to stop him.

Never had she seen a look so untamed. She couldn't tell if it was rage, panic or maybe insanity, as he struggled for control.

"Okay," she wheezed, "not hurt." Pushing farther away from him, she bent double and sucked in a half breath.

He watched her struggle for air, and the panic in his eyes hardened as he seemed to realize he was responsible for the problem, not the boys in the car.

He pushed himself away from her, sitting down on the sidewalk, his back against the brick wall. Slowly he folded his arms across his knees, the gun still dangling from his right hand. His harsh breath racked the air.

She took a hiccupy breath. It might have been deeper, but a half sob got in its way. "You could have killed those boys."

Finally Jason stood up while she still struggled to capture a few shallow breaths. He wiped his forehead on his sleeve and tucked the gun in his jeans. He had repainted some of his mask of composure, but his hand trembled where it touched her arm. "I'm sorry," he said.

With no more explanation than that, he let her go and walked off toward his Corvette.

He was sorry. She straightened up. For what? For overreacting? For aiming his gun at innocent teenagers? For slamming her against a brick wall so hard she saw stars?

How many times had her father said, "I'm sorry"? But he'd never been sorry enough to change. And he hadn't been around to tell Kelly he was "sorry" for his biggest mistake, had he? He hadn't been the one to tell her sister that she might never walk again, or to hold her hand through hours, months of grueling therapy. No, he'd left that to Lane.

And then Lane had been sorry. Sorry for trusting her father. Sorry for loving him. But the damage was already done. *Sorry always comes too late.*

Suddenly the pattern to Jason's behavior that she'd been searching for materialized in her mind. Its outline left a bitter taste in her mouth. The moodiness, the introversion, his distrust of others, even in his own agency, it made sense. Undercover work was the most stressful of all assignments. No one could hold up to that kind of pressure for long. Jason Stateler showed all the signs of a serious stress disorder. Burnout.

He'd told her she would regret agreeing to work this case with him. He was right. Just as soon as this case was over, she had to get as far away from him as possible. Because she knew, all too well, the havoc and heartbreak that came with being too close to a cop on the edge.

Chapter 7

Lane sat in the passenger seat of Jason's Corvette, watching him squint. As they pulled into the alley designated for the meet, she didn't think the pinched look on his face was due entirely to the bright sun.

"We don't have to be here," he said. "We could just stay out of sight until the bust Friday."

They'd already had this conversation twice.

"We don't want to spook them into changing their plans. If we suddenly drop off the radar, they might get nervous. Besides, this is a simple meet and greet—no money exchange or anything. What are you so nervous about?"

"There's no such thing as a *simple* meet." He spared her a glance and a frown. "I wish you'd have stayed home."

He could give a girl a complex, telling her all the time he didn't want her around. Still, she didn't let it irritate her this time. She knew his attitude was rooted in fear.

Last night he'd tried again to apologize for overreacting outside the restaurant. Then he tried again to talk her out of coming to the meet, but it had been a halfhearted attempt.

She'd barely spoken to him, and it obviously worried him. As she'd brushed her hair before going to bed, he crept up behind her so quietly that it had startled her when she'd looked up to find his image in the mirror behind hers.

"Are you sure you're all right?" he'd asked.

She'd heard the strain in his voice and knew what it cost him to ask.

"Did I hurt you?" he'd persisted quietly.

More than he knew. But she hadn't been able to tell him that. She hadn't been able to tell him that she'd thought he was a strong one. That she'd been curious about him because she had imagined him to be impenetrable.

It hurt to know he was only human.

She'd assured him in a dispassionate voice that she was fine, and had gone to bed.

She'd fallen asleep late in the night to the creak of his punching bag swinging from the ceiling and the rhythmic slap of fists against leather.

Jason killed the engine, and the sudden silence brought Lane back to the present. They were five minutes early. The seconds ticked away in silence until he pulled out his cell phone and punched in seven digits.

"Yeah, it's me," he said into the phone. "Have you got anything?" He grunted twice, made a noise that sounded like a groan once and hung up.

"Your hacker friend?" she guessed.

"Yeah. You were right, the records are a mess," he said.

She tried to keep her smile from looking smug.

With the air conditioner off, the heat in the car became unbearable. Minutes passed, and Alejandro and his boss were no-shows. She brushed at the damp hair stuck to her forehead.

Jason got out of the car and paced backed and forth a few times. Grumbling, he got back in the car and started the engine, switching the air conditioner on high.

"They're late," he said.

"Only a few minutes. Give it some more time."

He drummed his fingers on the steering wheel. "I don't like it."

Neither did she. Jason's nervousness bled into her system. A flight of bumblebees swarmed in her stomach, and her heart began to skip every third beat or so.

The Lexus from the other day pulled into the alley and stopped at the other end. The bees in Lane's stomach mutated into crows. Ugly, squawking, wing-flapping crows.

"No matter what happens, stay in the car," Jason ordered. "Slide over here and be ready to move this thing. If anything goes wrong, you get the hell out of here."

She should have chastised him for ordering her around again, but she didn't have the heart. Not when his face had turned such an unnatural shade of gray.

Lane crawled over to the driver's seat and put the car in gear. If things went bad, she wanted to be ready with as much horsepower as possible. She pulled her gun out of her bag and laid it on the seat beside her.

As Jason got farther away from her, the other car edged forward. Immediately, she eased up on the clutch and gave the engine a little gas. The Corvette rolled ahead, serving notice that she wouldn't tolerate them taking an advantage in this game.

Both cars stopped equidistant from her partner.

Suddenly she caught movement and a glint of light to her left, up high. Just as she laid on the horn to warn Jason, the window beside her exploded, and she squeezed her eyes shut against the glass shards stinging her cheek. The echo of the shot bounced off the surrounding buildings, making it sound as if there were nine gunmen.

She opened her eyes to see Jason running toward her with the other car in pursuit. They were going to run him down!

Lane stomped on the accelerator. The sleek black Corvette and the heavy luxury car careened toward each other in a game of chicken, with Jason in the middle.

He lunged right. The mystery car swerved to follow, fishtailing into Lane's path. More gunshots cracked out. Ignoring the sudden, searing heat across her shoulder blade, she raised her arms to protect her face as she broadsided the Lexus in a crunch of crippled steel and fiberglass.

The sedan immediately shifted into reverse and pulled away from the wreck, tires squealing. At the end of the lot, the Lexus stopped, and a man in blue coveralls ran from the building carrying a rifle. The man leaped into the car before it peeled away again. Lane's head fell back, and the world went dark.

She's not dead. She's not going to die.

Drawing strength from the silent mantra, Jason raced to the Corvette and pulled on the crumpled driver's-side door, his cries of frustration mingling with the groans of straining metal until it popped open.

Lane's head rested against the back of the seat, eyes closed. If it weren't for the tiny droplets of blood on her cheek where she'd been peppered by the glass, she could have been asleep.

Shakily his fingers reached for the pulse point along the column of her neck. Finding a steady beat, he craned his head skyward in silent thanks.

She moaned and shifted. Easing himself onto the edge of the seat, Jason had to nearly lie across her to get a better look at the welt rising on her right temple. The even rhythm of her chest rising against his reassured him she wasn't in any immediate danger.

He sat back when she moved again, raising her hand to her forehead as if to ward away the pain. Her eyes slowly opened, focused and then softened in recognition. When she fell against him, he welcomed her into his embrace.

His breath had finally freed itself from his chest and a relieved smile had crept onto his face before he felt it: the sticky warmth coating his fingers where they rested on her back.

She must have felt him stiffen. Her head tipped up. Brilliant green eyes reached out to him.

"Jason." Her lips trembled. She spoke so softly he thought he might be imagining her words. "I think I'm shot."

Please, God, not again. Not another woman dying in my arms.

She held on to him like he was her life line, burying her cheek at the base of his neck while he pulled her hair aside and leaned over her shoulder to see the wound.

There was a lot of blood and a tear in her shirt at the back. He pulled the torn cotton away, and she gasped, clutching him harder. "I'm sorry," he whispered, "I've got to get a better look." She nodded against his shoulder without raising her head.

Trying to be gentle, he eased the shirt away from her skin. Outrage flooded through him at the sight of her flesh flawed by a bullet's path. A shallow furrow ran across her shoulder blade, oozing blood steadily but not profusely.

He pulled back from her. Cupping her teary cheeks in his palms, he rubbed them dry with his thumbs and fought for calm. "There's no entry wound, Lane. It just grazed your shoulder blade. You're okay." His thumbs kept up their stroking.

"I'm okay," she repeated, as if saying it meant it had to be true. Already her voice was stronger, her hand steadier as it covered one of his. Her resilience amazed him.

The last evidence of her fear hung on her eyelashes in crystal droplets. He couldn't resist lowering his head and kissing them away. His tongue rasped her silky eyelids, tasting the saltiness and finding it powerfully erotic.

Like it had every time he'd touched her, his body responded with primal enthusiasm. This time, though, his desire was more than physical.

Her body enticed him, her mind intrigued him, but it was her spirit that captured him. This woman had experienced her share of tragedies and survived them all. Emotionally and physically she walked through fire and came out whole.

Her strength appealed to him like nothing else could.

He clung to that strength, relishing it, feeling it flow into himself. Until he stroked her hair and remembered, when the fine curls stuck to his fingers, that there was blood on his hand.

He studied his stained fingers, then clenched them into a fist. *Like a leech, drawing the lifeblood from anything it touches.* Disgusted at himself, he let her go.

She mewled in protest, then gasped lightly in pain as he lifted her and slid her over to the passenger seat.

''We have to get out of here,'' he said.

He tried the ignition. After sputtering a few heartbeats, the engine turned over and the Corvette coughed its way into the street. Something metal dragged on the ground, grating the pavement and Jason's nerves.

Every few seconds Jason's eyes flicked from the road in front of him to Lane's face, to the temperature gauge on the dash, then started the revolution over again. With at least ten more miles to their destination, the car was overheating. The air conditioner refused to push any breeze, warm or cool, through the car, and sweat beaded on Lane's forehead. Jason prayed it was from the lack of a breeze and not her injuries. Either way, she seemed oblivious to it.

The car gnashed along, topping out at thirty-five miles per hour. Halfway to their destination, she stirred, shaking off some of the daze she'd been in. ''Where are we going?''

''Somewhere safe.'' Glancing her way and seeing her dissatisfaction with that answer, he explained. ''I have a friend who is a doctor.''

''Hospitals have doctors, Jason.''

He shook his head, willing her to understand. ''No. They might come looking for us. I don't want to be sitting out in the open if they do.''

She looked tired. Too tired to argue, for once. He didn't know whether to be relieved or worried about that.

Lane breathed a sigh of relief as they pulled into the driveway of a modest suburban home. The Corvette choked one last time and died. She hadn't thought the wreck was going to make it. And she wasn't looking forward to hoofing it in this heat with her shoulder throbbing with pain.

She opened the car door, but before she gathered the strength to step out, Jason was there, scooping her out of the seat and into his arms.

"I can walk." She pushed on his shoulder in token protest.

"Forget it." He carried her like fragile glass up the few steps to the front door, which he swung open without knocking.

"Nick?" Jason's deep voice boomed through the quiet home. "Nick!" He kicked the door shut behind them and deposited her in an upholstered chair in the entryway. "Nick!"

Lane leaned forward, trying to avoid getting blood on the tapestry. Light footsteps sounded on hardwood and a man appeared at the end of a hall, wiping his hands on a towel.

Shorter than Jason, but more heavily muscled, the man wore very trendy fashions for a day at home. He wore a polo shirt, and khaki slacks, just a little baggy, that were immaculately creased. A snakeskin belt with a sterling buckle held them low on his narrow hips.

All in all, he was very good-looking.

And he had been smiling, until he took in the haphazard pair in his foyer. "What the hell?" he asked.

"I need your help, Nick." Jason's voice was low and soft, but imploring nonetheless.

"So I see," he said, quickly stepping forward. His eyes ran over Jason's shirt and hands, bloody from supporting her, and then assessed Lane.

She must look wretched, she thought as he knelt in front of her, obviously having decided she was worse off than Jason. Self-consciously she tucked a few strands of clotted hair behind her ear as Nick gently probed the lump on her forehead.

When his fingers hit the worst spot, she hissed. Jason flinched as if it had been him feeling the pain. He turned to stare out the window.

"Sorry," Nick said, rising up slightly to look over her shoulder at the wound on her back.

This time she clamped her teeth down on her lip to stop her gasp, wondering as she did it why it was so important to her not to let Jason know how much she hurt. *Because it hurts him that you hurt, and he's been hurt enough.*

She wasn't sure how she knew that, but she was as certain of it as she ever had been of anything.

Nick returned his attention to her face, lifting each lid slightly with his thumb and studying her eyes. He leaned so close she could smell his cologne. A little flamboyant for her taste, but it suited him.

Nick sat back on his heels and smiled. "Since it seems Jason has forgotten all of his social graces, I'll introduce myself. I'm Nick Motta, a friend of the big oaf, here." He grinned wryly as Jason ignored the dig, still watching out the window. "Although at times like this I forget why."

Lane liked Nick immediately. He was one of those people who could put you at ease no matter what the circumstances.

"Lane McCullough, the big oaf's partner." Nick's eyes widened. Lane couldn't quite read the reaction before he squelched it. Surprise, she thought, but it seemed like more.

"Pleasure to meet you, Lane. Now let's get that wound cleaned up." He took her hand and lifted, urging her from the chair. Jason immediately dropped the curtain and moved to her side to support her. Nick deferred to his friend, watching with a curious glint in his eye as Jason helped her down the hall.

Nick sat her down backward on a ladder-back chair. "Jason, I'm going to need the bag in my closet."

Jason returned in seconds, carrying an old-fashioned satchel like the one the crotchety old doc always carried in the Saturday Westerns. Nick snapped on a pair of latex gloves and then hesitated, holding a pair of scissors to the hem of her T-shirt.

"Jason, why don't you wait outside," he said quietly.

Jason's stoic expression never faltered. He stepped to her side. "I'll stay."

Nick spoke again, this time using that tone of voice unique to doctors, lawyers and schoolteachers. "Jason—"

"I said I'm staying."

Long seconds ticked away with the two men squared off, gazes locked.

Lane finally ended the standoff. "It's okay, he can stay."

Nick worked quickly and efficiently. Even with the local anesthetic he'd given her, the process of cleaning and disinfecting the torn flesh hurt terribly. At some point, Jason had taken hold of the hand on her uninjured arm. He clasped it gently as she cringed against the sting of antiseptic. She was tired, so tired that by the time Nick finished, her eyelids drooped like a sleepy owl's.

She was only vaguely aware of Jason carrying her into the adjoining bedroom and lowering her onto the bed. Somehow she registered the contrast of his warm body sitting next to her as she curled up in the cool sheets.

Someone tugged at her shoes. She didn't have the energy to protest, or even open her eyes, when one of them propped her back against his chest and slipped a fresh-smelling cotton shirt over her head. The same someone propped her against the pillow and applied a gentle pressure to her jaw, opening her mouth and placing something on her tongue.

A disembodied voice whispered, "Antibiotics," before she could clear her head enough to ask the question.

She felt a glass against her lips and drank thirstily, washing the drugs down with cool water. As she burrowed down under the covers, warm knuckles brushed her forehead, pushing the hair off her face and lingering at her temple.

A feathery kiss landed on her forehead.

She smiled into the pillow and eased into a peaceful sleep.

Jason left Lane sleeping and headed straight for Nick's bar. After pouring himself a glass of scotch straight up, he sank into one of the tufted armchairs in the study, brooding.

Nick watched silently, leaning against the door frame with his hands jammed in his pockets.

Jason downed half the tumbler in one swig then stared at the amber liquid vibrating in the glass. His hands were shaking.

He thought about what Lane had told him about her father. The lure of alcohol was strong when you were hurting. Just dull the senses until you could no longer feel the pain.

He set the glass aside roughly, propped his elbows on his knees and leaned forward until his face rested in his palms.

Nick ambled in and sat in the matching armchair, waiting. "You okay?" he asked.

"Hell, no."

"Anything I can do?"

"Hell, no."

The grandfather clock in the far corner ticked away the minutes.

"Talk to me, Jason," came the gentle urging.

Jason tamped down the emotions rising in his chest, struggling for control. Let it out a little at a time, he thought, like steam from a pressure cooker. Keep it under control or it will blow up in your face.

"It was just like last time." His voice cracked on the words, and he bit his tongue to fight back the vivid images that came with the memories.

"No, it wasn't. This time your partner is alive. She's okay."

Jason shook his head, his eyes fixed on the floor. How could she be okay? He had held her in his arms with her blood on his hands. "She was unconscious when I got to her in the car. I thought she was dead. Just like Karen."

"Just a bump on the head and a scratch on her shoulder, Jason. She's going to be fine."

Nick's even voice was a beacon, guiding him ashore from a dark sea. Nick was the only friend he could count on, had counted on, how many times? The only one he had been able to talk to when Karen died.

Others had offered their greeting-card sympathy, but only Nick had listened. Nick kept him on the straight-and-narrow when he might have ruined his life in the bottom of a bottle.

Nick knew the truth about Karen.

He met his friend's eyes, ready now to answer his questions.

"What's happening? Why are you working with a partner again?" Nick asked.

"She's Atlanta PD. We got our wires crossed and ended up investigating the same bunch." Jason's first encounter with Lane sprang back to his mind. Crossing wires was a good way to put it. Two very live, charged wires. "The system, in all its wisdom, decided we would be better off pursuing the case together."

"Are you all right with that?"

Jason's breath exploded from his chest. "Hell, no, I'm not all right with that!"

"The two of you seem to be getting along."

"What is that supposed to mean?"

Nick looked innocent. "Nothing. It's just that the way you were hovering over her, I thought maybe you'd finally quit beating yourself up about the past and decided to start living again."

Jason paced across the room, feeling like a caged beast. He couldn't escape the truth. Lane *had* started to make him feel things again. Things he had no right to feel.

"I'm working with her because I have no choice, Nick. When this case is finished, she's out of my life."

"That's too bad," Nick said quietly. "I think she might be good for you."

Jason felt his friend's disappointment. He knew Nick only wanted the best for him. Thankfully, Nick dropped the subject.

"So what went wrong today?" his friend asked.

"That's the $64,000 question," Jason answered honestly. There was only one reason why Alejandro and his boss would have turned against them. Their cover had been blown. But how? And by who?

Logically he should blame this on Lane. There hadn't been time to check her cover story in Macon. But she said she had contacts there who would vouch for her if anyone asked questions. Besides, he didn't have it in him to blame her for anything right now.

"I don't know. We set up an introduction with the head of the operation we're working, but we were ambushed," Jason said.

He leaned his head back against the creaking leather chair to stare at the ceiling. "Now the whole damned case—four months' work—is down the toilet. Our cover is blown, my partner's been shot and the bad guys are probably long gone."

"I'm sorry."

Jason heard Lane's words again, *Sorry always comes too late.* She was right. The damage was done, and it was his fault.

He'd let her get hurt.

"So what are you going to do now?" Nick asked. That was Nick: no platitudes, no false reassurances. Just take what life serves up and move forward.

Jason took a deep breath, appreciating his friend more than ever. "First I'm going to make sure she's safe, and then I'm going after those bastards."

He took his glass to the bar, poured out what remained of the liquor and put the bottle back under the counter. He needed to be sharp tomorrow. Turning back to Nick, he explained. "This time, I got a license plate number."

The sun set late in the summer sky. Lane woke to a room engulfed in darkness. She blinked, forcing her eyes to focus on the red digits of the clock beside the bed—8:54. She had slept nearly six hours.

Sitting up, she tested her shoulder. Not too bad, as long as she didn't lift her arms up high. A little stiff, and the skin around the wound felt tight, puckered. But all in all, much better than she had expected.

A shard of light from the hallway glinted underneath the door. Voices, close enough to identify as Jason's and Nick's, but not loud enough to make out what they were saying, drifted in from elsewhere in the house.

The hardwood planks were cool under her feet as she padded quietly down the hall toward the kitchen. She turned the corner in time to see Jason set the handset to the phone back in its cradle. His eyes jumped to hers, seeming to drink in her presence as if she were a fountain and he a man too long in the desert.

She looked at his hand, still resting on the phone. "Have you got something?"

"No. I was just checking in with our hacker. He's still working."

The look on his face gave away his lie, but she let it go. Tonight she didn't have the energy to fight his mistrust.

Nick's light voice broke the quiet. "How are you feeling?"

"Much better." She grimaced, sitting down while he leaned over and pulled her T-shirt away from her back to check her wound. "I can't believe I slept so long. You'd think I got hit by a tank or something."

"Shock will do that," Nick said. "You needed the rest." He straightened up from his examination, apparently satisfied. "And now you need some nourishment."

She sniffed the air appreciatively. "Do I smell chicken?" Lane hadn't realized how hungry she was until he mentioned food.

Nick smiled and pulled a casserole dish out of the oven. Both men watched silently while she devoured the man-size portion of chicken and rice he'd served. By the time she finished, the quiet had grown uncomfortable.

"So, Nick," she said. "Do you have a practice nearby?"

Jason and Nick exchanged a glance.

"No," Nick replied, sounding uneasy. "I don't actively practice medicine anymore."

"That's a shame." From what she'd seen, Nick was a caring and skilled physician. "Why did you give it up?"

Lane noticed Jason's eyes narrow and darken in a cautious look she hadn't seen before.

Nick hesitated, then tipped his chin up a fraction. "I got my medical training with the navy. Some years later they decided my life-style was unsuitable for the military and discharged me."

Why was Nick's life-style a concern to the navy? Unless— Realization dawned. She looked at Jason, now recognizing his expression. She imagined hers wasn't so different when she introduced people to Kelly, when Kelly had still been in a wheelchair. People could be hurtful sometimes, even when they didn't mean to, and it was hard to watch someone you cared about be hurt.

With an easy smile, she turned back to Nick. "You're gay?"

He nodded.

For a moment she wondered about Jason and his friendship with Nick. But no, she'd seen the way Jason looked at her, felt the way he kissed her and responded to her kisses. No way did he share Nick's life-style.

"But you could still practice," she said to Nick as she stood up to put her plate in the dishwasher.

"Officially I'm still licensed, but with the AIDS scare and people's attitudes," he raised one corner of his mouth in chagrin, "it just seemed easier to get a job at the medical research lab down the street."

Lane laid her hand on Nick's arm as she walked back to her chair. "Well, it's lucky for me you were here." She planted a light kiss on his cheek. "Thanks for taking such good care of me."

Suddenly she felt a yawn rise from the depths of her belly. She couldn't quite cover her mouth in time, and the yawn stretched into a laugh.

"You're welcome." Nick swatted her backside. "Now back to bed with you. Doctor's orders."

Lane groaned. After a six-hour nap, sleep should be the last thing on her mind, but a full stomach had her feeling lethargic again.

"Is it all right if I take a shower first?"

Nick nodded. "Just don't let the spray hit the injury directly, and keep the soap away from it. Call me when you're done, and I'll put some more antibiotic cream and a fresh dressing on it." She thanked him again, then smiled and yawned as she returned to the bedroom. Jason stuck his head in and handed her a clean T-shirt before she stepped into the bathroom and turned on the faucets.

The warm water caressed her aching body, swirling the last of her tension down the drain with the runoff. She stayed in longer than she should, rolling her neck back and around on her shoulders and then letting it hang straight down in front of her.

She grinned, studying her wrinkled toes. Poor Nick wouldn't have any hot water for hours. With a sigh, she twisted the faucets closed. He must be tired, too, and was probably waiting for her to come out so that he could dress her shoulder and get to bed.

She slid a clean T-shirt over her head and wrapped a towel turban-style around her hair. The last of the steam wafted out around her as she opened the bathroom door.

It wasn't Nick waiting for her. Jason sat on the edge of the bed next to turned-down covers and freshly fluffed pillows.

She'd seen a look like his once before, on the cover of a wildlife magazine. The award-winning close-up captured the eyes of a gray wolf stalking its prey.

He patted the bed beside him. "Come sit down."

Chapter 8

Lane was drawn to the bed like a marionette, with Jason pulling the strings. Lowering herself to the mattress, she licked her lips, suddenly dry as picked cotton.

His strange power over her fascinated and frightened her. She hadn't forgotten the kind of man he was—exactly the kind she shouldn't get involved with. The kind who was too out of control to be safe.

But he'd kissed her three times now—once inside the warehouse, an act and not an act; once outside the warehouse, as much a punishment as for Alejandro's benefit; and once in the car, comforting her when she was hurt. Each kiss had been different, stamped on the surface by its own emotion, and yet the same, charged with an undercurrent of passion.

He wasn't like any man she'd known before. Not that she'd known all that many. At least, not intimately. Her previous relationships had all been so…rational. Carefully calculated. She prided herself on keeping a level head, never losing control.

She was starting to think control was overrated. None of

those men made her feel so needy. Looking into his amber eyes was like sitting in front of a fire on a winter day. From a distance, it made you feel safe, protected from the cold. Up close, it left you flushed and hot, like tinder ready to ignite.

Gently he turned her so that she faced away from him and then scooted close behind her. A ceiling fan spun lazily above them, circulating cool air over her bared shoulders as he pulled the T-shirt away from her back.

"Don't let me hurt you," he said. His voice flowed slow and thick like molasses, sounding more like a plea than a warning.

It made no sense to her. He would never hurt her. Then his fingertips brushed the edge of her wound, spreading ointment, and fire engulfed the raw flesh under his touch. She jumped.

"I'm sorry." His torment landed softly on the back of her neck.

She kicked herself mentally. He'd tried to warn her, but she'd been too deep in the spell of his nearness to understand. Now he thought he'd hurt her, and somehow she knew that's what he feared most.

"It's okay. I just wasn't ready." She prepared herself with a deep breath. "Go ahead," she encouraged. "Try again."

This time his touch was light as cotton candy. His shadow fell over her shoulder as he leaned close. Underneath the medicinal tang of the ointment, she could just make out his unique scent.

She'd never been more aware of a man. Or of her own desire.

Jason pressed a gauze pad gently to her wound with one hand and taped the corners with the other, then eased the shirt back into place. His palms lingered on the curve of muscle at the base of her neck. "Are you sore?"

"Just a little." Was that her voice? It came out as deep and throaty as his.

The bedsprings creaked as he shifted his weight. Still resting on her shoulders, his thumbs rotated, biting deep into the tissue then easing back as his fingers squeezed the tension away. Her head fell back at the sheer pleasure of it.

"There?" He wrapped his left hand around her throat to steady it and pressed his right into a knot of muscle just below the base of her skull.

"Umm." She felt the massage clear to her core. Lord, what he could do to her with a single touch. It made her wonder what he could do if he really applied himself.

His hands moved steadily, pushing into her muscles then pulling back. She arched into his hands, matching his motion stroke for stroke.

"Better?" he asked, never stopping the slow kneading.

"Mmm..." She breathed in time to the rhythm of his hands. Everything else was lost in the onslaught of sensation.

"He sent up some pills to help you sleep, said to take them before you went to bed."

"Hmm—who?"

Jason's hands went still. "Nick? Our host for the evening?"

"Oh," she fumbled, flushing as her mind cleared. "Of course. I mean, I don't think I'll need it."

Jason picked up the massage where he left off, moving his attention to her upper back. "He likes you."

"I like him, too." Floating on the languid river of sensation his hands created, she could barely form the words.

One of his hands rested on each side of her waist, on her hipbones. His thumbs probed her spine along her lower back, rubbing up, then down. More pressure, and then less.

She needed a distraction, something to focus on to keep her from drifting too far away. "How did you two meet?" she managed to ask.

Jason hesitated, then chuckled. "At a gay bar."

Despite his shock tactic, "Hmm?" was all she could manage to say as his hands slipped down her arms and he devoted his attention to her forearms and the tendons of her wrists.

The texture of his voice folded itself around her. "I'd been watching gay bars for about a week, looking for a suspect known to frequent them. It was winter, and I nearly froze to death sitting in my car all night, but every time I tried to move my stakeout inside, I got, um, distracted.''

Lane smiled, getting his meaning. ''You mean you got hit on?''

''Something like that,'' he said drily. Lane laughed and he let go of her long enough to poke her in the ribs.

''Anyway, one night I was sitting outside when Nick walked out. I had seen him there a few times. He seemed like a nice guy—at least he hadn't been hitting on me. A group of guys hanging on the street corner followed him from the club. It didn't look right to me, so I went after them. Sure enough, as soon as they got around the corner they jumped him. He held his own at first—his military training, I guess—but there were three of them, and it turned ugly pretty quick.

''Luckily I got there before they did any real damage and managed to chase them off with my gun. Nick ended up helping me with the case. We hit every bar he knew looking for my suspect. With him, I could get inside without being, um, distracted.''

She felt him shrug behind her.

''It took us a while, but we finally got the guy, and we've been friends ever since.''

She liked the way he said ''friend,'' easy and smooth, without the sharp edge of mistrust usually riding just underneath his words. ''I'm glad you have a friend.''

His hands stopped moving. In the stillness the day's events finally sunk in. Her mind reeled as images flashed through it: Jason running toward her, a cracked window with a perfect hole through the center, blood on her shirt and on his hands. Unable to resist the temptation any longer, she sank back into his warmth. For three long breaths she rode the rise and fall of his chest, reveling in the feel of his heart thudding against her back.

''Lane?''

She squeezed her eyes shut against the nightmares and

worked to steady her breathing. Seconds passed until he hooked a finger under her jaw and turned her to him.

"Someone really tried to kill me today," she whispered into the self-imposed darkness.

His body tensed. "Yeah. They did."

"But why me, in the car? You were out in the open. Why didn't they shoot at you?"

"I don't know."

"What are we going to do now?"

His hesitation reached out to her. Opening her eyes to his, her breath caught. Everything he felt, everything he wanted, blazed there for her to see.

"We're going to make sure the bastards never get another chance," he said. His throat convulsed with more words, but they never found voice. His head dipped toward hers and stopped, a hairbreadth away.

Her tongue whorled over her lips, a silent invitation.

As if her movement woke him from some dream and he'd just realized where he was and what he was doing, he reared back, tearing his hands and his eyes away.

She shook at the abandonment.

Levering himself off the bed, he gulped air like a drowning man. "I shouldn't have started this," he said, more to the wall than to her.

Struggling to understand, Lane resisted the urge to scream out her frustration. A thousand questions rushed through her mind, but she didn't get to ask one.

He stopped at the door on his way out, his eyes meeting hers again briefly. "I'm sorry," he said in a voice full of rust and nails. Then he left.

Lane flopped back on the bed, her body slow to relinquish the natural buzz he had created. In a flash of anger, she punched the pillow and crawled under the covers. He was sorry. Humphh. *Sorry always comes too late.*

She'd have her answers, yet.

Setting the sleeping pills Nick had sent up for her aside, she switched off the bedside light. Gradually the crickets' melancholy chorus calmed her troubled mind. Outside her window a lightning bug sparked against the dark background of night. Its yellow flare burned brightly, reminding her of the fire lit so briefly in Jason's eyes, the burning desire. And then the insect's light snuffed out. Just like his eyes.

Maybe Jason's suffering ran deeper than simple burnout. She remembered the heavy scars she'd felt on his body the night of his nightmare. Like the tip of an iceberg, were those scars the visible warnings of much deeper injuries underneath? Had his body healed itself on the outside while wounds still festered within? If so, she had to crop these growing feelings she had for him. She couldn't afford to put her future, her happiness, in the hands of a man who had none.

Heaving a deep breath, Lane pounded her pillow into shape. Truth be told, she was as afraid of him as he was of her. And still she wanted him. She needed him, to feel safe, if nothing else. He was her protector.

Sometime later, she held her breath as she felt a presence in the room. Booted feet trod across the wood floor, and cane creaked as someone settled into the old ladder-back chair in the corner.

In the dark she smiled, knowing he couldn't see. He'd come back. A dark angel to watch over her.

A rumpled afghan lay over the empty chair in the morning. It was 7:00 a.m., and already sunlight streamed through the window leaving a trail of heat and dust motes behind that predicted another scorcher for Atlanta.

On the other side of the bathroom door, the shower was running. For a moment the image of a brooding Jason Stateler, surrounded by steam, with hot water pounding his naked flesh, flashed in her mind, forcing her to catch her breath.

She should be ashamed of herself, throwing herself at her partner like a horny teenager. There were rules against that. In her department and in the FBI as well, she was sure. He'd been right to break it off last night.

She dressed quickly in the shorts, freshly laundered, and clean shirt someone had left on the dresser for her. The same someone, she guessed, who had thoughtfully brought her purse from the car for her.

Lane studied her image in the mirror over the dresser. Her collision with the steering wheel had left a golf-ball-size bruise, colored lilac and lime, in the center of her forehead. She had no makeup on, and her hair, unstyled, had sprung to life wilder than ever this morning. She dug through her purse until she found a green ponytail holder and used it to collect the unruly curls behind her head.

Checking her image in the mirror again, her eyes lingered on the reflection of the door behind her. Stalling, she realized. Waiting for him to walk out, take her up in his arms and finish what he started last night.

The bathroom door stayed closed. With a shrug at her mirror image, she followed the sizzle of frying bacon and the sound of a badly hummed version of ''Good Morning, Sunshine'' to the kitchen.

''Morning, Nick.'' The table was set for three, with large glasses of orange juice at each place and a turkey platter heaping with eggs in the middle of the table.

''Good morning, sunshine,'' he replied, in time with his hummed verse as he flipped the bacon onto another platter, carefully avoiding splashing grease on his loafers.

He spun the spatula with a flourish and threw a grin her way. ''How's the arm this morning?''

''Better,'' she replied, setting the plate of bacon he'd dished up onto the table.

Still he insisted on a cursory examination of her wound. Apparently satisfied, he smiled as he picked up a bottle of pills on the counter, instructing her in a very professional tone to take two per day until they were all gone, to prevent infection.

"There you go." He slapped the bottle in her hand. "A few days on these, just to be safe, and you'll be good as new."

"Thanks, Nick." She shoved the bottle through the drawstring top on the purse slung over her shoulder. "Can I ask one more favor?"

"Anything."

"Can I use your phone? I need to check on my sister."

"Sure." He handed her a portable model and sat down at the end of the table.

Lane dialed the number, anxious to talk to Kelly. Her spirits flagged when the recorder picked up. She left a brief message, just that she was okay and wanted to make sure Kelly was okay, and hung up.

"Everything all right?" Nick asked.

"Mmm-hmm. I guess so. She wasn't there." She frowned and picked at the eggs on her plate.

Nick studied her a long minute. "You look worried."

She laid the fork on the table. "I'm a worrier." She shrugged and smiled dimly, trying to look confident. "She's probably just out running errands."

"Probably."

Lane toyed with the eggs on her plate. "Nick, can I ask you something?"

"Anything, darlin'," he drawled, scooting his chair closer to the table.

"Have you ever been Jason's doctor?"

His face turned guarded. "Why do you ask?"

"He has some pretty serious scars."

Nick raised his eyebrows, a grin raking his face. "Seen those already, have you?"

Lane felt the blush creep up her cheeks and did her best to tamp it down. "Do you know what happened?"

"Yeah, I know what happened," Nick answered softly.

Lane took a bite of eggs. She twirled the fork in her hand, hating to ask him to break his friend's confidence, not to mention doctor-patient confidentiality. Still, she had to ask. ''Does it have anything to do with Karen?''

Nick looked up in surprise. ''He told you about Karen?''

''No, not exactly.''

Nick studied her over his plate. ''What did he tell you?''

Lane stared miserably at her food. ''Nothing.''

He stabbed at some eggs, the steel silverware plinking against the plate. ''Then you'd best leave it alone.''

''I just want to help him,'' she added. ''I feel bad, like somehow this all has something to do with me.''

''No. It's not your fault.'' Nick waved his fork to emphasize his words, but said nothing more.

Jason stumbled into the room. Next to Nick's puppy-dog good looks, he looked like an alley cat spoiling for a fight. The white T-shirt tucked into his faded jeans must have been one of Nick's. It was a size too small, accentuating every hard muscle where it stretched across his chest.

''I need to borrow your bike.''

Nick looked up, put on a killer smile and said, ''Good morning to you, too, Jason.''

Jason huffed and shuffled like a petulant child. ''Yeah, right.'' He held his hand out for the keys.

As the door slammed behind Jason, Nick shook his head and shoveled more eggs onto his plate. Within seconds an engine roared to life in the garage. Its whine rose and fell as it was throttled up and down several times, slow, then faster.

The noise died, and Jason's head poked through the doorway a few moments later. His scowl had dissipated to a mere non-smile. ''Bike sounds good, Nick.''

''It should. I've spent all month tuning it for a race next weekend. You damn well better get it back to me in one piece before then.''

Jason turned to Lane, but his eyes avoided hers. ''You ready to go?'' He slid his arms into his black leather jacket.

''Yes,'' she answered, pushing her half-eaten plate of eggs away. ''I'll get my—''

The slamming screen door cut off her words. He left before she could even finish a sentence. Irritated, she slung her purse over her good shoulder and stood up.

As she shoved the door open, Nick stopped her with a hand on her arm.

"It's not you, remember that," he said softly.

Jason's strong hand shot back through the door, clamped onto her elbow and swung her outside. "Nick," he said, his voice growling with warning.

Bewildered, Lane looked from one friend to the other. Nick stood tall under Jason's glare, then acquiesced, turning back to the table to collect the plates.

Jason took a deep breath and nudged Lane toward the driveway. Turning back to Nick, he said, "Thanks," then added quickly, jangling the keys, "for the bike."

Jason ignored the brush of Lane's thighs against his as she settled herself behind him on the motorcycle. She put her hands on his hips, hooking her fingers through his belt loops for security.

He released the clutch, and the bike lurched into motion, unbalancing Lane. She let go of the belt loops to wrap her arms securely around his waist. Her hips snuggled closer to his as he cornered without slowing. The contact did nothing for his sour mood.

Each breath pushed his chest into her arms. His heart thudded against her palms. With each beat he pushed the bike harder, looking for release in speed. Release from the anger. Release from the guilt. Release from the fear that Lane McCullough was going to force him to face aspects of his life better left buried.

Last night he'd wanted her, plain and simple.

The wind whipped tears into his eyes as the suburban Atlanta landscape blurred past. Lane clung to him like his shadow, and he gradually relaxed in her grasp.

From the way she rode, he knew she'd been on a motorcycle

before. She leaned into the curves, hugging his body, relaxed and limber.

Another surprise. Motorcycles, especially those peeling down the freeway like a bullet train like this one, terrified most women.

She laughed at the speed. Not only was she not afraid, she seemed to be enjoying the rush almost as much as he was.

"Jason?" Her voice was hoarse, his name pushed back in her throat by the wind. He craned his head around until he could see her from the corner of his eye.

"What?"

"Slow down."

"What?"

"Slow down!"

The corner of his mouth crooked up. "Too much for you?" He knew he was well over the legal limit and pushing his luck.

"No," she shouted. "But if you keep it up, I'm going to have to arrest you—"

Over his shoulder he saw the edge of her grin.

"Again," she finished.

His heavy mood lifted. What was it about her that eased his spirit? He slowed the machine to a more reasonable, if not quite legal, speed. The morning's turbulent emotions settled to a vague uneasiness deep in his gut.

Lane sat forward. "Where are we going?"

She wasn't going to like it, he knew that. But he was relieved. At last he had the excuse he needed to end this farce of an undercover assignment. So why wasn't he happy about it?

One of her hands disentangled itself from his belt loop and rapped on his helmet. "Hello. Earth to Agent Stateler. I asked if you know where we're going."

He looked over his shoulder again and caught a flash of green eyes. It made his gut tighten. "Relax. I have a plan."

"This is your plan?" She couldn't believe he would do this, after everything that had happened. They stood on the curb outside her precinct, the motorcycle sitting in a No Parking zone.

Jason stalked toward his own image reflected along with the morning sun in the building's glass facade. Skipping to keep up with his long gait, she followed. He plowed through the detectives' bullpen without slowing, oblivious to the stares of her friends and coworkers.

Dan North stopped her near the watercooler, holding a stack of computer printouts. "I think I got something on the company that owns that Burl Street location, Lane. You want to see?"

"Later, Dan." She breezed past him without stopping.

Jason was waiting for her at her desk. All the arguments she'd been building flew from her mind at the sight of his wind-tousled hair and sun-ruddied cheeks. A day's growth shadowed his jaw.

With his hip propped on the corner of her desk and his arms folded over his chest, he stared at her, looking perfectly at ease in his work boots, jeans, white T-shirt and black leather jacket.

From the jut of his chin, she guessed he was prepared for battle. Her hesitation let him get in the first shot.

"It's over, Lane."

"Like hell."

"You think they would have shot at us if they didn't know we were cops? Face it, our cover is blown. Our investigation is over."

"There's still the two Neanderthals at the warehouse. And Alejandro."

"Small potatoes. I can take care of them," he said, leaving.

She hurried behind him, her heart pounding. It couldn't be over yet. Too much had been left unsaid between them. There was too much she still didn't know about him. "There's still the payoff."

He snapped around, his lips pressed in a narrow line, and covered the distance between them in two giant strides. She backed into the door frame behind her and he moved in close, towering over her.

"Keep your voice down, damn it."

"You're not quitting, are you? This case isn't over."

He glanced over his shoulder nervously. The bullpen buzzed with activity, as always, but no one seemed to be paying particular attention to them.

His voice lowered to a growl. "They don't know that we know about the payoff."

"Exactly. We'll call in the troops and have the whole place covered. We've got him—whoever he is."

Jason's face twisted as he leaned closer, pressing his physical advantage. "No. No more cops, Lane. You've got to keep this quiet, you hear me. Don't tell anyone."

His words sank in slowly. What he really meant was he didn't trust her. Even after everything they'd been through.

"You think it was me. You think I blew your cover?"

"Lane," his low voice vibrated through her, shaking her to the core. "My cover was solid for four months. Two days after you come on the case, it's blown to hell. What does that tell you?"

She felt the blood rush to her cheeks and for once didn't care that she was blushing. Let him see her anger. "I did not blow your cover. I was the one who got shot, remember?"

He shifted uneasily. "Believe me, I remember." For the first time, some of his confidence and determination seemed to wane. "I don't think you blew my cover, Lane. But someone did. Other people here knew where you were and what you were doing."

"No." She shook her head, denying the possibility that someone here would betray her even as the truth of what he said wound its way inside her heart.

"Yes." He held her shoulders firmly. "I need you to make them think it's over. That we've given up. Go back to your normal routine. Stay here, where it's safe. File your reports—shuffle your papers. But leave the payoff out of them. Please."

Uncertainty clouded her thoughts. He made some sense. Somehow someone must have discovered they were not who they pretended, or they wouldn't have been attacked. But to suspect her own department was more than she could accept.

She looked over his shoulder at the men she worked with every day. Busy, in their normal hubbub of activity, they were answering phones, typing forms, studying files. They were her friends. They were her family. They would never betray her, she would bet her life on it.

But would she bet Jason's life on it? If there was even a slight chance he was right, she couldn't take the risk.

"All right. No reports on the payoff." She met his eyes, fighting back the tears that threatened at the thought that this really was the end for them.

"Lane—" He halted, looking unsure of his next move, then straightened his shoulders. A cock-eyed grin raked his face. It was the loneliest thing she had ever seen.

"It's been fun." He smoothed out the slight hitch in his voice. "I'll see you around."

Her stomach tied itself in knots as he walked away. It wasn't supposed to end like this. She couldn't let him leave without even saying goodbye.

Lurching away from the door frame she leaned on, she started after him and ran blindly into her captain as he emerged from the interrogation room across from her desk.

Suspicion rippled through her like quicksilver. The door had been open, the room easily within earshot of her conversation with Jason. Had Roland overheard? Why hadn't he let them know he was there?

She loathed the suspicion growing within her. She loathed Jason for planting it there. No way would Roland Bowling ever do anything to hurt her. So why couldn't she look him in the eye?

Roland's head swung from Lane to Jason's retreating figure, and back. "Let him go, Lane. Come tell me what's happening."

Roland listened intently to her story, minus the information about the payoff, looked appropriately shocked that she had been hurt and asked all the right investigative questions. She saw no signs that his reaction was anything but genuine. Disgusted at herself for not being honest with him, she was tempted to tell him everything. But she didn't.

"So he's gone. The case is over," she lied to her trusted friend, finishing her story.

Roland leaned back in his chair and rubbed his chin. "To tell the truth, I'm glad."

Lane looked at her captain quizzically, mistrust rearing its ugly head again. Why would he be happy to have her off this case, especially before it was solved?

"I've been worried about you," he said.

His tone wasn't right. Her investigator's instincts chanted warnings in the back of her mind. That wasn't just vague concern in his voice. He knew something.

"Why?" she asked.

"I have a few friends over at the Federal building, so I checked this guy Stateler out. I wanted to see what you were getting into, out there with him." His fingers thrummed a brown folder on his desk, then pushed it over to her. "I didn't like what I found out."

When Roland left her alone in his office with the FBI file, she suspected that what she would find inside wouldn't be pretty. It turned out to be worse.

In his six years with the FBI, Jason had lost two partners to violence. The first, Jim Sturman, the supervisor she'd met the other night, had suffered a minor, but disabling, injury in a drug raid Jason organized. That explained the man's limp.

Lane swallowed a lump the size of a charcoal brick when she read the name of his second partner: Karen Bastille. She'd been killed while working undercover with Jason. Lane flicked through the gruesome pictures of her death.

No wonder he had nightmares.

Since Karen, he'd worked alone. He had an amazing solve

rate, which had earned him several commendations for bravery, and an equally amazing number of reprimands for not following procedure, for taking too many chances.

Any third-rate shrink could interpret the psychology at play. Jason Stateler was a man doing penance, offering his own life as atonement for his sins. He didn't need to kill himself with alcohol the way her father had; the way Jason worked, one of the miscreants he pursued like an avenging angel was sure to do it for him.

Lane closed the brown folder with a heavy heart, knowing what she had to do. Outside the office window, Captain Bowling barked orders and waved an unlit cigar. He had once told her that reporting her father's alcoholism to the department was the hardest thing he ever did. Sitting here now, she believed him.

Recommending a fellow officer for psychological evaluation was never easy. Especially if that officer was your partner. But that was what she now had to do.

Chapter 9

The man in the starched shirt and perfectly pressed suit across the desk from her bore little resemblance to the rumpled character she remembered from the precinct the other night. Today, she found herself wishing for a little less formality and a little more approachability.

Chewing her bottom lip, she stared at the insignia on the wall behind him. The banner under the logo's scales of justice read: Fidelity, Bravery, Integrity.

What about compassion?

She hoped to find that in Jim Sturman when she'd decided to go to him earlier. That he had once been Jason's partner should work in her favor. Jason had said that Sturman cut him slack. She hoped that meant they were friends.

''Detective McCullough, this is a surprise.'' His cane lay propped against the desk beside him. ''How can I help you?''

She sat stiffly, wondering where to start. ''You were Agent Stateler's partner once, weren't you, sir?''

''Yes,'' he answered. ''Before this.'' He swept his hand over his crippled thigh.

Lane let her gaze roam around the well-furnished office. Law books were carefully arranged by size on the shelves that lined one wall. The chairs were real leather. ''But you've done well in the Bureau despite your disability.''

Sturman scowled. From the time she'd spent with Kelly at the rehab center, Lane knew some people never accepted their physical limitations. She suspected Sturman was one of those.

''If you call being chained to a desk, pushing paper all day 'doing well.' But getting hurt is a risk we take with the job, isn't it?'' He sat back in his chair. ''Since you're obviously up and around, I take it your wounds were not so serious.''

''How did you know I'd been hurt?'' she asked, surprised.

''Agent Stateler called in this morning. He said you had been injured and were no longer available to work on the case.''

Relief washed through Lane. He had called for help, after all. ''Then he's not out there alone? You've assigned other agents to help him?''

Sturman's eyes snapped up from the silver letter opener he'd been fidgeting with. ''Your cover was compromised. There is no further avenue of investigation in this case. Jason is taking a few days off to recover from this latest—'' he waved the letter opener ''—fiasco of his.''

Fiasco! The cold-hearted fish. He had to know what it would do to Jason to see another partner hurt. So much for him being empathetic.

He turned the letter opener toward her. ''Are you telling me that Jason is still pursuing this case, without my authorization?''

Jason had lied to Sturman. He didn't trust his own boss.

Sitting under the man's cold, gray stare, she could see why. ''No, I just thought, that is, his state of mind—''

''And what state of mind is that?''

She wavered. This was where she should tell Sturman that Jason was out there risking his life in a misguided attempt to assuage his guilt over Karen's death. That Jason needed help.

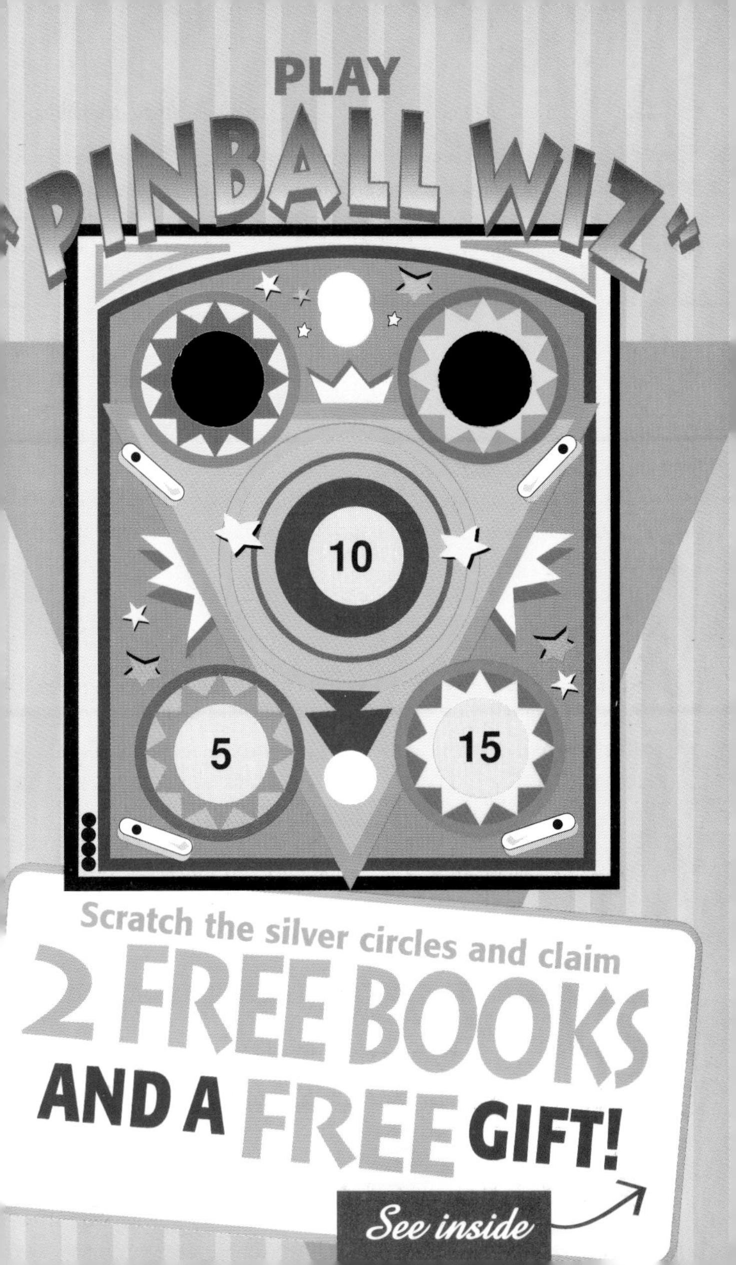
PLAY
"PINBALL WIZ"
10
5
15
Scratch the silver circles and claim
2 FREE BOOKS
AND A FREE GIFT!
See inside

That he wasn't competent. God, was that what she was really saying? That Jason was mentally incompetent?

Nonsense. His willingness to take risks had saved her life in that warehouse, and he'd kept his head during a crisis when she'd been shot. He might have some problems, maybe they were severe enough that he needed help with them—who wouldn't after what he'd been through—but he wasn't over the edge. Not yet.

Suddenly this visit didn't seem like such a good idea. Jason would never get any help here. But if the Bureau that was supposed to protect him wouldn't help him, then who would?

The answer sneaked into her heart. She would. She was his partner now. "I—he seemed overly concerned that I had gotten hurt."

A sick feeling grew in the pit of Lane's stomach as a sparkle of something like satisfaction lit Sturman's eyes.

"Then why are you here, Ms. McCullough?"

"I just wanted to reassure Agent Stateler that I'm okay."

His silver eyes dulled to cautious pewter. He must have figured out where she'd been going with her intimations before, and he wasn't buying the change in her story. "Maybe I should check it out, just to be sure. Why don't you tell me what the two of you had on the case, where you think he might go."

Lane pulled on a false smile. "That's not necessary. I'm sure you're right. Jason just needs a few days off. He's probably holed up somewhere cool, waiting for this heat to let up." She lowered her eyes in what she hoped was a convincing display of self-deprecation. "Besides, I'm really not sure where he might go. He wouldn't let me help much with the case."

Excusing herself quickly, she headed down the hallway. She felt the weight of his stare on her back until the elevator doors closed, swallowing her whole.

At least she had her own car back again, she thought. The officers sent to retrieve it the other night had left it right in her usual parking place at the station. She hadn't liked being dependent on Jason for transportation.

The feeling that someone was watching, though, stayed with her as she drove. Easing into a left-turn lane, she vowed she wouldn't look in the mirror again. *There is no one back there*

The light changed. Lane made her turn, glancing in the rear-view as the dark Bronco behind her continued straight and out of sight. *See,* she chastised herself, *no one there.*

She turned off Burl Street a few blocks from the distribution center and parked her car in the half-full lot of a twenty-four-hour Laundromat. If Alejandro or his goon were lurking about the distribution center, she didn't want them tracing her plates to uncover her real identity.

Not that it mattered. Jason was right—their cover was already blown. Why else would anyone shoot at them? Still, walking down the sidewalk so close to one of the truck hijacker's bases gave her the creeps. She didn't like being out in the open, feeling unprotected.

Who was paranoid now?

When she finally reached the crumbling building she and Jason had used as a base before, she let loose a relieved sigh. She saw no sign of Jason, or Nick's bike.

Inside the tenement they had used as a base before, she called out. "Jason?" There was no answer. Caution kept her from calling any louder. Resigned to the fact that he wasn't there, she wondered what to do next. Where would he go?

As she made her way back through the building, a hand shot out from underneath the staircase, drawing her into the darkness. Strong fingers clamped brutally over her mouth, crushing her scream. The barrel of a gun bruised her rib cage. She couldn't breathe, could hardly move. Her lungs burning, she stomped her heel where she hoped the arch of his foot might be.

Her captor grunted. Contact! The hand slipped from her mouth, and she stumbled forward.

"What are you doing here?" He made no attempt to come after her.

She had recognized him even before she turned around, be

ɔre she heard his voice, rough as crushed glass. She knew the ɜel of him, the scent of him. Even knowing, her heart still ıced, the terror coursing through her veins replaced with tremlous desire.

And then anger.

Jason had held her long past the point when he must have ɜcognized her, too. He had wanted to scare her. And he'd ucceeded. She was very frightened, but not in the physical ense. What scared her was the fathomless fear she heard in is voice. The depth of his dread. Most of all she was scared f how badly she wanted to help him and the possibility that he might not be able to. That anxiety cooled her anger.

On knees just now quit wobbling, she faced him, struggling or calm over the emotions battering her from within. "We ave to talk."

His head shook violently. "I told you it's over. You don't ave a part in this anymore."

"You can't do this alone, Jason."

"I have to." His body looked tighter than a coiled spring as e took her elbow and propelled her toward the window that erved as their entryway.

This wouldn't be easy; she knew that. He'd locked the twin lemons, guilt and grief, inside him for too long. "Why, Jason? Vhy are you trying so hard to push me away?"

As he looked at her, for a moment he softened. The conection between them pulled her into his eyes, two swirling ools of tortured, molten gold, until he jerked away with a trangled moan.

Leaving her chilled and shivering in the Georgia heat, he rawled alone through the window. She followed him over the ill.

She hated being the source of his pain. Didn't want to cause im more. But if she let him walk away now he might never ace what he was doing to himself. "Is it because of Karen Bastille?" she asked.

He whipped around, his eyes ablaze, and his heat washe over her once again. ''How do you know about her?''

''I know.'' Her heart flip-flopped at the anger twisting itse into his features. ''It doesn't matter how.''

He crossed the distance between them in three raging step ''The hell it doesn't. Where did you get that information? An why were you snooping into my business?''

''I wasn't—I—'' she stumbled over her words, thrown b the sudden turn in the conversation. ''Roland had a file.''

''Your captain has a file on me?'' He leaned close enoug for her to see the red lines webbed across the whites of hi eyes.

''He has friends at the Bureau. When I was assigned to wor with you, he called in some favors to find out more about yo He was worried about me.''

Jason made a derisive snort. ''Yeah, I'll bet he was wo ried—that his little operation here was about to be blown wid open.''

Somehow he'd turned the conversation completely aroun twisted it in his dementia. This was about him, not Roland.

''This is *not* Roland's operation.'' She could see he didn believe her. He wouldn't say it, but his eyes mocked her na iveté.

No matter how she tried to get through to Jason, she couldn make a dent in his protective armor. All the psych texts in th world couldn't prepare her for six foot plus of wounded mal Especially when it came in a body like his. All she wanted wa to help him, but it was hard to concentrate, to stay detache with him standing so close. She took a step back as she stare up at him, recognizing the suspicion simmering in his expre sion.

''Is she the reason you don't trust anymore, Jason? Becaus you trusted her, and she let you down by dying?''

''No.''

His denial came too quickly, was voiced too sharply. Not

bull's-eye, but she'd hit somewhere near the mark. He glanced up and down the alley.

He lowered his head, squeezing his eyes shut as if the scene of his partner's death was replaying before him. It had been an alley just like this one, Lane remembered from the pictures in his file. Just him and his partner, alone in the open, just like now. He probably *was* reliving it.

Why couldn't he just admit he needed her?

Reaching out to him, she touched his forearm and felt the bunched muscles beneath his sleeve. "Then why won't you let me help you?"

He jerked back. "Because I don't want you in my life."

Damn him. It was a blind strike, just another attempt to push her away, but the words stung, and she lashed back, anyway. "You don't have a life, Jason. You threw it away four years ago, when your partner died. All you have now is a cover. You hide out with the criminals because being a tough guy, without any emotions, is easier than being the real you and facing your feelings."

So much for cool, professional detachment. Some psychologist she was going to make. She should stop, but once she'd started down this road she couldn't turn back. She had to have her say while she still had the courage, while she could still stand under the dangerous expression that darkened his face.

"You play the big, heroic FBI agent, working alone, taking on the scum of Atlanta single-handedly, like some kind of martyr for the cause of justice, but really you're just afraid. Afraid to let anyone onto that emotional island you're marooned on, because then you might start to care about them. And sometimes it hurts to care about people, especially when they die."

She finished her tirade and stood deflated, shaking and shocked, wondering if her outburst had done more harm than good. What if she bungled this and made things worse for Jason?

He stood silently for a moment, breathing heavily, his gun, still in his hand, hanging slack at his side. Slowly he raised the weapon to her shoulder, not pointing it at her, just nudging her with the barrel turned sideways. "Don't play amateur psychologist with me. You're not my doctor. You're not anyone's doctor, yet."

His words fertilized the seeds of doubt already planted in her mind. He was right, she didn't have her degree or any practical experience. Her lower lip trembled and she pulled it between her teeth to stop the quivering, but not soon enough.

They both knew he'd won.

It made Jason sick to see the hurt his words caused her. He'd let himself get too close to her, let himself care too much. Last night was proof enough of that. He should never have touched Lane. He knew from experience the devastation that could lead to.

But her skin, glowing like candlelight, and the dark, wet spirals of her hair had enticed him. Enchanted him. Spun a web where the past didn't matter and danger couldn't touch them.

Last night he had wanted her; he still wanted her.

For an instant, when he'd seen her creeping into the abandoned building this afternoon, his heart had jumped. Not in fear, but in joy. Despite the danger, he wanted her with him. And recognizing that had mustered the anger he needed to push her away again. He wouldn't let his weakness be her death, too.

Her mouth twitched like she was trying to figure out what to say, but squealing tires kept him from ever knowing what she decided on.

A black Lexus—the same one that had been at the meet where they'd been ambushed and Lane had been shot, the same one he'd seen Alejandro leaning over in the alley—raced toward them from the end of the block. Even before he saw the gun barrel looming out the half-open window, Jason lunged at Lane. He drove her backward, out of the street, shielding her body with his own.

He and the sidewalk collided with a grunt and then he was

on his feet again, pulling her up and into the shallow entry of a nearby doorway.

"How did they know we were here?" she asked shakily.

The sedan overshot, careening past them and stalling in a barely controlled one-eighty. "From your partner, most likely. The one you told about this place. Damn it, now do you believe someone in your department sold us out?"

With Lane's hand in a death grip, Jason bolted from the stoop. Their feet pounded the pavement in a frantic beat. Behind them the stalled engine roared to life. As they stumbled around the corner of the building, something thunked the cornerstone, and flying bits of brick stung Jason's ankles. Great, a silencer, he thought.

Now that they were momentarily out of the line of fire, Jason slowed a half step to dig the key to the motorcycle out of his jeans. Lane rammed into him from behind, and he saw that she had somehow pulled her gun as he dragged her along, and was covering their backs as they ran.

Just as he pulled her into the toolshed where he had left the bike, the sedan rounded the corner. Lane exchanged shots with them, covering Jason while he swung a leg over the saddle and started the engine. Swerving to avoid Lane's volley, the car skidded into a rusted trash bin, buying them a few seconds.

Lane slid onto the seat behind Jason, and he gunned it, heading away from the sedan. Over the machine's engine, he heard the peel of the sedan's tires as it followed. They were close.

In his rearview mirror Jason saw a lethal-looking automatic pistol followed by a black-sleeved arm emerge from the passenger-side rear window. He couldn't hear the silenced shots, but they had to be firing.

He swerved to the driver's side of the car, painfully aware of staying where the shooter couldn't get a clean line of fire at Lane's exposed back.

Her arms squeezed him so tightly he had to fight to draw a breath as he swerved between cars, nearly clipping the fender of one, but putting a little more space between them and their assailants. When Jason was forced to slow down to dodge a taxi, something brushed his sleeve at his elbow and dinged off the handlebars. That bullet was too close.

He jumped the bike over the curb and sped down the sidewalk in a crazy path. Behind him the taxi turned off the street and the black sedan raced after them once again. The area was getting too crowded. He needed a way out.

They came up fast on an empty lot with a cement block wall in back. A pedestrian-size chain-link gate opened to the street on the other side. Jason skidded into the lot, almost losing control as the rear tire spun from pavement to gravel. He gunned the bike straight toward the open gate. It was wide enough for a person, he only hoped it was wide enough for the bike.

"Too late to worry about it," he grumbled into the wind as the sedan pulled up to the curb behind them. A foot before they reached the gate, several slugs plugged the cement wall above Jason's right shoulder. Gray dust showered around them. Lane ground her cheek into Jason's back and squeezed him even tighter.

They flew through the narrow opening without slowing. One handlebar scraped the fence post, sending them into a sideways skid for a heartbeat. With a grunt of effort, he righted the bike and veered left, out of the line of sight of the black sedan.

Jason checked and rechecked over his shoulder for miles after they'd lost the sedan. Finally letting himself believe they were safe, he pulled over and unwound Lane's stiff arms from his waist. She hadn't let up her death grip or said a word during the wild ride.

She was white as a ghost. His heart thundered as he searched her face for signs of pain. His hands roamed over her back, dreading what he might find, but having to know. "Are you okay?"

Lane took a deep breath and nodded, but her eyes hadn't yet lost their glazed look. She pushed his hands away and slid off the bike.

What was she doing? With one foot down on either side of the bike, he rolled it along beside her as she walked away. "What are you doing?"

She shrugged, her shoulders jerking awkwardly, almost convulsively. "I'll go now."

"Go where?"

"Away." Her voice was as uneven as her gait. "You said...you wanted me...out of your life."

His laughter sounded as raw to him as his gut felt. "*Now* you're willing to leave me alone?" Didn't she get it? This unprovoked attack changed everything. She couldn't just walk away.

When he grabbed her elbow and stopped her, turning her to him, he understood her malaise. Her pupils were huge, the green fields around them had shrunk to thin rings. The color still hadn't returned to her cheeks. She was in shock.

He lightened his grip on her arm. "Lane, you can't go."

She stared at him uncomprehendingly.

"They're escalating this, Lane, actively coming after us. They tried to kill us both, out in the open, with witnesses. They won't be satisfied anymore just to have us off the case."

Slowly her pupils returned to normal size. He could see her mind begin to work the puzzle. "We have to be dead?"

He nodded, nearly choking on the walnut-size lump that hung in his throat when he thought about how close she'd come to being shot down in that alley. "Until we figure this thing out, you're stuck with me."

Thankfully she didn't argue but climbed on the bike behind him. When she'd wrapped her arms around his middle, a little more loosely this time, he kicked the engine over and pulled out into the road with no particular destination in mind.

He just needed to be moving; it didn't matter where.

Lane was surprised when Jason turned the bike off the expressway and onto a two-lane highway. She wanted to ask where they were going, but knew he'd tell her when he was ready. For now, she was content to hold on and go where he took her, letting the sun on her back pound the chill out of her bones.

Soon the concrete gave way to unlined blacktop, and they passed the entrance to one of Georgia's national battlefield parks. She remembered the place from grammar school field trips. It was the sight of one of the bloodier skirmishes that preceded Sherman's march on Atlanta.

The blacktop eventually became a dirt trail, and Jason steered the bike through a break in a wire fence that must mark the back of the park property. This entrance was definitely not on the tourist map.

They lurched through ruts and over stones on a narrow ribbon of red clay that could barely be called a footpath. Soon enough even that disappeared, and they entered what looked like virgin territory.

The forest closed in. Towering pines blocked the sun with their high branches, while still allowing room for a lush thicket of undergrowth at ground level. Branches reached out, snatching at her legs as she passed.

Jason parked the bike under the shelter of a dead pine, its trunk scorched from a long-ago lightning strike, bent double like a mortally wounded soldier fallen over a fence line.

Without a word he pushed his way through the bushes on foot, climbing farther up the hill. His passage disturbed a hundred unseen creatures. Lane heard them skitter this way and that, though they were too quick for her eyes to catch. While she hesitated, considering whether any of the wildlife might be of a species she'd rather avoid, Jason pressed forward.

When she caught up, she found him perched on a flat boulder that hung off the side of the mountain like it was the end of the world.

The view of the valley was beautiful. At the bottom of the slope, green plains stretched as far as she could see. The scene was so peaceful and so remote that it was hard to believe a major metropolis like Atlanta lay just out of sight.

"You know this place?" she asked.

He pulled the blade of grass from his mouth and studied it. "I used to come here sometimes. To think."

So this was his safe place. It suited him. So peaceful and yet with a history so violent.

Silence as wide as the cotton fields in the distance stretched between them. She waited, happy that he had chosen to share this place with her.

"Come here." He held out his arm invitingly, opening a small space beside his body. She filled it unquestioningly. His arm behind her, hovering near her shoulder but not touching, he pointed down the ravine.

"Look. See it?"

He leaned closer to point more accurately. Her skin tingled where his breath feathered across her neck. Inhaling the sweet pine-laden air around her, she concentrated on the direction of his extended arm, squinting to search for some break in the pattern of foliage. Whatever he wanted her to see should stand out against the green blur.

Finally, she spotted it. "A cannon." The rusty artillery stood in stealth, nearly covered by brush, about twenty yards down and to her right. It sat on a ledge much like the one where they sat, positioned to decimate troops approaching through the fields below.

"I don't know how they got it up the mountain, but it's a great position. From here, they could kill anything that tried to cross the fields. When I was a kid, I used to come here when the park was really crowded." He threw her a grin that melted her heart. "I'd sit up here and kill all the tourists."

"I thought you were from Michigan."

"Moved here with my mom when I was thirteen, after my parents divorced. She had family in Marietta." His hand absently rubbed his thigh. "I was angry at her for taking me away from my dad, so I avoided her by spending all my time up here. I crawled all over this mountain and the fields around it.

I found lots of things—miniballs, buckles, canteens, even a sabre."

She smiled at the thought of his boyhood adventures. "Removing artifacts from a national battlefield is illegal," she teased.

"I never took them. I just liked knowing they were here, had been here for a hundred years. Who was I to take away all that was left of the soldiers who dropped them? After a while, I started bringing a bedroll and spending the night up here."

A corner of his mouth ticked upward. "And yes, camping in a national battlefield is also illegal. But this place was all I had. It was the only part of Georgia that felt like home for the first couple of years."

"So what brought you down from your mountain, Mohammed?"

"First, my mom freaked and sent park security after me. I guess I didn't realize how much I was hurting her by staying away. And then," he flashed a killer grin, but it never quite reached his eyes, "I discovered Southern belles."

Lane tried to imagine him as a teenager. She'd bet he was hell on wheels in those days. But everyone moves on, some people just travel rougher roads than others. Unfortunately, Jason's road had been a minefield.

He'd taken a big step, bringing her here, opening the door to his past, even if only a crack. Dare she hope he would let her swing it wide?

"I'm sorry I pushed you so hard earlier. You're right, I'm no doctor, I had no right. But if you want to talk about it, I'll listen."

He shuffled to his feet stiffly and stood with his back to her, staring out over the valley. "There's nothing to talk about. I made a mistake. She died because of it."

She tried to keep her voice gentle. "The report said you were cleared of any wrongdoing."

"Not everything is in the report."

"Jason, you can't blame yourself—"

"Leave it alone, Lane." Even pitched as low as it was, the tone of his voice told her the conversation was definitely over.

Disappointment settled over her shoulders like a scratchy blanket. He wouldn't talk to her. Not today. Maybe not ever.

Before she could decide what to do next, he turned on her. With a deep breath he pulled his shoulders back. "Who did you tell, Lane?"

The question caught her off guard. She hesitated, not sure what he was asking at first. Then she understood. He thought she'd told someone that he was still working the case. That he might be at the distribution center, after she'd promised not to.

The core of her that had softened toward him hardened instantly. "No one." Ice crystals hung on her voice. After all they'd been through, he still didn't trust her.

"Then you were followed."

"We were at their site. Maybe they just saw us."

He shook his head. "There hadn't been a soul there all day. I was getting ready to leave when you showed up. Whoever came, came with you."

Her heart lurched. Maybe she had been careless. She'd been so preoccupied with...what? Convincing herself that he needed her?

She'd been so sure that he'd created the idea of an official leak out of his own paranoia, that she'd forgotten she could be leading their enemy right to him.

Despite the afternoon heat, she shivered and rubbed her arms. "It's possible."

He blew out his breath. Instead of the anger she expected, she heard only worry in his voice. For her. "I have to get you somewhere safe, out of the reach of your *friends* at the precinct."

Thinking it was one thing. Hearing him say it was another. "Only Dan and Roland Bowling knew anything about the distribution center, and I just can't believe either one of them had anything to do with this."

Still, Roland had been nearby when Jason had dropped her off. He might even have heard Jason's warning for her not to tell anyone about the distribution center. And Dan had certainly been interested in what she was doing, more interested than he generally was in anything other than the latest box scores.

What Jason didn't know was that there was another possibility. She hadn't gone straight from the precinct to the distribution center. "If I was followed, it could just as well have been from your office as mine."

"What do you mean, my office?"

She chose her next words carefully. How do you tell a man you had almost ruined his career? That you would have, if his boss had been a little better listener, had shown a little more compassion for the man who was supposed to be his friend?

Suddenly her world tilted. As if she'd been standing on a platform that shifted twenty degrees, throwing her off balance. Like a kaleidoscope, the world turned. Colorful bits and pieces of nothing fell into a new pattern.

"After I read your file, I went to see Sturman," she said evenly, not wanting to set him off until she'd had her say. Her mind reeled with new ideas, half-formed, but potent.

Jason's quiet didn't bode well for her.

The rest of her words tumbled out in a rush. "I went there to ask him to help you. After I learned everything you'd been through, I was afraid for you, out there alone, in your state of mind. I didn't know what else to do. But I didn't tell him anything, Jason. He gives me the creeps." She took a deep breath and forced calm into her voice. "He was so dispassionate. I kept thinking he should have been worried about you. And upset at what I implied."

"And what was that? That I'm unstable? That I'm not fit to be on the street? Is that what you went to tell Sturman?"

Lane lowered her eyes, a flush tingling her cheeks. "I only wanted to help."

"Thanks, but that kind of 'help' I can do without."

She had to make him hear her out. "I *don't* think you're unstable."

"No? Then what do you think?" If his glare had been any sharper, it would have bored a hole in her.

"At the time, I *thought* you were overly suspicious—"

"Paranoid."

"That you'd been working undercover so long, you'd lost touch with who you really were—"

He lifted an eyebrow, egging her on. "Delusional."

"That you took too many risks—"

"Ah, suicidal."

When she didn't go on, he did. "You forgot depressed, neurotic, obsessive—"

She slapped her hand down on the rock beside her. "Stop it!"

"Stop what?"

"Putting words in my mouth."

"Why? Am I not using all the correct clinical terminology?"

"No. I mean, yes." He had a unique ability to get her turned around inside her own mind. "I mean, none of that is what I'm saying."

"Then what are you saying?" he asked hoarsely. She could see the pain of her words, her betrayal, on his face.

"That I was wrong. You were right to be suspicious. Someone is leaking information, at the very least. And maybe even directly involved in this. But maybe it's your office, not mine."

"No way."

"What, you don't hesitate to accuse my department, but there can't be one bad apple in the almighty FBI?"

Jason hesitated, then shook his head, but not as emphatically as he could have. "If someone inside the Bureau was involved, they would have shut me down a long time ago. I worked on this case without a hitch before you showed up."

"Yes," she said, getting up to confront him eye to eye. "And look how close you were getting. How long could they string you along before they ran out of excuses for denying you a meeting with the boss? Think about it. You were standing in the open at that first meet, but the shooter fired at me, in the car. I imagine a dead agent draws a lot of attention at the Bureau, a big investigation that could be uncomfortable for someone with something to hide."

She rested a hand on his shoulder. "Someone doesn't want you dead, just distracted." Imploringly, she spread her hands out to her sides. "That's me, one convenient distraction."

Waiting, Lane counted the seconds by the number of buzzing insects she brushed from the air around her. She knew she'd made him doubt his friends the way he'd made her doubt hers.

"You're right," he finally said, turning around to her. "We can't trust your people or mine."

"Then we'll trust each other."

Chapter 10

Jason hardly breathed when Lane curled her arms around him and pushed her head against his chest. She was right, and he knew it. Whoever wanted them out of the picture could be from the Bureau as easily as they could be from her department. Instinctively, he'd known that all along. That's why he used the hacker and handpicked his own drivers from local talent rather than going through official channels. But what could he do about it? He should demand she go away, or take her somewhere safe. But where would that be?

If he kept her with him, could he live with the consequences? Sooner or later she was going to find out what a bastard he really was. He owed her the truth about Karen because, God help him, he was afraid he was going to make the same mistake again.

He doubted he could stay close to Lane for any length of time without taking everything she was willing to give. Even now his body hummed with awareness at her closeness. She rested her cheek on his shoulder, and her skin on his was a caress.

A week ago he hadn't thought he was capable of the feelings she stirred in him. He still wasn't sure he was capable of living with them.

Turning his head, he skimmed his lips across her hair then gently eased her back a few inches. "We need to get away from Atlanta. Somewhere they don't have any contacts and no one will think to look," he said.

She thought a moment. "I know a place, not too far away."

As Jason swung the motorcycle back onto the blacktop road and accelerated, he let his mind clear, allowing the miles, the heat and the blurring landscape to hold his emotions at bay.

Lane rode in silence. He supposed she was as tired as he was. Too tired to push words past the wind rushing around them.

Only when she pointed to a country road diverging from the main one did she break the quiet. "There," she said.

Kudzu vines covered the pines lining each side of the road, giving the impression they were driving between two solid green walls. Like mice in a maze, Jason thought, pushed inevitably forward.

Up ahead, in a niche in the tangled vines, sat a country gas station. Jason eased off the accelerator and pulled in next to a pair of ancient red-and-white pumps. The buzz of a thousand invisible insects replaced the hum of the bike as he switched off the engine.

Lane's thumbs were still hooked in his belt loops. Still straddling the bike, he glanced over his shoulder at her. "How much money have you got?"

She fumbled in her pockets a minute. "About three dollars." She looked up, embarrassment and worry shading her cheeks pink. "My purse was in the car."

"What car?" he asked. In the rush to escape, he hadn't given a thought to how she'd gotten to the distribution center. That could be a costly mistake!

"My own," she said. Lane must have read the concern on his face because she quickly said, "Don't worry. It's parked in a lot three blocks away with lots of other cars around. Besides, only my cover ID was in there.''

Jason relaxed a little. He didn't want to give these guys any more information than they already had.

Lane sighed and shifted in the seat, her hips rubbing briefly against his backside. The contact sent a rush of heat racing up his spine. No, make that down his spine, where it settled between his legs. He eased away from her, hoping she wouldn't notice his growing discomfort. And hoping it didn't grow any more.

''What're we going to do, rob the gas station?'' she asked.

A grin crawled onto his face. Only her humor could turn around his mood like that. He shifted around to where he could face her squarely, liking the way she looked with windblown hair and ruddied cheeks. Alive.

''Naw, I've got about two hundred bucks,'' he admitted.

She arched her eyebrows.

''I always carry emergency money.''

''You would.''

He realized she was pointing out his paranoia again, but her tone was joking, so he put on his best patronizing look for her. ''My emergency money is going to buy us a roof over our heads tonight. So if you want to sleep in a nice, warm bed with me instead of out in the woods with the critters—'' he spider-walked two fingers up her bare arm for effect ''—you'd better act grateful.''

He'd never seen a pair of pupils grow so large so fast. Too late, he realized the innuendo imbedded in his words. Blood that had just begun to dissipate rushed again to his groin. Stifling a groan, he swung his leg over the seat and headed for the pump. ''We need gas.''

What they needed was a fire extinguisher.

He stared resolutely at the gauge as he filled the tank, then hung up the nozzle and headed for the restroom on the side of the cinder-block station. When he came out, Lane was nowhere in sight. Swallowing his fear, he knocked on the women's room door. Unlocked, it swung open. Sunlight splayed across an empty room as unclean as the men's room had been.

He hurried around the building. He'd check inside, he told himself, before he completely lost his mind.

Peering between the peeling paint letters on the glass storefront, he saw her. She stood in front of an oscillating fan, her arms over her head, holding her mass of black, wavy hair off of her neck. She let the hair sift through her fingers, blowing in the artificial breeze, then lifted it again off her nape. Her head tilted back so the current from the fan hit her throat.

Jason swallowed painfully and ignored the pulse in his groin as she rotated her head, exposing each side of her neck to the rushing air. Her eyes were closed. The look on her face was…rapture. Cool relief from the stifling heat.

Outside, Jason had no relief. He was on fire, mesmerized. When she turned her face away from him, he swayed slightly, then took a step forward, pulled to her like a snake to a charmer's flute. He took another step forward, then recoiled when he saw the other man.

The gas station attendant, some three-hundred flaccid pounds of him, sat on a stool behind the counter stripping Lane with his leer. Condensation slipped down the side of the bottle of soda in his left hand and puddled unnoticed on his thigh. There were two unopened drinks and a brown paper sack next to the cash register.

Anger, and jealousy as green as Lane's eyes, surged through his chest like an electric shock, causing his heart to clench. Shoving the door open, he cleared his throat to break up the scene, but the sound came out more like a growl.

Lane opened her eyes and turned to him, smiling, all innocence and seduction, then frowned. She probably had no idea what she could drive a man to with a display like she had been putting on.

Ignoring her for the moment, Jason threw a twenty on the counter and scowled at the attendant in a look every male on the planet understood. The expression plainly said, "Mine."

He crammed the change in his pocket and gave the confused-looking Lane barely enough time to grab the drinks and the sack from the counter before he hauled her out by the wrist.

As soon as they were outside, she yanked her arm away and stopped. "What is wrong with you?" she asked.

Four perfect red imprints marked her wrist where his fingers had held her too tightly. His stomach cramped at the sight of what he'd done to her, what she'd made him do.

"What was that?" he asked.

"What?" She put her free hand on her hip, the other still held the things she'd bought.

"That." He waved at the store, and his voice rose a half octave. He hated to fight. Especially with her. But he couldn't stop himself. "In there. That little erotic dance in front of the fan."

She looked angry now. Maybe it was better that way. Get her good and mad so she wouldn't let him anywhere near her.

"Erotic! I was just trying to cool down. It's a hundred degrees out here, in case you haven't noticed."

"You might have been cooling down, but you were making the big guy in there very hot. We're supposed to be keeping a low profile here. We don't need to draw attention to ourselves. Believe me, that guy won't be forgetting you anytime soon. In fact, you'll probably play a starring role in his dreams for quite some time."

Lane stepped up to him. Her lips quivered, but her gaze was strong and steady. Good, let her blast him.

Lazily her eyes drifted down his front, gliding without reaction over the still noticeable bulge behind the fly of his jeans.

She smiled sweetly up at him and said, her voice syrupy with sarcasm, "It looks to me like the gas station attendant wasn't the only one who got a little overheated."

With that, she handed him a soda and left. Jason watched the sway of her backside until he realized he wasn't doing his already-over-stimulated body any favors.

With a violent jerk he twisted the cap off the bottle and chugged the drink to the bottom. It didn't help much.

The vibration of the bike had become part of her. She felt it even when they stopped, like when the world keeps spinning even after you get off a carnival ride. Jason killed the engine on the bike.

A blackberry thicket full of nearly ripe berries almost obscured the faded wooden sign advertising the Red Peak Lodges—summer cottages for rent by the day and week. Special weekday rates.

Jason glanced at her over his shoulder. "This is it?"

She nodded.

They followed the red arrow on the Red Peak sign down a gravel lane. Red Peak, a spot Lane remembered from childhood vacations, wasn't too far from Jason's mountain. When he convinced her they needed to get away from Atlanta, she thought the secluded cabins here would be perfect. Looking at the place now, Lane wasn't so sure.

Eleven depressingly abandoned-looking bungalows sat in a semicircle ringed by a pothole filled drive. In the center, knee-high grass strangled an empty playground. Only one swing hung on the set. The handles were missing off the teeter-totter. The other twisted contraptions of metal that she and Kelly had once so enjoyed climbing over and under looked more like salvage yard refuse than sources of endless, mindless entertainment.

The middle cottage, Number 6, was slightly larger than the five on each side of it. As Lane remembered, it served as both the office and the manager's house.

Jason surveyed the property with the same intensity he had studied the gas station. "You used to come here as a kid?" he asked.

Lane winced. "It didn't used to be like this." She remembered the place through the eyes of a child: bright bungalows that, to a miniature body, seemed like grand palaces. Moms and dads drinking lemonade on the porch while the kids scampered across the jungle gym. All that was left of them now were their ghosts.

This wasn't the place she remembered, the haven where even her father could escape, for a while, the demons that tormented him. "We should go somewhere else."

"No. It'll do. The more deserted, the better."

Already striding off, Jason nodded back over his shoulder. Lane hurried to catch up to him, and together they circled the grounds. The forest and brush encroached far closer on the circle of cabins than Lane remembered. No more than twenty feet behind Number 10, a path wound off into the wilderness.

"Where does that go?" Jason asked, stepping a few feet down the trail.

"To the lake." She followed him, pushing branches out of her way and praying that wasn't poison ivy brushing against her ankles.

"How far?"

"About a mile and a half."

Jason looked surprised. Lane grinned ruefully. "That's why my family stayed here—Dad couldn't afford lakefront on a cop's salary."

Afraid he would want to make the hike right now, she added, "It used to be a lot wider and clearer. I'm not sure I could even find the way anymore."

Thankfully, Jason looked satisfied and turned back to the cottages. An old sedan, painted tan in the areas that hadn't rusted through, sat parked beside the office. A dog the same tawny color as the car lay on the steps, attached to the porch post by a heavy chain.

As Jason stopped and leaned in the car's open window, the dog picked up its head, rolling its lazy eyes toward them. Jason shook his head. "Keys are in it. Someone isn't very cautious."

No one was as cautious as Jason Stateler. She was ready for a cool room and a soft bed, but he seemed intent on taking his time, still checking the place out as they strolled toward the office.

The yellow dog, most likely a mutt, but with a squashed face and cropped ears that hinted at pit bull lineage, slapped its tongue over the sides of its muzzle while it studied them. Strings of drool leaked out the corners of its mouth and puddled on the stairs. It barked twice.

"Shush, Sam, I'm a-comin'" a woman's voice called out the screen door. The dog flapped the flies off its head, slinging drool Jason's way, then put its face back down between its paws with a lonely whimper. Jason grimaced and wiped the slime off his jeans as he skirted around the mutt and into the office.

From an attached room in back came a gray-haired woman, looking over her shoulder as if she couldn't tear herself away from something in her quarters. Lane heard the theme song from a popular soap opera playing on a TV with a lot of static.

"Nice dog you have," Jason said when the woman finally made it to the counter.

"Humph." The woman shrugged. "Sams's better'n a doorbell at lettin' me know when folks is about."

"It must be nice having him around when you're here alone."

"Her."

"Ma'am?"

"Sam's a her. Short for Samantha."

"Oh." Jason looked amused. "Well, it must be nice having a big dog around when you're here alone."

The woman shrugged indifferently, but the soft look in her eyes said the dog meant more to her than she let on.

"Can I help you?" the woman asked, wiping her hands on her cotton frock. "I'm Dora."

While Jason rented them a cabin, paying in advance for two nights, Lane stared out at the deserted playground, remembering Kelly, before her accident, running, squealing with delight as she leaped onto the monkey bars. The place was full of ghosts, all right.

As Dora pulled a key from a drawer, Lane turned her back on the playground and her memories.

"Here you go Mr. and Mrs. Timmons," Dora said, handing Jason the key. "Number 7. It's got clean sheets and towels."

Mr. and Mrs. Of course, Jason would have signed them in together, and under an assumed name. Luckily this wasn't the kind of place that asked for ID.

He put his arm protectively around her waist. His embrace was nothing more than part of the cover, she told herself. It didn't mean anything. Still, she relaxed into the light touch of his hand on her waist.

Jason put the key back on the counter. "Could we have Number 10? If it wouldn't be too much trouble."

Dora looked puzzled.

"It looks a little more private." He squeezed Lane tightly to him. "I'm sure you understand." Looking up at Jason, Lane could see he had turned on a blazing gets-me-what-I-want smile.

Dora blushed and tucked a wisp of hair back into her bun. Pulling open a drawer, she exchanged the keys. "Bed's not made up in 10. I'll be along with some fresh linens directly."

Jason turned up the wattage of his smile. "Don't bother yourself over it. I can see you're busy."

Lane glanced through the open door behind the woman, where she could see enough of the black-and-white TV to see a doctor and a nurse in a clinch.

"Oh, it's all right. I was just watching my dailies." She looked longingly over her shoulder.

Jason patted her hand where she laid the key on the counter. "Well, why don't you just give us the linens, we'll make up the bed. We don't want to put you out since you seem to be here all by yourself."

That was the second time Jason had mentioned Dora being

alone. So, he was fishing to find out who else might be lurking around. Not a bad idea, given their situation.

"Well, thank you, if you don't mind, that would be real nice." She glanced over her shoulder at the TV, her gaze lingering long enough to take in the action.

On their way out, the dog barked twice. From inside, Dora shouted. "Shush, Sam, leave them nice folks alone. Them's paying guests."

Jason stooped over and put his palm down for Sam to smell. When she didn't bite it off, he patted the animal on the head and scratched behind her ears. "Good dog, Sam," he praised before walking away. Lane trailed behind him, having grabbed an armload of sheets, bedspread and towels from the pile Dora had directed her to.

After reaching the cabin, Lane made the bed while Jason paced the pine-slat floors. The efficiency unit only had two windows, one in front and one on the side facing the woods. Jason tried them both, sliding them up and down repeatedly.

"Are you worried about someone coming in through those, or us being able to get out them?" she asked, meaning it as a joke.

"Both," he answered, way too seriously.

Next he checked the locks on the door. Twice. She half expected him to check under the bed for bogeymen.

She smoothed the cotton bedspread over the end of the mattress. "Jason, relax. We're safe here."

He picked up the telephone by the bed and jiggled the hook, listening for a moment as if to be sure it worked before setting it back on the nightstand.

"You're sure no one knows about this place? Not even Bowling?"

She didn't let herself get angry at his insinuation that her captain was the one trying to kill them. They'd both agreed that the leak could be in either one of their departments. "No. My father may have told him about this place, years ago, but

Roland wouldn't have any reason to think I'd come back here now, even if he does remember it."

She finished the bed and crossed the room to put away the bath linens. Leaving a washcloth on the edge of the vanity outside the bathroom door, she took the towels inside the little room that contained the shower and the john.

When she came back out, Jason was staring out the side window at the trees as if he could see into the depths of the forest. She put a hand on his back for balance as she stood up on her toes, looking over his shoulder. Leaning closer to the window, and leaning harder on him, she tried to see what he saw.

There was nothing there.

She knew he was worried about her. About them. Staying with her had to be hard for him, after what he'd been through with Karen.

"We should clean up and get some rest," she said, her hand still resting on his hard shoulder.

"You go ahead." He slid away from her touch. "I'll...keep watch." He pulled the single chair in the room up to the front window, but didn't sit. He looked like a man with his mind in overdrive. The way he rubbed his forehead every few minutes, she'd bet he was working on a killer headache.

She hated being the source of his pain, but, what to do about it? There had to be something she could do to get him to relax. Pondering the question, she headed for the shower.

Jason swung the chair around in front of the window and straddled it, staring out at nothing. In a vain attempt to tune out the sound of the shower running in the other room, he focused on the melody of the forest: birdcalls, the breeze rustling the pines, the first of the evening crickets beginning its song.

It was no use. The steady pounding of the shower beat its way into his consciousness, bringing with it images of water sluicing over bared feminine curves. Lane McCullough's bared feminine curves.

What was he going to do now? He couldn't solve this case sitting out in the woods fifty miles from nowhere. And the last thing he needed was to be holed up in a twelve-by-twelve cabin with his alluring partner for any length of time. Every man had his limits, and he feared he was fast approaching his.

But he couldn't leave Lane alone, either. Not while her life was in danger from a pack of truck hijackers that had suddenly turned as aggressive as a wolverine with its hackles up. The hunters had become the hunted, and that didn't sit well with him. Not well at all.

He crossed his arms over the back of the chair and propped his chin on them, sighing. What the hell was he going to do now?

Fifteen minutes later, when she stepped out of the bathroom, he wasn't any closer to an answer than he had been when she'd stepped in. He turned around in time to see the last tendrils of steam follow her into the room.

She stopped in front of the vanity, clutching her wadded-up clothes to her chest with one hand and steadying a towel piled turban-style on her head with the other. The towel wound around her torso from her breasts to her thighs left her decent, but exposed far too much creamy skin for his comfort. He turned his stare back out the window before he embarrassed them both.

"I don't suppose you see a shopping mall out there?" she asked.

"Sorry. Just pine trees and lightning bugs." He glanced back her way. "What's the matter, afraid you're missing this week's blue light special?"

"No. I'm afraid I'm going to have to put this disgusting T-shirt back on." She wrinkled her face and dangled her T-shirt, pinched between her thumb and index finger, out in front of her.

"Well, there's always the bedsheets," he joked.

Her eyebrows shot up. "Good idea." Dropping the dirty shirt to the floor, she snatched the pink-flowered spread off the bed. Holding it shoulder height, she simultaneously dropped the towel and spun the coverlet around in a sleight of hand that would have made Houdini proud. He swallowed his groan just before it escaped.

"If you want to shower, I think I left you some hot water," she said. "I can wash out our clothes in the sink."

The flower-covered spread hung around her like a sari, hugging her body in just the way he wanted to. Ten pink toes wriggled out underneath the hem at the floor.

"Thanks," he replied, working hard to suppress his smile of appreciation, "but we only have one bedspread. Besides, I don't look good in peonies." Lane's laughter reverberated through him, rattling his resolve, but not quite shaking it loose.

She picked up the forgotten paper sack from the gas station. "Well, then, how about some supper." Her arm disappeared into the bag, searching, while he turned his chair around to face the bed.

"What have you got in there?"

"Why, sir, a fine seven-course meal. Gourmet, of course."

He leaned a little closer. "Seven courses?"

"Mmm-hmm." She rattled the bag, finally coming up with two canned drinks. "First course, ice tea, minus the ice. They're warm, but they're wet. Unfortunately, these are the only two we have, so you have to make it last for the six remaining courses."

He popped the lid on the can and took a long swallow. When he lowered the can, it was half-empty. "Course number two?" he asked hopefully. His stomach had started to rumble painfully.

Lane grinned, sat Indian-style on the now-unmade bed, and rummaged in the bag again. "Let's see. Salad would be next." Triumphantly she threw him a cellophane bag of raisins.

"Salad?"

"Well, you have to use your imagination. I doubt Blain's gas station is famous for its cuisine."

"I doubt Blain's gas station is famous for much of anything," he mumbled, his mouth full of raisins.

Lane opened her own bag, and they both chewed in silence a few moments. While the sweetness of the raisins still lingered on his tongue, she passed him course three, crackers and processed cheese spread with a little plastic tab to do the spreading. Course four, the "vegetable," Lane claimed, consisted of a bag of king-size corn chips, which they shared.

He crumpled the empty bag and launched it into the wastebasket for a three-pointer.

"Showoff," she complained without a hint of malice in her voice.

He hooked a finger over the brown sack and pulled it toward him. "I don't suppose you have a steak in there for our main course?" he asked.

She snatched the bag back, rolling her eyes. "You don't ask much, do you?"

He shrugged. "I'm a meat and potatoes man."

"In that case, you're in luck. Meat, I have." Reaching again into her bag of goodies, she pulled up two long plastic packages of beef jerky. "Well, at least I think it used to be meat."

His smile sneaked up on him and spread itself across his face before he realized it was there. He was enjoying playing this game as much as Lane seemed to be enjoying staging it. Even though he hated jerky, he opened the plastic package and ate every bite.

"And for dessert," Lane said when the jerky was gone, "we're having my very favorite."

She reached into the bag, and Jason found himself relishing the anticipation. Not because he was still hungry, but because whatever she had next was her favorite. He wanted to see her enjoy it.

She tossed him a package of yellow cakes. He burst out in laughter.

''Umm,'' she said, licking the last of the cream filling from her fingertips. ''That's definitely the way every gourmet meal should end.''

He set an uneaten half of his cupcake on the table, more interested in watching her lick the last of the cream filling from her fingers than he was in eating. ''End? But that's only six.''

''Six?''

''Courses.''

She thought a moment. ''So it is.'' Leaning across the bed, she turned on the ancient-looking clock radio on the nightstand. Static crackled through the air while she fiddled with the knobs, turning this and twisting that until the soft wail of a saxophone filled the night air with jazz.

Holding out her hand, her eyes mated with his. ''Well, I'm all out of food, so I guess the seventh course will have to be me.''

His heart stopped beating, and he couldn't swallow.

She took pity on his condition. ''A dance, Jason. I'm just asking you to dance.''

The twin green seas of her eyes drew him in, deeper and deeper, until his limbs felt heavy and his lungs burned. Oh, how he wanted to dance with her. How he wanted to hold her close, feel her warmth pressed against the cold walls of his heart. He wanted to feel her softness against his hardness.

Only the strength of his memories, vivid reminders of why this couldn't be, gave him the will to rip his gaze away from the emerald depths of her eyes before they pulled him under for good.

Sucking in a deep breath, he managed to turn his head unevenly side to side. ''I don't think so.''

Her hand fell to her side. He shut his eyes against the hurt he read on her face, but it didn't help. He couldn't block out the hurt he heard in her voice.

''That's too bad,'' she said softly. ''For both of us.''

Both of them jumped at the sharp rap on the door. Jason leaped from the chair, reached for his gun, pushed her behind him in one motion. When no one kicked the door in, he asked, "Who is it?"

"It's Dora, Mr. and Mrs. Timmons."

Jason shoved the gun in the back of his jeans, but still kept Lane behind him as he cracked the door open a few inches.

The lodge manager stood on the porch with her dog panting at her heel. "Just wanted to be sure you had everything you needed before I turn in for the night."

"We're fine here, Dora. Thank you for checking," he said.

Dora's gaze curved past the edge of the door and around Jason to where Lane stood. Remembering what Lane was wearing, he understood the slight flush that rose in the woman's cheeks.

"I'll leave you two be, then," Dora said.

"Good night," Jason called as she stepped back.

"Good night," she answered.

"Oh, just a minute," he called. Reaching back to the table by the door, he picked up the remnants of his half-eaten cupcake and tossed it to the dog, patting the mutt's head as she gobbled it up. "Good dog, Sam."

Blowing out a breath, Jason shut and locked the door and then turned around. Lane was still close behind him. Too close. His turn put her right in his arms, and him in hers. This time she didn't look at him. She stood stiffly in his arms, waiting.

Waiting to be pushed away again, he realized. Rejected. Waiting for him to kick her in the gut one more time.

Another jazz number came on the radio, a trio this time, and he fought the waves of longing that washed over him with the music.

He fought and lost.

Their movements were jerky at first, out of sync. Then he pulled her closer and let his body telegraph his direction. They swayed together like two souls in one body while the haunting harmony surrounded them. Another song started and ended. That made two. Or was it three?

He should stop now, while he still could. But he didn't. He

lost track of the world around him until he realized Lane had stopped. She stood in his arms, looking up at him, her eyes shining, questioning.

He knew what they were asking. Her position put her intimately against him. She had to feel the throb of his desire almost as strongly as he did.

"I'm sorry," he said automatically.

"For what? For being attracted to me? For wanting me the way I want you?"

"For wanting something I can't have."

"Can't have? Or won't let yourself have?"

The fire of an old anger once again leaped to life within him. He couldn't explain it to her. He was too ashamed. "I think I'll take that shower now." He had to get past her to get to the bathroom.

She stood her ground. "My God, you won't allow yourself even a few moments of pleasure in that desolate life of yours, will you? Your partner died, and now you can't forgive yourself even that long."

It wasn't fair for her to talk to him like that. She didn't know. Didn't know what he'd been through. Didn't know what he'd done.

"What was this big mistake you made, Jason? What could you have possibly done that was so bad?" It was more a challenge than a question, he recognized.

He clenched his fists to stop his hands from shaking. He couldn't do anything about the rest of his body. He pushed his way around her, but her words stopped him before he got through the bathroom door.

"Why are you still punishing yourself for her death? Because you feel guilty?"

He propped his hand against the door frame to steady himself as a sharp pain stabbed beneath his ribs.

"Because you should have protected her?"

The pain grew, expanded like a balloon inside his chest.

"Because it should have been you and not her?"

The bubble finally burst and spread fire throughout him. "No," he ground out between teeth clenched against the pain, the memories. "Because I loved her. She was everything to me, and I let her die."

Chapter 11

How could she have been so stupid? She should have seen it. Partners in law enforcement shared a special bond. They were friends, mentors, brothers and sisters, and, occasionally, lovers.

All departments had rules against that sort of thing, of course. But rules don't mean much to the human heart.

She should have realized his pain was too deep to have been caused by anything less than love. The death of a partner could devastate any cop, for a while. But Jason was a strong man; he would have bounced back. The death of a lover, though, was another matter. Especially if a man felt responsible for that lover's death, as Jason did.

Suddenly Lane felt cruel for treating him as she had. She had teased him, tempted him, then taunted him for not giving in to her seduction.

She knew he had feelings for her, no matter how hard he tried to cover them up. Finally she understood why those feelings frightened him.

She had feelings for him, too. New feelings, turbulent and

powerful, rushing deeper and stronger inside her than anything she'd felt before. She wanted to explore those feelings. To find out how far and how fast those rivers ran.

Maybe they both needed to run those rapids. How could Jason get on with his life if he didn't confront his fears? And who better to help him face them head-on. She could teach him that history didn't always repeat itself.

Her mind wandered. Images of the two of them tangled together in a rumpled bed heated her blood and made her heart pound.

How long had it been since his sheets were damp and sweaty from love, rather than night terrors?

The water ran a long while before the bathroom went quiet. The moment of truth: did she have the courage to go through with it? Dora had only sent two towels in the stack of linens she'd given Lane when they checked in. And Lane had them both in her hands.

She heard him slide the curtain aside and step out of the shower. It was now or never. Sucking in a deep breath, she rapped a white knuckle twice on the door, twisted the knob and pried it three inches open. All she could see was blue linoleum and a sliver of the ancient commode.

"Jason?" She pushed the door another inch, catching a glimpse of honeyed skin, lightly furred with the same pecan-colored hair as his head. "I, uh, seem to be hogging all the towels," she confessed. He quickly stepped out of sight behind the door.

Lane waved the white cloth inside like a flag of truce.

"Thanks," he said huskily as a muscular forearm emerged and a hand snagged the swatch of terry.

She hesitated, her courage waning. This always sounded so easy in Kelly's novels. Her heroines never worried about rejection. But then, they'd never tried to seduce Jason Stateler either.

Resolutely she let the bedspread she'd been wearing fall to

the floor, then pushed the bathroom door wide-open and stopped, stunned by the magnificence of his body.

He stood with his back to her. His hair was plastered, dark and damp, to the back of his neck. His broad shoulders tapered to a trim waist and taut butt. Even at his height there was no awkwardness or gangliness about him. Each part fit, proportionate to the whole.

The towel he'd been rubbing over his back stopped midstroke as she moved up behind him. This was it. Do or die.

"Let me help you with that," she suggested. Instead of taking the towel dangling in his hand, she used the one she carried in hers, stroking it down his neck and across his shoulders.

His skin felt cool to her touch. She ran her fingers over his spine, feeling the chilly droplets clinging to his skin. It struck her then that there was no steam in the room. He'd taken his shower cold. Frigid, if the gooseflesh puckering his arms was any indication.

"Oh, Jason..." she said, rubbing the towel over his biceps and leaning close to warm him. She planted a kiss above his shoulder blade, molding his skin between her teeth, pulling gently, then releasing and soothing the spot with her tongue.

"You're going to make that cold shower good for nothing, aren't you?" he asked, unmoving.

"I hope so," she breathed in his ear. Lane smoothed the towel over his hips, around the firm mounds of his butt, and then dropped to her knees, drying each chiseled thigh and calf with infinite care.

She traced the towel over the length of him as she got back to her feet, letting her nipples, already hardened to tight peaks, brush against his back.

She felt the battle raging within him as she looped the towel, and her arms, around him, and dried his chest in slow circles. His body turned to steel beneath her palm as she circled his own hard nipples, the heel of her hand lingering over them, pressing and massaging before moving on. His chest swelled with an expansive breath as her right hand strayed up, then down. Higher, then lower. Her fingers swirled over his navel, felt the hair arrowing down from there.

He groaned like metal twisted in a vise. His left hand shot out and grabbed her wrist. "No." His voice was heavy, and sandpaper grainy.

Before she could lament the rejection, he spun on her, her wrist still captured in his hand, caught between them. He plastered her palm to his chest, where she counted the erratic beat of his heart.

"No," he said again, more softly this time. His eyes were on fire. The flames of desire. "It will be over in a hurry," he explained gently, "if you touch me like that."

Her smile was slow in coming. As slow as his mouth descending to hers. He wasn't rejecting her. At least not yet. His lips rested lightly against hers.

Need pushed against her skin from the inside out, threatening to split her at the seams. Still she held back, letting him lead the way. It seemed like they stood that way an eternity, so close, but barely touching. Their harsh breaths marked time between them. She'd give him all the time in the world.

Finally his hands slipped up to cup her face. The wait was driving her insane. She wanted to taste him, to drive her mouth against his and drain him. The craving made her dizzy, but still she waited. When she thought she couldn't stand it another second, he moved.

He rubbed against her mouth, moistened her lips with his tongue, sucked on her tenderly, then plunged inside.

His tongue was heaven in her mouth. He was rough and salty on top and sweet and silky underneath.

He drew back for a breath and then surged forward, not just with his mouth this time, but with his body, crab-walking with his legs alongside hers, pushing her out the door of the bathroom and against the edge of the vanity.

Without warning, she was lifted, set on the counter, and his mouth left hers to attach itself to her breast. He leaned over her, suckling, one hand holding her shoulders back against the cool glass of the mirror, the other sliding along the hot inside of her thighs, pushing them apart. She gasped as his fingers pressed into her moist channel, first one, then two, crossed.

He swallowed her first gasp, and several that followed it, with open, probing kisses. He shifted to stand with one leg between her thighs, one of hers between his, and pulled her up from behind with a hand on the small of her back, urging her to buck into his other hand as it worked magic inside of her. Crooking his head into the hollow of her throat, he whispered exotic encouragement into her ear.

Her heartbeat thundered, his touch shaking her to the core before she could stop him. Before she could tell him this was a journey she wanted them to make together. Wave after wave rippled through her, leaving her boneless and weak.

When she opened her eyes he was still leaning over her, supporting her, the only thing keeping her from sliding right off the counter. But he'd pulled his head back and was watching her. She knew from the dark look in his eyes that he had been watching her the whole time.

"Is that what you wanted?" he asked roughly.

The bite of his words shocked her. She'd expected fear, maybe. Sorrow. Guilt, even. But not anger. Not now.

"No." The blush she knew already stained her cheeks deepened in intensity.

"And if I don't have any more to give?"

"I don't believe that."

At least he hadn't pulled away. In fact, his hand had drifted up to cover her breast. Achingly. Tenderly.

She found enough hope in that to nullify the hurt his words caused. She sat up close to him on the counter. "I don't think you believe it, either."

He smiled a smile devoid of happiness. "Still trying to figure out what's going on in my head, Doc?"

"It's not what's going on up here that matters." She tapped his temple with her index finger, then trailed it down his neck to his chest and left it resting over his heart. ''It's what's going on in here that's important now.''

His false smile cracked and fell, leaving behind an empty look, as if he were a hollow shell, waiting to be filled. He swayed slightly, leaning into her touch.

Lane had the feeling he was on the edge of a great divide. One nudge and she could push him over. The question was, what would the fall do to him? What if she pushed him into something he wasn't ready for? Something he couldn't live with. The decision to leap had to be his. She owed him that much.

''Tell me what you want, Jason. What you really, really want.'' She took his hand from her breast and placed it on his own chest over his heart, covering it with both of hers. ''In there.''

He squeezed his eyes shut. After a second he pushed her hands away and straightened up. She panicked, tried to hold on. She couldn't lose him now, when she'd come so close to breaking through.

Firmly but gently he set her away from him and took a step back, revealing his whole self to her.

Her eyes took him in piece by piece. The wide chest she'd seen before. The flat stomach with the scars riding just inside his hipbone. And at the juncture of his legs stood his fully aroused sex, as finely sculptured as a Michelangelo marble, hard and begging for the attention of more than her eyes.

His eyes followed the tracks of hers. ''I think what I want is pretty obvious,'' he said.

She brought her gaze up to his, shaking her head. ''No,'' she said, barely breathing. She had to be sure. She had to know he was sure. ''Tell me.''

He closed the gap between them. She couldn't see him anymore, but she could feel him. His heat against her thigh.

He placed her hand back on his chest. ''I want you to make my heart race.''

He landed a soft kiss beneath her ear. ''I want you to touch me until it burns.''

The tip of his curled tongue drew a path along the underside of her jaw, his whiskers roughing her face. Lane still hadn't touched him back. Holding off her natural responses was killing her. But she wanted—she needed—to hear the words.

He rolled his mouth over hers and said it to her lips. ''I want to make love with you.''

Like a bird uncaged, her hands flew to him. She caressed his back, massaged his chest, memorized the contour of his hips.

Desire spiraled tight within her as he lifted her off the counter and deposited her in the center of the bed. She pulled him down with her, loving the weight of his body on hers. He lay cradled in her hips, poised on the brink of entry.

His hands pillaged her hair. ''I've wanted to do that for so long.''

''What?'' she asked, breathless.

''Bury my hands in this wild hair of yours.''

With her hands low on his backside, she pulled him closer. ''Now bury yourself somewhere else.''

He held himself away, gulping air like a drowning man. ''Lane, wait. Slow down.''

She tried to ask why, but the electrical storm brewing between them interfered with her brain's ability to send the appropriate signals to her mouth. Her eyes locked on his and she saw he was just as desperate.

''It's been a long time for me. I need—'' he shuddered ''—I want it to be good for you.''

She swallowed the lump in her throat and let her fingers skim over his body to the point he needed her most. ''It's perfect,'' she said, encircling him and guiding him home.

The roar of the wind they created together drowned out everything until there was nothing but the sensation of him thrusting inside her. Each time he withdrew, he took away her hope. And then on his return he gave twice as much as he'd taken.

He loved ferociously. Unrestrained. Uncivilized. There was no more facade. This was too primitive, too natural.

The force of their passion buffeted her, each gust making her momentarily weightless. She clutched at him, irrationally afraid he would be swept away when the storm's crescendo peaked.

He drove deeper and faster within her. Touching her heart. Piercing her soul.

Her climax lifted her on gales of shivering pleasure. Jason followed her immediately, calling out to her as the muscles in his back and legs contracted rhythmically.

The tempest gradually calmed to a gentle breeze on which Lane floated back to reality.

She wanted to say something witty or something reassuring. Anything to lessen the impact of what they'd done. As if anything could lessen the impact of having the most incredible sex of your life in the arms of a man who was little more than a stranger. It didn't matter, anyway. The experience had left her speechless.

At least he seemed just as affected. He hovered over her, his body still joined to hers, with his eyes closed. His breath cut the silence in ragged gasps. Finally he broke the connection between them and rolled onto his back, taking her with him. Relieved of his weight, she pulled in a deep breath. They lay together a long time like that before he opened his eyes.

For the first time, when she looked into those eyes, she found them unfettered by the anger, the hurt, the guilt of the past. He looked almost…happy. Peaceful, at the least.

Womanly pride unfurled in her breast. She'd done this. Made him forget. But for how long?

His forehead came to rest on hers and his tongue danced along her lips, seeking entrance. She felt his body stir. So soon?

She turned her head aside, suddenly unsure.

Forgetting wasn't the same as healing. How long would it be before he remembered? When would the doubts creep back in, and with what vengeance, at having been temporarily displaced?

He cupped her chin and eased her head back toward him, studying her. "That didn't take long."

"What?"

"For you to start having regrets."

"No...I—"

"Liar." He slid his hand across her shoulder, down her torso and over her hip to rest on her thigh, pulling her leg over his body.

"It's just...so soon. You can't already—"

"I told you, it's been a long time."

"Since Karen?" She felt him soften. Her question effectively squelched his renewed desire.

With a sigh he shifted her to his side. "No."

"But you did have a relationship with her? That's the big mistake you think you made?"

He tucked his hands under the back of his head and stared at the ceiling. "Yes."

Lane propped herself up on one elbow, studying the care lines etching themselves onto his face. She resisted the urge to try to smooth them away.

"We can't help who we fall in love with, Jason, even when we know it's dangerous." Someone should be giving her the same counseling. She was falling in love with Jason Stateler, and that love put her heart at risk. What kind of future could they have if he couldn't live with his past?

"You don't want to talk about this now, not like this," he said.

She supposed it was morbid to lie in bed with a man, after you had done the things they'd just done, and ask him about his dead lover, but she had to know. "Now, more than ever, I need to hear it."

He rolled out of bed and into his jeans, then paced the length of the room, his back to her. She pulled the bedsheet up under her arms and sat up.

When he spoke, his voice echoed a hollow tone. "Karen wasn't my first partner, you know. Not even the first one I lost. My first partner was shot in a drug raid. The bullet fractured his femur and damaged the sciatic nerve, so he was stuck behind a desk."

"Jim Sturman?"

Jason nodded. "Then Karen was assigned to me. By the time we had worked together a few months, we knew each other better than most married couples. We threw ourselves into the job and built a great solve rate. We spent so much time together, working and traveling, that it just seemed natural to be together off duty, too."

Jason stopped pacing. Dragging his hand through his hair, he turned around and faced her. "I'm not sure exactly when my feelings for her changed, I just know one day I looked at her and realized she was beautiful and smart and I wanted her."

"But she was your partner." Lane knew the words were ludicrous as soon as they left her mouth. She was his partner, too—even if only temporarily—and it hadn't stopped her from having feelings for him far beyond the professional, or from acting on those feelings. Her thighs still ached from the intensity of their coupling.

He rocked back on his heels, crossed his arms over his chest. "I knew it was wrong. I tried to deny it at first. Then I tried to ignore it. It nearly drove me crazy being so close to her without telling her how I felt." He shrugged, and his voice became a little less even. "So finally I gave in. The day I told her, I was so nervous. I was afraid she would laugh at me—think I was joking."

"But she didn't laugh?"

"No." A tiny glimmer of remembered joy flared in his eyes, then snuffed out. "Except when she called me a fool for waiting so long to tell her."

His gaze leveled on Lane, boring into her as if seeking something deep inside her. His eyes begged silently. For what? Understanding? Forgiveness?

Her stomach turned queasy. She honestly didn't know if she was ready for this.

"We were so damn arrogant," he said. "We knew there were rules against what we were doing, but we wanted it all. We were a great team, there was no reason to ruin that just because we were sleeping together." He shook his head. "So we pretended the rules weren't meant for us."

His chin snapped up and his eyes narrowed. "We kept our minds on the job while we were at work, though. There were no supply room encounters or make-out stakeouts. Hell, we even slept in separate hotel rooms when we traveled on Bureau business. It was never anything sleazy. Ever."

"I never imagined it was," she said softly.

He dropped his eyes, mollified or ashamed, she didn't know. "We thought we could handle it. And we did, for a while."

"A while?"

He seemed reluctant to continue. His Adam's apple bobbed as he swallowed hard.

"A long while. We stayed partnered for another two years. It wasn't always easy, but we were discreet, and careful never to let our personal relationship interfere with our work."

"So what happened?"

"I guess we never considered that the reverse might happen—that our work might interfere with our personal relationship. Karen was a terrific agent, but she was really aggressive on a case. To be honest, sometimes she was downright reckless. I was always bailing her out of some scrape or another and it scared me. She thought I was too conservative. I thought she took too many risks. Things got…complicated."

"You broke up?" The only thing that Lane imagined would be harder than working with someone you loved was working with someone you used to love.

"No, but I was afraid that was where we were headed. I told Karen that I was going to request a transfer so that we could go public with our relationship. I probably would have done it earlier if it hadn't been for Sturman."

"Sturman?"

"He was our supervisory agent by then. I wanted the paperwork put through quietly so Karen's reputation wouldn't be trashed."

"You didn't trust Sturman to do that?"

Jason shook his head, dragging a hand roughly through his hair. "To be honest, Jim wasn't a very good agent, and he was a worse supervisor. He never should have been given that job. Never would have been if I'd told the truth about the day he was shot. He made himself out to be a hero. Let's just say that isn't quite the way it happened. We didn't talk much after that."

That explained a lot to Lane about why Jason didn't depend on his office for support when he worked a case.

"Anyway," he continued, "I told Karen I was going over Sturman's head to the director. She was furious that I wanted to quit and that I was going to break the chain of command. She never liked the thing between me and Jim. We had a fight about it, and things got really tense between us for a couple of days.

"I did call Sturman, but to ask for a few days off to sort things out, not for a transfer. But Karen and I had been working a gun-smuggling operation, and we were getting pretty close. Sturman wanted me to set up a meet with one of the suppliers, then we could let it sit for a while. I was so mad at Karen that I set it up alone. I didn't even call her and tell her about it. I just wanted it over with. I never thought she'd show up there. She had no reason. But while I was waiting for my contact, Karen drove up."

He had to clear his throat to continue. Even then, his words were gravelly, and each one seemed to require an enormous effort.

"I don't know why she came, but I don't think she knew there was anything going on, so she had no reason to be concerned. She got out of her car and smiled at me like the whole world was turning her way. Like things had never been better between us. I just stood there, frozen. I knew something was wrong, but I couldn't move. Then all hell broke loose. There were shooters on the roofs of buildings on either side of the street. We had no cover. I was hit, and I must have blacked out for a few seconds, because the next thing I remember, the street was quiet. Karen lay a few feet away, with a puddle of blood around her. She was still breathing when I got to her. For a minute I thought she might make it. I prayed she would."

He stopped talking, but Lane couldn't tell if he was done or just needed to catch his breath, which was coming in broken gasps. He took up pacing the floor again, then stopped when he came to the corner of the bed. He sat down there, his head bowed, elbows resting on his thighs and his hands dangling between his knees.

She almost hoped he wouldn't continue. She knew how this story ended; she didn't need to hear it.

He needed to tell it, though. "It's a hell of a feeling, Lane."

No, no, no, sounded in her head in time to the thrumming of her heart.

His voice lowered to a reverent whisper. "Holding the woman you love while she draws her last breath."

The horror of what she'd heard congealed in Lane's bloodstream. She drew the sheet up higher and pulled her knees to her chest.

She'd expected the truth to be bad; what she got was worse. Jason and his partner hadn't just been casual lovers. He'd wanted to marry her, to spend the rest of his life with her, until violence ripped that dream away without reason or warning. And she suspected the story didn't end there. Losing someone you loved was tough enough. Having to hide the truth, to deny the full extent of what you lost, could be crippling.

"All these years," she asked, "you've never told anyone at the Bureau?"

He scrubbed his hands over his face, and when he pulled them away his cheeks were damp with the tears he wouldn't let fall. "They wouldn't have understood. And I didn't want them to remember her like that."

"Then you had no one to talk to about it?"

He shrugged. "Nick."

Thank God for Nick, she thought.

He continued. "For a while after she died, I was lost. I thought the way to get over it was to find someone else. Anyone else. I went through a string of drinking binges and one-night stands that I'm not very proud of. If it hadn't been for Nick, dragging me out of the bars and threatening to kick my butt if I didn't pull myself together, I might still be lost."

He edged up the side of the bed until he sat next to her, his big hand covering hers on the mattress. "That's partly why I fought this so hard. I didn't want to use you like that, in a one-time thing."

What they'd shared hadn't felt like a one-time thing to her. In fact, it felt very much like the kind of thing she could never get enough of. The kind of thing she might not be able to live without.

A chill danced down her spine. For all her thinking, she hadn't thought past tonight. She should be ecstatic. Jason had just admitted he wanted them to have a future together. Why did the thought leave her so unsettled?

Maybe because he wasn't ready for a future, and she knew it. Not when he had yet to deal with his past.

He tucked a strand of hair behind her ear, but didn't let go of the curls. "You scared the hell out me yesterday."

"When I got shot, or when I kissed you?"

"Both," he whispered, and she heard the old agony in his voice, stronger, if that was possible, than ever. He pulled her against his chest and ground his cheek against the top of her head.

She'd done this to him. How could she have thought sex would solve anything? She'd thrown herself at him, tempted him and aroused him until his body's physical demands shorted out his mind's better judgment.

She'd told him he could trust her. And then she'd led him back into the nightmare from which he'd spent four years trying to wake up.

Stupid. Stupid. Stupid.

"Can't you see?" he asked. His breath hitched and he held her even tighter. "It's just like before. It's happening all over again, and I can't stop it. I can't stop myself."

It wasn't like before. She had seduced him; it was her fault. Couldn't he see that? If not, maybe he was blind to other differences as well. Maybe making love had blurred the line between past and present beyond his recognition.

Suddenly she felt chilled, and it wasn't from the air-conditioning. Pushing herself away from his chest, she scooted across the bed, tugging the sheet tucked under her arms with her. "I'm not Karen."

He held out his hand after her, deep crevices furrowing his brow. Then his hand fell. "Is that what you think, *Doc?* That you're some sort of substitute for her?" His voice shook. In frustration…or fear of the truth?

She didn't answer him. She couldn't even look at him.

After a few seconds of her silence, he lurched off the bed and stalked to the door. Before walking out, he turned and looked over his shoulder at her, his eyes sharp as knives. "Believe what you want, but I know exactly who I made love to tonight."

Chapter 12

Jason woke to a pain in his neck like he'd been hacked with a dull ax. The half-moon had traversed the sky and dipped into the tree line, leaving a cloak of black velvet in its wake.

He must have slept for hours on the hard wooden porch.

Rolling his head around his shoulders, he kneaded the knotted muscles with his thumb and forefinger. His rear was numb. Pressing his back against the cabin wall, he shifted his hips until the pins and needles of restored circulation pricked his backside.

That's what you get for making love to a woman you weren't supposed to touch. A pain in the neck and a pain in the a—

Worse yet, they both might just get a lot more than that out of it. He hadn't used any birth control protection; hadn't even thought about it. Not that he had anything with him, if he had thought about it. He'd never done that before. Not even in his lost days.

He should never have told Lane about Karen. She couldn't just let things be; he knew that about her. She had this need to fix everything, everyone. Even the unfixable.

Somehow, though, he found himself revealing things to her that he'd never told anyone. Letting her into the secret places where he'd buried the truth, buried it deep before it had destroyed him. For her, he resurrected it.

Surprisingly, he found the memories' razor edges had dulled over time. They still hurt, but they no longer had the ability to lay him open like a gutted fish. Because of her?

Ironically, near her—the place that most unhinged him, that inflamed his deepest fears—was also the place he found the most peace. The only peace he'd felt in years.

A sound that didn't quite fit jolted him to attention like a slap in the face. Movement on the far side of the grounds caught his eye. A shadow shifting near the trees. It could have been a cloud crossing.

Cloud, hell. Clouds did not make the hairs stand up on the back of his neck.

He got to his feet soundlessly and turned to the door of the cabin, hoping Lane had not locked him out. Across the playground Sam barked twice.

Calculating how long it would take an intruder to work his way across the compound, Jason twisted the doorknob. Thank God, it opened. He leaned into it, willing it not to squeak. In the dark, his eyes found Lane's outline, sitting up in bed. He was pretty sure that was his gun she held out in front of her.

It was a sign of his confusion last night that he'd left the room without it. A sign of his carelessness. The kind of mistake a cop makes when he's involved with his partner. The kind of mistake that gets people killed.

"I heard the dog," she whispered, her voice uncertain.

Jason took the gun from her and shoved it in his jeans. "We have to go."

Lane pushed the covers away and swung her legs over the side. Sometime after he'd left last night, she'd put her dirty clothes back on. He didn't even want to think about what that meant. Only her feet were bare. She scooped up her sneakers while he checked the intruder's position out the front window.

A run for the woods would be risky, but they didn't have much choice. He waved the barrel of his gun toward the side window, which faced the forest. "That way."

She stood clutching her shoes to her chest while he opened the window. "It could just be vagrants looking for someplace to stay."

He nodded, motioning for her to climb up on the sill. "Could be."

She swung one leg out and looked back at him. "Or thieves, looking for something to steal."

That was Lane, refusing to believe the worst, even when the truth of it stared her in the face. She couldn't accept that someone she trusted had betrayed her, even now, when intruders here ruled out the possibility of the leak being in his department. No one at the Bureau could know about this place.

Only someone close to Lane could have betrayed her, someone who knew her family very well. Reciting in his head a litany of curses reserved for the man who had broken Lane's trust, Jason prodded her forward. "Go."

Hunching his own body through the small opening, he leaned back in and snagged his T-shirt off the floor, then slipped to the ground outside, grabbed her hand and tugged her toward the back of the cabin. At the corner, he stopped and peered around the edge. The silhouette of a man, a second interloper, moved along the back of the cabins, near the tree line.

Jason recognized the apelike walk. Grumman. So it was probably Morales in front.

He needed a diversion. Leaning down, he felt around the ground and pulled up a clod of dirt and grass with his fingers. It might just work, if his aim was good.

Pushing Lane back toward the front of the cabin, he pantomimed his intentions, praying she understood and would, for once, do what he said without question.

When the man working the front of the cottages leaned forward, hands cupped around his eyes, to look inside the cabin three doors down, Jason stepped out and heaved the grass clod toward the porch of the office.

Bingo! The dirt made only a soft thud, almost imperceptible if you weren't listening for it, but it was enough to rouse Samantha. Two barks.

The man peering in the cabin jerked toward the sound, and Jason shoved Lane toward the trees. As soon as she started forward, her bare feet brushing soundlessly through the grass, Jason stepped into the open, his attention focused on the man in front of Number 7. If the man turned, Jason's big outline should draw his attention away from the twenty feet of open ground Lane had to cross to get to the woods. She would get away, he hoped.

Gun ready and feet planted in a firing stance, Jason waited for the man to realize the noise was a ruse and turn. He counted the seconds it would take Lane's long legs to reach the woods. Four. Three. The man out front twisted slowly toward them, searching. Two. Jason checked over his shoulder just in time to see Lane dissolve into the black forest.

As Jason jumped for cover behind the building, the man completed his turn and faced the spot where Lane had entered the trees. Not daring to breathe, Jason waited for the prowler's reaction. Had he seen her escape?

While the seconds ticked off, Jason flexed his grip on his handgun. Nothing. The silhouetted man continued his cabin-by-cabin search, and Jason filled his starving lungs, then blew the breath out silently.

If he had to, he would take on both men to cover her getaway. But, knowing Lane, she would be right back in the middle of things if it came down to a fight. Besides, it was becoming important to him that they *both* live through this.

He checked the progress of the man in back. Two houses down, and closing. Lane should be a fair way down the path to the lake by now, but Jason was trapped. No way was he getting past the intruders without being seen.

He returned to the front of the cabin, edging his nose around the corner just far enough to catch a clear profile of the prowler in front. Alejandro. Then where was Morales? Grumman rarely worked without him.

Jason's hopes took a nosedive. He might be able to take two men, if he could get to them one at a time, but three? And what if Morales had been in the shadows somewhere and seen Lane dash into the woods?

Alejandro's footfalls on the walkway in front of Number 10 reminded Jason he didn't have time to worry about it. Just as Jason was about to launch himself toward the sound, a light glinted into the center of the semicircle of lodges. A door squeaked.

"Who's out there?" Dora asked.

Jason peeked around the corner. Alejandro had flattened himself against the porch, in the shadows. Dora stood in the spotlight of her own porch, pulling the belt of a housecoat tight across her middle.

"Mr. 'n' Mrs. Timmons, that you?" Her voice pitched higher on each word.

Jason had to pull back when Grumman slunk around the corner to hunch next to Alejandro. "It ain't them," he heard Grumman say. "Maybe the old bag knows where they are."

Alejandro grunted an affirmative. "Go find out."

While his partner waited in the shadows, Grumman swaggered across the open ground in front of the office, a gun held loosely behind his back.

If Jason slipped around to the back of Number 10 now, he could make it to the woods. He wanted to go after Lane. He was still afraid Morales was out there somewhere, stalking her. The image of him sneaking up on her in the woods almost prompted his feet to move, but Dora's shaky voice stopped him. He watched her back into her doorway. "Can—can I help you?"

He closed his eyes. Damn. Why didn't she lock the door? Why didn't she have a gun? Even in rural Georgia, times were changing. A woman couldn't just open her door to strangers in the middle of the night.

Sam sensed the danger. After her habitual two barks, she stood growling. Jason heard the clink of metal as she pulled at her chain.

He flattened himself against the wall. Sam snarled and he heard her teeth snap. *Good girl.* Then came a thunk and a whimper.

Dora's gasp broke through Jason's indecision and started his feet pumping. He hurried around behind Number 10 and past the next three cabins. He stopped behind Number 6, listening. He heard Grumman's rough voice barking questions and Dora's shrill one, denying that she knew anything about an FBI agent and a cop.

Beside the office, beneath the window, Jason crouched in the darkness while Alejandro rattled the doorknob of Number 10. When it swung open, and the man stepped in, leading with his gun, Jason figured that gave him about thirty seconds to get in Dora's cabin, disable Grumman and get Dora out before Alejandro finished searching Number 10 and came to find Grumman.

Moving to the front of the bushes planted around the office, Jason heard Sam whine from where she cowered underneath a boxleaf shrub. If she announced his arrival, he was dead. Reaching out into the dark, he offered his palm. "Shh, girl. You know me." He scratched her ear, feeling a sticky blob of blood from Grumman's blow, but her tail thumped the grass. She must not be hurt too badly. He hoped her owner would fare as well.

Jason moved on, creeping up the stairs. A shower of adrenaline-induced sparks tingled his skin. His heart raced. He raised his foot to kick in the door.

And nearly fell over when a thunderous roar split the night in two. He recovered his balance and leaped for cover as Grumman flew out the office door, searching for the source of the sound. Deep in the bushes, next to Sam, Jason fought to restart his heart.

He knew that engine. At any second he expected the big motorcycle to come barreling out of the woods, Lane perched on the saddle, in a crazy rescue attempt.

Grumman jumped down the steps, cursing, and hurried across the walk to meet Alejandro, who had also run out when the noise started. They jogged toward the sound—and the exact spot where Lane had disappeared into the forest.

Jason repeated Grumman's curse in triplicate, watching them disappear into the woods. Rushing into the office, he grabbed Dora and propelled her to the door. "You've got to get out of here. Go. Fast."

He nearly fell over her when she stopped at the bottom of the steps. He tried to push her on, but she bent over to unclip Sam's chain and coax the dog out of the bushes.

The engine noise stopped. Jason herded the old woman and the dog into her sedan and slammed the door behind them. Thank God the keys were still in the car. "Drive, and just keep driving. Go."

Dora fumbled with the ignition a second, but soon the old engine choked to life. Jason ran toward the woods as she spun gravel, pulling around the circle drive and onto the county road.

He entered the forest where there was no path, hoping to get an angle on Grumman and Alejandro and cut them off before they got to Lane, but the undergrowth slowed his progress. The darkness of the woods clawed at him, distorting all sense of direction, distance and time. He knew only the burning of his lungs and the chafe of sweat-drenched clothing on his skin.

He forced himself forward against the thick foliage for what seemed like hours, but he knew it couldn't have been more than minutes. Finally he stopped. Fighting for control over the swelling panic, he slowed his breathing and calmed his racing heart. Losing his head would not help her.

When the pounding of blood against his eardrums quieted, he listened. Hearing nothing but the buzz of insects, he stepped forward again, moving more slowly this time, more quietly. He angled again for the lake, and the trail he prayed Lane had taken.

Another mistake, he realized. He should have set up a contingency plan, a place to meet if they got separated. He had let himself get distracted, fallen for his partner and failed to do his job. Again.

He clenched his jaw until it ached. He had to be the only man alive stupid enough to make the single worst mistake of his life *twice.*

When he thought he might give in to the panic after all, he heard the unmistakable sounds of another animal crashing through the vegetation. A human animal. It had to be Lane.

Jason put himself on an intercept course with the noise and grabbed her as she ran by. Fast as a cat's strike, she spun around and connected a fist with the side of his face.

He reeled backward from the blow. ''Ow!'' Mercifully the solid trunk of a tree behind him had kept him from going all the way down. His ego had been bruised enough tonight without being knocked down by a woman.

Lane must have realized who it was as soon as she hit him, because she hadn't run. She stood in front of him, nursing her knuckles. ''Ow, yourself.'' She shook her hand in the air. ''That hurts.''

He grunted an affirmative as he tentatively probed the rising welt on his cheek. Over the knuckles in her mouth, she asked, ''Are you okay?'' She stepped forward and touched his cheek.

He pulled his head back and took her hand, too overwhelmed at seeing her alive and well to be mad about a little thing like a black eye. ''I'll live.''

He rubbed his thumb over her palm, staring at her like an idiot. The discomfort was still there between them, but he didn't care. He wasn't letting her go again.

She glanced over her shoulder. ''We have to go. They might still be following me.''

Jason listened and then shook his head. ''I don't hear anything. I don't think they'd chase you this far into the woods. The darkness makes it too much of a fair fight. From what we've seen, they prefer ambushes. They're more likely to be waiting for us on the road."

She considered him for a moment, then her shoulders relaxed. God, he admired her resiliency.

"So what now?" she asked.

"We go in the opposite direction."

"The lake?"

He nodded. They needed to get moving, but he needed to know something first. "What did you do to the bike?"

Her impish grin cut through the darkness. "I rolled it over a log so the back wheel was off the ground and lashed the throttle back with my hair band."

He stared at her in disbelief. "A hair band?" She'd saved his hide with a hairband.

"It worked for a few seconds, until it jumped the log and crashed. Then I ran like crazy."

She looked far too pleased with herself.

"Stupid stunt. You were supposed to be running away."

"And you were supposed to be right behind me, not making yourself a target."

"I was covering your back."

She stepped up into his face, so close to him he could see the starlight twinkle off her eyes. "And I covered yours, *partner.* You needed a diversion."

Game, set and match: McCullough.

Never one to be a sore loser, he tried to match her grin. "All right, but you're going to be the one to tell Nick you wrecked his bike."

Lane's expression turned satisfyingly sober. "You think he'll be sore?"

He squeezed her hand, inexplicably happy for the small favor that she didn't pull away. "Furious."

As they plunged farther into the darkness, he kept a firm

grip on her, determined not to lose her to the darkness. They had a lot to talk about later.

They trekked along in silence, Jason pulling Lane along behind him as he broke a path for her as best he could through a world full of smells and feelings and sound, but no sight. When they emerged on the waterfront, the clear air over the lake refreshed him, lifting the shroud of the forest from his shoulders.

Cool waves lapped at the beach as they walked through the sand. Jason worried over the way she dragged her feet. Not that his own steps were much steadier. It would be morning soon, and they were both exhausted.

When she stumbled, her toe digging into the sand, he caught her before she could fall. She righted herself without comment and tried to move forward again, but he held her back.

''Wait.'' He scanned the area. ''There.'' He pointed to an inlet just ahead. Sitting her down under the wide branches of tree, he tipped her chin up with his hand. ''You rest a few minutes. I'm going to go find us some transportation.''

She nodded and leaned her head back, eyes closed. ''Lane.'' Her eyes gradually opened. ''Where's your gun?''

''Here.'' She pulled it from the small of her back.

''Keep it handy, okay? Stay put, and keep your eyes open. I'll be back as soon as I can.''

She looked so tired, but she nodded and sat up a little straighter.

''Be careful,'' he thought he heard as he walked away. He hated to leave her, but he needed to find some way to get out of there. Something to take them farther and faster than they could go by foot.

He walked nearly a mile, much farther than he had intended. His angst at leaving Lane increased with each step he took. All the boats moored along the shore were too new, too expensive. He wasn't that good with wiring engines. Especially boat engines. Finally he found something he could handle. A small, flat-bottomed rubber raft with oars. It would be slower than a motorboat, but quieter.

He released the nylon cord that attached the raft to the dock, jumped in and sank the oars hard in the water, impatient to get back to Lane. Rowing steadily, he began to relax when the quiet inlet came into sight. Until his eyes searched the shore and the tension hit him like a hammer.

She was gone.

He felt his throat contract, but he couldn't swallow. Not daring to call out for her, he paddled harder. Reaching shallow water, he jumped out, frantically scanning the shore for any trace of her. Footprints in the sand, anything.

At the sound of sloshing water behind him, he spun, instinctively bringing his gun up, then immediately lowering it. Lightning flashed straight to his loins at the sight before him. Lane rose up from the water near an outcropping of rock, her face turned up to the stars, her hair swept back from her face. Her T-shirt clung to her, outlining every contour he remembered so well.

Had it really been just a few hours ago that he had touched the breasts outlined so clearly beneath the translucent cotton?

Rivulets of water ran across her face, beneath the neck of the shirt, down her bare thighs.

Envy clawed at him. Once, he had touched her like the water now did, easing itself over her, around her, inside her. Then, it had been his heat, not the chill of the lake, that had made her shiver.

She was startled when she saw him. "You're back."

He turned away from her, unable to form words with her standing there like that, and afraid, even in the dark, that she would see him. He couldn't control his body's natural reaction to her, but he didn't have to like it.

Lane watched silently as Jason pulled a raft to the beach.

"I told you to stay put," he said as he turned around stiffly.

It didn't take much to guess that she was the source of his

irritation. This time she hadn't meant to do that, to turn him on. Lord, had she gone crazy? First throwing herself at him, then closing herself off from him, and now this?

Men have killed women for less.

She picked up her gun from the rock next to her and met him on shore. "I just wanted to wash up. The bug bites and the scratches from the brambles in the woods were driving me crazy."

"Fine. You could have been killed, but, hey, at least you'd be a clean corpse."

She fought back her impatience. "My gun was sitting on the rock right next to me. I was perfectly safe."

"Uh-huh, there's no way anyone else could have sneaked up on you, the way I did." He left the raft lying on the beach and propped his back against the tree he'd left her sitting under earlier.

She followed him. Couldn't he see she hadn't done it on purpose? "You told me to stay awake. I was getting tired. I thought the water might revive me a little."

His eyes raked her wet shirt, lingering over the peaks of her breasts, pebbled from the cold water. "I guess it worked."

Her cheeks burned. She crossed her arms over her chest. This was ridiculous. What did he want from her? "You were gone a long time!"

"And you were so worried about me that you took a bath?"

"It wasn't a bath, I just waded in by the rocks and rinsed off. And I wasn't worried. I knew you would be back. I was just...restless."

"Restless. That's why you nearly gave me a coronary?" He stalked back to the raft.

She gave him, and herself, a few minutes, then sidled down to the water. He was right, as usual. She owed him an apology, but she couldn't bring herself to say the words. She hadn't said them in years.

Jason stood by the raft in knee-deep waves, lifting cupped palms full of water to his face.

The urge to go to him pulled her to the shore's edge, but she didn't go in. It probably wasn't a good idea to get that close to him right now. He might drown her.

Lane inhaled the clean air, filled with the scent of pine and red clay, trying to think of some way to make him understand what she was feeling. How could she, when she wasn't sure she knew? "You must think I'm either stupid or insane."

"Why would I think that?"

"Because I didn't listen to you when you told me how much danger we were in at the lodge. And then I did it again out here."

He shrugged and lifted a fistful of water to the back of his neck.

"Because of the way I treated you last night," she added quietly.

The starlight reflecting off the water changed the usually golden cast of his eyes to silver. Mercury. She couldn't tell if it ran hot or cold.

"Don't worry about it. One of us had to come to our senses."

Cold. Definitely stone cold.

He pushed the boat toward her. "Are you coming?"

She waded out to him, climbed in as he picked up the oars and took a seat. Taking up an even stroke, he kept his face averted from hers in the predawn light.

"Please, Jason, I need you to understand."

He jerked the oars out of the water. The boat glided soundlessly across the lake's glass surface. "Then explain it to me, Lane. Explain why you've played me like a yo-yo the past two days."

She knew she'd hurt him. Now she knew how badly. He had given a part of himself to her, a part he'd been terrified to give, and she had thrown it back in his face. "I wanted you to see that we could be together and the world wouldn't end. I wanted you to know you could care about someone again. I thought I was helping."

A low, tortured laugh burst from his lips. "That's classic. You slept with me for strictly *therapeutic* reasons."

He cocked his head to the side, the oars poised for rowing again. "Well, Doctor McCullough, you're going to be a very popular counselor if you offer that service to all of your patients."

Lane's cheeks burned. "That's not what I meant." But she realized that's how her words had sounded, so she quashed her retort. "Oh, God, I'm making it worse, aren't I?"

"Yes. You are." Jason set the oars in the water and started rowing. Twice, he seemed about to say something, and then bit it back. Finally he sighed and let the oars go still again. "None of that explains that bull about thinking I had you confused with Karen. You pushed me for the truth, and when you got it, you shut down on me, and I don't know why."

Elbows on her knees and face propped on her fists, Lane searched for the reason and came up empty. "I didn't mean to hurt you."

He shook his head and rowed in long, hard strokes.

She was growing irritated with this game. What did he want from her? *The truth,* a little voice in her head chided, sounding remarkably like Kelly. *Like he gave you.* Lane wished she could talk to her sister. Kelly would know how to sort this craziness out. She had tried to call her earlier from the cabin, after Jason walked out, but Kelly hadn't answered.

With each plop and whoosh of the oars, Lane's misery increased. "I was scared," she finally admitted.

His even rowing faltered. "Of me?"

"A little." She examined her hands, not able to bring herself to meet his eyes. "And of whoever is after us."

"Is that all?" From his tone of voice he had already figured out that it wasn't.

When had he come to know her so well? The connection between them had become more than physical. Sometimes it was like their minds touched.

"No. I guess I was mostly scared of me."

"Why?"

Lane wished she knew. What was this great truth that she couldn't admit, even to herself? She reached for it, fought for it, until it made her head pound. Rubbing her temples, she surrendered with a sigh.

"I don't know. I guess I just don't handle stress well," she said.

He looked up, surprise cracking his unreadable expression for an instant. She knew she wasn't being honest with herself, or him. The half truths tasted bitter in her mouth. "I guess I'm my father's daughter after all." She held her hand up, watching it tremble in the starlight. "Lord knows I could use a drink right now." Her voice tripped over the sob bubbling in her throat.

Jason let the oars go still and scurried to her on hands and knees. The little raft, like her stomach, pitched and rolled with his movement.

"Stop," he said, capturing her shaking hand and pulling her to him. She went unresisting to his chest.

"Just stop. You're fine. You handle stress better than anyone I know." His hands soothed her back as he murmured the words in her ear.

The tremor from her hand spread throughout her body, rippling through her in waves just under her skin. "Then why am I shaking like a leaf?"

He rustled his cheek in her hair. "You're just tired. You need some rest. That's all. You're the strongest person I know, Lane McCullough. And you're safe. I won't let anything happen to you."

Lane nestled herself against him and allowed herself, just for a minute, to believe him. But reality sneaked past even his strong embrace. "They'll find us again, won't they?"

He tightened his arms around her. His silence was answer enough.

She suppressed a shiver. "This means it's him, doesn't it? It's Roland. No one else could have known about this place."

His caresses settled into a gentle rhythm, in time with the waves licking the side of the raft.

"I've been thinking about that," he said.

She didn't like the tone in his voice. He sounded too much like a parent saying, "This is going to hurt me worse than it hurts you" just before pouring disinfectant on an open wound.

"What about Kelly?" he asked.

She blinked in shock. Kelly? "You can't think—" She couldn't make herself say it.

"She would remember the lodge, probably more so than Bowling," he persisted.

"She's not involved in this." Anger sharpened Lane's tongue. As if his mistrust of her friends in the police department wasn't bad enough, now he was accusing her sister.

"Someone could be using her for information."

"No," she said, strangled. "Kelly wouldn't tell anyone anything that could put me in danger. They could put bamboo shoots under her fingernails and she wouldn't—oh no."

The blood drained from Lane's head, leaving her dizzy.

"What?" She heard the concern in his voice.

"I called her."

He shook his head, confused. "When?"

She leaned forward, rushing now, giving in to the panic thrumming throughout her. "Tonight, from the cabin. After you went outside."

His eyes shuttered half closed. "There's a caller ID box in the office at your house."

She felt dazed, out of control. "They traced the number with a reverse directory. They're in my house. Oh, my God, they have Kelly."

Chapter 13

Lane stared at her feet as she walked. Roadside dust billowed over her sneakers with each step, weighing her down, holding her back as it had for the past hour. The morning sun burned against eyes that already felt scoured, dry and gritty from worry and lack of sleep.

"We can't walk all the way to Atlanta," she grumbled.

"I told you, we are not hitchhiking," Jason said.

She clucked in disgust, kicking up another cloud with her toe and feeling more petulant with each stride. It didn't help that he was right. They couldn't stand on the side of the road with their thumbs out when Alejandro could be cruising the area, looking for them.

Scuffing her feet deeper in frustration, she walked on in silence.

"I'll get us a car," he finally said, followed by a sigh.

She looked at him speculatively. "How?"

"Same way I got the boat."

"You're going to steal one?"

"Have you got a better idea?"

"No," she admitted.

"Good. Because I think there's a house around the next bend."

Crouching behind a hedge, they studied the brick home and the car parked in front of it.

"It can't be," Lane said.

"It is."

Dora's old car sat in the driveway, with Samantha tied to the door handle. Apparently, Dora hadn't run too far when she'd rushed away from Red Peak last night.

Jason grinned at her. "We got lucky. Very lucky."

Lane rolled her eyes. "Oh, yeah, we've had all the good breaks on this case."

He chuckled. "I'm glad to see you're feeling more like yourself."

She didn't even know who "herself" was anymore. "What's so lucky about that old rust bucket? We'll probably have to push it to Atlanta."

"It'll get us there. And Dora has a very bad habit of leaving her keys in the car. If she followed her usual pattern, we're out of here."

Lane craned her neck over his shoulder to get a better view. No one moved around the house. Even the dog seemed to be asleep.

"Keep your fingers crossed," Jason said. Motioning for her to stay put, he crept down the driveway. Looking in the window near the dashboard, he waved for her come on. Maybe they had found just a little luck.

Lane followed Jason's path down the driveway while he untied Sam, her tail thumping, and refastened the leash to a tree trunk. Before he walked away, he gave the dog's head a sound pat. "Sorry, girl, I don't have anything for you this time."

He slid into the seat next to Lane. "Dora really needs to learn to take the keys out of her car."

"Poor Dora, after the night she's had, then to wake up and find her car stolen."

''Would you feel better if I left a note?''

''Yes.''

''Good,'' he said, starting the car and throwing his arm over the seat back as he looked behind him and backed Dora's rust bucket out of the driveway. ''Then pretend I did.''

She didn't have to see the smirk on his face; she heard it in his voice. She groaned, realizing he was trying to take her mind off Kelly. It wouldn't work, but she appreciated the effort. ''I'm going to have to add that to your diagnosis, you know,'' she said without meeting his eyes.

''What?''

''Predilection for thievery. No social conscience.''

She glanced at him sideways to make sure he hadn't taken her seriously. They were still on rocky ground when it came to her assessment of his mental state. When he barked out a good, healthy laugh, she relaxed.

Scenery whipped by in a teary blur as the wind popped Lane's hair into her eyes. Twenty minutes into the drive to Atlanta, the air conditioner in the ancient car had succumbed to the heat. Rolling down the windows provided little relief.

When they finally pulled into the subdivision where Lane and Kelly lived, it didn't look like a neighborhood where women weren't safe in their own homes. A couple of kids played in-line hockey in the street. A sign proclaimed it a neighborhood-watch community and asked citizens to please dispose of their litter properly.

''Go in the back way, through the alley,'' she told him, after they'd parked a few houses away. ''We can get into the house through the laundry room window. The lock's been broken for years.''

Lane slid along the fence, gun drawn, focused on Jason's wide shoulders and back. She never thought she'd be breaking into her own home, but they had to find out if Kelly was all right. And if there were intruders in the house, she and Jason needed the element of surprise on their side.

Jason started to duck in the window, and she stilled him with a hand. Their eyes dueled silently over who would climb in first. Finally, after poking in his head and checking the room, he relented and hoisted her up until her hips rested on the sill. She crawled in and covered the door while he followed her.

Counting one, two, three, on his fingers, he pulled the laundry room door open and swung into the back hallway in a fighting stance, with Lane on his heels.

Room by room, they checked the house. The living room, the bedrooms, the kitchen, all appeared in order. Standing in the dining area, Lane lowered her gun and turned to Jason. "She should be here," she said, fighting down a swell of panic.

"Everything looks okay. Maybe she went out."

Lane's gaze traveled out the dining room window and zeroed in on the blue Taurus in the driveway. "Her car's here."

"Neighbors?"

Lane shook her head. "None she socializes with—or that she would go to if she was in trouble."

As Jason holstered his weapon, Lane turned back to the living room, her eyes filling with tears at the sight of Kelly's beloved plants throughout the room. Who would take care of them now?

She spun around at the sound of a thump behind her. *Kelly!* Before she'd completed her turn, she saw that Jason had retrieved his gun and had his hand on the doorknob to the one room they hadn't searched: Kelly's office. It was so small, Lane had thought it pointless.

She hurried back toward Jason, but he didn't wait for her backup. When she saw what he was going to do, she started to run.

He took a deep breath, lifted his foot and kicked, letting out a gush of air as soft sneaker connected with hard wood.

The door flapped wildly on its hinges as Jason flew through it. A screech, an unearthly howl, nearly split Lane's eardrums. There was a grunt and a thud that could have been Jason falling, or being knocked to the floor, and then thrashing sounds. Objects crashing to the floor. Limbs connecting with furniture.

The pandemonium continued as Lane's clammy hands grabbed the door frame to stop her momentum outside the office. She swung into the room in a crouch, her gun ready in her outstretched hands, set to face whatever monster, human or otherwise, threatened her partner.

Lane thought she was ready for anything when she burst into the room. She was wrong.

There were no evil miscreants. No masked hit men.

Jason lay on his back, prying a squirming ball of white and orange fur from his chest. Hissing, the cat sank his claws through Jason's shirt. Jason hissed back. Thin streaks of red on his cheek and neck guaranteed that it wasn't the first time the feline had grappled with more than just cotton.

With a quick check around the room to be sure there were no more surprises waiting, Lane tucked her gun into her waistband and knelt to disentangle cat from man.

"Are you all right?" she asked, pulling J.D.'s hind claws out of Jason's shoulder.

He sat up, firing a lethal glare at the cat, who had immediately calmed and now nestled comfortably in Lane's arms. "I'll live." He raked a hand through his hair and reached for his gun, which had slid across the floor and under the desk. "Kelly didn't tell me he was an attack cat."

"He's not, usually. Something must have upset him." Lane smoothed the hair down on the back of J.D.'s neck. "It must have something to do with Kelly. She loves this cat, and the cat loves her. Something must have happened to her."

"Don't think the worst yet. We don't know what happened here."

She didn't answer. She couldn't. Transfixed, she stared disbelieving at the blue and white screen of Kelly's computer:

I have what you want. Let's make a deal.
Tomorrow. 9 a.m. Burl Street.
No uninvited guests—I'll be watching.

A.

"The distribution center?" she muttered to herself.

Having leveraged himself off the floor, Jason peered over her shoulder, his eyes narrowed against the glare of the monitor, or maybe against the words he read. "That can't be. That's when they're supposed to get their big payoff."

Her stomach quivered and pitched. "But it's signed 'A.' Alejandro. Why would he invite us right into the middle of a payoff?" None of this made sense to Lane. "What kind of deal could he possibly want to make?"

"None. Not when he's holding all the cards."

"Those aren't cards he's holding. It's my sister." In a moment of pure fury, she struck out, knocking the computer monitor from the desk. Jason grabbed her arm before she trashed the room any further.

"What could he possibly hope to gain by taking her?" she asked, her head bowed.

"Only one thing I can think of."

Her shoulders trembled under his touch as she raised her head. "What?"

His eyes darkened to amber, like good whisky. "Us," he answered softly.

At last she understood where he got his face of stone. Grief carved it. And fear so strong that it had to be masked to be controlled. In the past few minutes her own face had petrified into the same rocky expression.

As he watched her, she had the feeling he was taking stock of her. Weighing her strength. Gauging her fortitude.

Oh, she wanted to break down. She wanted to rage and sob and run away and cover her head, and let someone else face Alejandro and bring Kelly back to her, safe. Except that would be giving up. And giving up would mean she had finally become her father's true legacy.

That, she would never do.

She wrestled her heart into a steady beat. "Then 'us' is what he will get. But not on his terms. He came after us, now we've got to go after him, *before* he has a chance to spring his little trap tomorrow.''

Lane knew she had measured up when the corners of Jason's mouth crinkled. His eyes shone with admiration, maybe even pride. She couldn't say why his approval was so important to her, just that it shot a much-needed jolt of confidence to her beleaguered faith.

His fingers trailed down her arm to take her hand in his, and it felt good.

Jason led Lane back to Dora's car and held the door open for her. As she lowered herself into the seat, she looked up at him with such faith that he felt wholly unworthy. He closed the door gently behind her and hurried around to the driver's side.

''Where do we start?'' she asked as he settled himself behind the wheel.

He wanted to start by tucking her somewhere safe until this was over. But that wasn't possible now. This case had suddenly become very personal. Her sister was missing. Lane had been deceived, betrayed. Probably by someone close to her. Her trust had been violated. He wouldn't violate it again by doing anything that might lessen their chances of getting Kelly back safely. And that meant he had to stop holding information from her.

He shored himself up with a deep breath. ''I got a license plate on the Lexus the day you were shot.'' She opened her mouth to say something, but he stopped her, holding up his hand. ''I know I should have told you. But I didn't know if it would lead anywhere or not. I called my hacker from Nick's that night, and he's been trying to trace the car ever since. Yesterday he called me back just before you caught up to me at the distribution center. He traced the registration back through a couple of dummy corporations to a parent company.''

''You think someone in the parent company is involved?''

''The same company is also in the maze of ownership of the

distribution center.''

Hope lit her eyes. ''Do you have an address?''

''It's on the east side of town. About twenty-five minutes from here,'' he told her, bile rising in his throat at the thought of leading her into the den of the vermin trying to kill her.

Like a lamb to slaughter.

She had a right to know, he told himself. She had a right to *do* something, or at least try.

Lane was as much a victim in this abduction as Kelly. She might be the psychologist, but he knew the helplessness and hopelessness that came with being a victim. She had to reestablish control over her life to overcome those feelings.

She needed to fight back.

Maybe if he'd been able to fight back four years ago against the nameless bastards that killed Karen, things would have been different for him. But by the time he got out of the hospital and hit the streets, the leads were cold. He had never found the man who pulled the trigger.

So he had fought back the only way he could. He threw himself into the job in the hopes that somehow, someday, he would save another Karen. He took on the ugliest cases, went after the worst of the wackos, played undercover games that other agents wouldn't touch.

For four years, fighting back had relieved the pressure. Kept him whole, or at least sane. Or so he'd thought. Since meeting Lane, he'd begun to wonder. Had he been fighting, or hiding, like she'd said? He didn't know anymore.

Now she was the one who needed to fight back, and no matter how badly he wanted to protect her, he had to help her. If she died because of it, then he would put a pistol to his head and pull the trigger himself.

There wouldn't be another four years like the last four.

Jason didn't really expect to find anyone at the east side office. Seeing Morales's T-Bird parked in plain view out in front sent warning bells peeling in his head.

When Lane saw it, her eyes widened. ''They're here,'' she whispered, but the hope faded from her face as quickly as it had arrived. She was a good cop. Jason knew her instincts would warn her this was too easy, as his had.

They rolled slowly past the older, red brick office building once in Dora's car, then parked a few blocks away and hiked back, hanging close to walls of the buildings they passed. It wasn't much, but some cover was better than none.

A trickle of sweat rolled down from his temple and caught in the corner of his eye. He blinked it away.

''The door is open,'' Lane said, crouching beside him at the corner of the building across the street from their target. The buildings on either side of it looked vacant.

She started toward the office. Jason pulled her back. ''I don't like it. That door is like a formal invitation. Like they want us inside.''

''Do you think it's a trap?''

He wished he knew. Nothing about this felt right. ''I don't know. If they wanted to ambush us, why wouldn't they have set it up at your house?''

''Maybe we aren't the only ones being set up.''

''Maybe. Then again, they had no way to know we'd find this place.'' An old, familiar feeling stirred inside him. It took a few moments, but he finally placed it.

It had been a long time since he'd had anyone to share ideas with. To evaluate the possibilities of a case and draw conclusions on what they knew. It had been a long time since he'd trusted and respected anyone enough to be a partner. ''Okay, so what do you want to do?''

When she turned her head to him, her eyes sparkled with the green fire he'd come to love. ''Whatever their reasons, it's their game. We'll play by their rules, for now. There's something in that warehouse they want us to see. Let's go find it.''

He jerked his head once in agreement, then gave her an

impulsive kiss on the cheek. "Just for luck," he lied.

The sun illuminated the first twenty feet down the hallway. Beyond that, darkness engulfed the interior.

Lane took a cover position and aimed her weapon at the door while Jason ran toward the portico. The birds, lined up on the edge of the roof and chirping gaily, scattered when he approached in a headlong rush and threw himself against the wall to the right of the open door.

Taking a second to catch his breath, he peered around the edge and down the hall. Seeing nothing, he signaled for Lane to follow. While she ran across the open ground, he couldn't generate enough spit to swallow.

When she reached his side, he released the breath he had been holding and lowered his weapon. Together they crept into the building and checked each suite. The place was empty.

"Nothing," he muttered, closing the door to the last office behind him as they headed for the stairs to the second level.

The first door at the top of the stairs opened easily. "Still nothing," Lane said. She leaned against the wall outside the second door and reached around to push it open. No sounds. No movement.

It looked as uninhabited as all the others, except for a bare desk and an empty filing cabinet with the drawers hanging open. Lane moved around the edge of the steel desk and gasped. Before she drew her next breath, Jason was beside her.

She turned and buried her head in his shoulder, clutching his T-shirt in her fists.

At her feet, Morales lay dead, a neat hole in the center of his forehead. A dried band of blood circled his forehead and pooled beneath him. Next to him lay Grumman, in the same condition, except Grumman's mouth was open, his gray teeth bared as if his last words had been a curse on his killer.

Over her shoulder, he saw the two round holes in the glass window that marked the fatal bullets' paths. The view led directly to the boarded-up, four-story building next door. One window was open: the one directly across from where they stood.

Lane's gaze followed his to the window. "They were ambushed...just like us."

Neither Lane nor Jason felt the need to check for pulses, but they quickly searched the dead men's pockets for any scrap of information that might indicate where the hoods had been, or where they were going.

Finding nothing but car keys, matches and a few coins, Jason sighed in disgust. "Let's check the car. Maybe they missed something there." He doubted it, though.

The car had been cleaned. From the fresh smears on the windows and door handles, Jason figured it had even been wiped for prints.

He leaned back in the driver's seat and rested his eyes a second, but only a second. This was ridiculous. They were sitting in the open, in the broad daylight. He swore and pulled her out of the vehicle. "We have to get moving."

"Where to?" she asked, stumbling as he pulled her along.

"Doesn't matter, just away from here." He glanced over his shoulder at the warehouse. "We've seen what they wanted us to see."

"But what does it mean? And where is Kelly?"

Jason wished he knew. Trying to think of something comforting, but not patronizing, to say, he turned onto the street where they had left the car and then quickly jumped back, pressing them both into the rough brick building.

"What?" Lane mouthed.

"Cops. They're all over Dora's car."

Lane's sharp breath pressed her chest into Jason's damp back. He felt her heartbeat gallop in counterpoint to his own as she leaned around him to peer down the alley for herself.

"Oh, my God," she gasped, jerking back.

"What?"

"That's Dan with those officers," she said, her face creased with confusion.

"Dan, your partner?" He never had liked that guy. Now the feeling grew closer to hate. "This is a long way from your precinct's territory."

"Dora must have reported the car stolen by now," she said. "Maybe they somehow connected it to us. Or maybe he found this place the same way your hacker did. He tried to tell me he had a lead when we were at the precinct, but I didn't stop to listen. It has been so long since I reported in, maybe he got worried and decided to check it out himself."

"Or maybe they're part of the cleanup crew that took out Morales and Grumman."

Lane's bright eyes faded to a dull green patina. He hated being the one to quash her faith in her department. "Or maybe not," he added, squeezing her hand in his. "Either way, it's time to find a new ride."

She squeezed his hand back and squinted up at the sky and the white-hot circle of sun beating down on them. With her other hand she swiped at the fine hairs, dark and damp, sticking to her forehead. "Morales's car? We have the keys."

He nodded, and they jogged, until they slid into Morales's T-bird. As she buckled up, he couldn't help winking and grinning at her. "I think my predilection for thievery is wearing off on you. This is the second car you've been an accomplice in stealing. And this one was your idea."

"Doesn't count if the owner is dead." Lane deadpanned, leaning forward and stabbing at the controls on the dash until a blast of air exploded from the vents. She leaned back and sighed blissfully. "Besides, at least I picked one with air-conditioning."

Jason flexed his fingers on the steering wheel as he drove. *Don't look at her. Just don't look at that proud face.* Fighting back was one thing, but this was insanity. Lane wanted to go to the distribution center, to try to track down Alejandro.

What Jason needed was calm reasoning, an objective analysis of their tactical situation, a logical entreaty as to the futility of running all over Georgia without a plan.

What came out was a rough, "It's a waste of time."

His eyes flicked over at her before he could stop them. It was only a glance, but he had plenty of time to see the pink rage rising to her cheeks and the astonished purse to her lips.

Nice going, Stateler, way to control the situation.

"My sister has been kidnapped, and following our only lead is a waste of time?"

"We're not getting anywhere."

"We can't give up."

"I'm not suggesting we give up, just that we step back and take a look at where we're going."

They rolled to a stop in front of a red light.

"Fine. You step back." She pulled on the door handle. "I'm stepping out."

He snapped up her wrist. "What are you doing?" God help him, he didn't know what he'd do if she got out. If she walked away.

Last chance, Stateler. Don't blow it.

The light turned green, and still Jason let the car idle in the intersection. He loosened his grip on Lane's wrist, rubbing his thumb over the pulse point there. "Look at us, Lane. We're both exhausted. It's not each other we want to fight."

Blaring horns harmonized from all sides of the intersection as irate motorists wove around them. Slowly he let his hand fall away from her, relieved when the door handle clicked back into place beside her. "It's over a hundred degrees out there. You haven't had much sleep, neither one of us has eaten in almost twenty-four hours. We aren't going to do Kelly any good like this. On top of that, we just left the scene of a double murder in one of the victim's cars. FBI agent or not, that could be a little hard to explain."

"But Kelly..."

Jason leaned toward her, pushing against his shoulder harness, resting his left hand on her knee and draping his right arm across the backrest. "They're not going to hurt her, Lane, at least not yet. They need her to get to us. We can go to the distribution center, but you know we won't find anything. We got too close, so they shut the operation down. They're cleaning up. All we can do is wait. That's what they wanted us to see back there. The best thing we can do for Kelly is to rest and try to come up with a plan for tomorrow."

Lane knew he was right. If she hadn't been so tired, she would have seen it herself. She couldn't help Kelly like this. But what choice did they have? They had nowhere to go. Was anyplace safe for them now? "Where can we go?"

He put the car in gear and mingled with the flow of traffic. "A safe house."

She rubbed her eyes. Maybe she was even more tired than she thought. He wasn't making sense. "You're going to ask the Bureau for help?"

"No, not a Bureau safe house. My safe house."

"You have your own safe house?"

He shrugged like he didn't seen anything abnormal about that. Did he really not see how paranoid that was?

"More or less," he said. "Officially, it belongs to Nick's grandmother. I helped him clean the place up after she moved to a retirement community in Florida a couple of years ago, and ended up buying the place."

So it was more a house than a safe house. What would Jason's house be like? Cold and sterile, like the apartment? She desperately needed more than that tonight. She needed warmth and comfort and security. "You don't think they'll find us there?"

"No. Nobody knows about that place except Nick. I paid cash and left the deed in his grandmother's name. The address isn't on file in any of my Bureau records, and I've never had any Bureau buddies over there. I don't even go there myself very often."

Despite his reassurances, Jason made Lane wait in the car

until he checked out the little row house. Parked down the block, she waited until he gave the signal from the window, then pulled Morales's car into the driveway and waited. The garage door groaned open, and she pulled in and cut the engine.

The car's courtesy lights shut off as the garage door lowered behind her. At least they wouldn't have to worry about the car being spotted by a patrol. Once those bodies were public, the T-bird would be on the top of every squad car's hot sheet.

Her nose wrinkled at the oily smell in the garage. Before her eyes adjusted to the darkness, Jason opened a door and sunlight slanted past him, lighting her way around a dusty Jeep and into the kitchen.

''The house is clear. It doesn't look like anyone's been here,'' he said.

What she saw as she stepped into the house pleased and surprised her. Everything was inviting and permanent feeling.

Her footsteps knocked on a gleaming hardwood floor, worn glass-smooth by the passing of many years and many feet. In front of her, a family area stretched so large that it must have made up most of the ground floor. A huge brick fireplace and its hearth covered most of one wall.

Her imagination created snapshots of cozy evenings cuddling with Jason while the fire licked away the chill of an early fall. She wet her lips, which had suddenly dried as if she really could feel the heat of the flames.

She glanced at Jason, who stood leaning against the doorjamb, his arms folded across his chest and his ankles crossed. The way he watched her taking in the place, she had the feeling having her here made him uncomfortable. Like she'd invaded his inner sanctum.

He followed her path through heavy-lidded eyes, his hazel irises nearly hidden behind thick lashes. The effect was a guarded, dangerous look. And downright sexy.

She rubbed away the gooseflesh that had risen on her arms and continued her tour of the room, stepping across a thick oval rug, braided with bands of earthy brown and rich russet, offset by threads of hunter green. Her fingers trailed along the back of a leather couch, butter soft and just a shade lighter in color. The room had a decidedly masculine atmosphere. ''You redecorated after you bought the house.''

''Had to. Nick's grandmother had a penchant for floral prints that I just couldn't stomach.''

She stopped on the far side of the room in front of floor-to-ceiling shelves stacked with books. Tilting her head, she scanned the titles.

He twirled his keys around his index finger, stopping them in his palm with a solid smack on every rotation as he watched her.

The eclectic nature of his reading collection impressed her. There were contemporaries of all genres, classics, even a few ''alternative'' fiction works she wouldn't recognize if Kelly hadn't told her about them.

''Have you read all these?'' She looked back at Jason, and the keys went still.

''Most. Sometimes I come here between cases to—'' he shrugged again ''—decompress, I guess. Reading helps.''

Lane turned her attention back to the shelves and felt her face light up. ''You have one of Kelly's.''

''I do?''

She stretched to pull the novel from one of the higher shelves. ''Kelly's publisher makes her use a male pseudonym for science fiction. She says male sci-fi writers sell better, which Kelly thinks is bunk. But, 'you gotta make a living,' she says, so she picked Kevin Kellog because it kind of has the same sound as Kelly McCullough.''

Jason shoved himself off the door frame and walked over to her. He took the book from her and thumbed through the pages. ''I remember this one. I really liked it,'' he said, turning it over in his hands.

''I'll have her autograph it for you,'' she said, smiling, before she realized what she'd offered. The smile froze on her face, then shattered.

It might be too late. Her sister might never get the chance to scrawl her name inside one of her books for a fan.

She took the novel from Jason. Before he could see the tears in her eyes, she turned her back to him and reached up to put the book back into its place.

A warm hand on her wrist stopped her. He gently loosened her grasp on the spine of Kelly's novel and pulled it down.

"You hang on to it for me." His voice swelled and dipped like a rough sea as he spoke. Lane swayed like a small boat on the tumbling waves. "When we get her back, I want that autograph." His eyes tethered her to shore. "We will get her back. I promise."

"I wish I could believe you."

"Then do. Believe me."

She wanted to believe him. She wanted to believe *in* him.

But he was the same troubled cop he was yesterday, and last week, and the last four years. If she took the comfort his eyes offered now, he would sneak into her heart forever. Then someday, when the pain got to be too much for him, he would break it.

Lane couldn't live through that. Not again.

Easing out of his grasp, she took a step back. Disappointment shadowed his rugged features. Awkwardly they faced each other, intimate strangers. Three feet apart, but a world away.

Chapter 14

Jason moved first. He couldn't stand there while she looked at him like that, lonely and hurting and afraid. If she would let him, he could make it go away, at least the lonely part.

He should never have brought her here. This place was too personal. Too close to his dreams of a warm home and a willing wife. But what choice had he had?

He cleared his throat and tore his thoughts away from what might have been. "The bathroom is upstairs, first door. You clean up, and I'll see what I can scrounge up to eat," he said, leaving her standing behind him clutching her sister's book.

When he heard the water stream on upstairs, it sounded like she was filling the bath instead of running the shower. Good. She could use a nice long soak, and he could use some time to shore up his defenses.

Lane McCullough had really gotten to him. Why couldn't she just admit that she needed him?

He pulled open the refrigerator and groaned at the contents. Or lack of contents.

Systematically he rifled through the cupboards and cubbyholes for anything edible, trying to keep his thoughts from wandering to a certain beautiful, infuriating, passionate, stubborn detective he knew. He slammed a few of the cabinet doors behind him. Childish, he knew, but it made him feel better to let out his hostility in some harmless way.

The water cut off upstairs. He surveyed the loot he'd gathered on the table. Not exactly gourmet, but it would have to do. He popped the frozen dinners into the microwave on thaw and fidgeted with the silverware he'd set out.

With nothing else to distract him, his overactive mind pictured Lane sinking into the tub, waves sipping at her skin. There were rose-scented bath salts in the cabinet under the sink. They'd come as part of the set with the towels and other accessories. He wondered if she'd found them.

His blood heated at the thought of her, still damp from her bath and smelling like a rose, stretched out on cool sheets with her hair fanned around her head on the pillow. The dusky tips of her breasts would be the same color as the comforter in the guest room.

No, he didn't want her in the guest room. The image shifted immediately to his room. The antique pine, king-size bed—

Damn. He slammed the fork he'd been twirling onto the table. This wasn't getting him anywhere. She had made it perfectly clear she didn't want him for anything other than getting her sister back. He wasn't a teenager, for God's sake. He was capable of having two consecutive thoughts that weren't about sex.

If he was honest, he had to admit it wasn't about sex anymore, anyway. He would want to be with her, even if all he could do was sit next to her on a bus.

It was only because he felt responsible for her that he couldn't get her out of his head, he told himself. Feeling protective was natural, given his history. As soon as the case was over and she and her sister were safe, he'd forget her.

He held on to that thought tenaciously, grumbling it all the way to the tiny service bath off the laundry room, where he let a chilly shower try to convince him it was true.

It didn't help; he knew a lie when he thought it.

Lane stretched, feeling like a new person without the layers of dust and sweat she had been carrying around. Stepping out of the bath, she pulled the drain plug. The tepid water swirled away with a contented gurgle.

Baths always made her feel better. Warm water worked wonders on her mind as well as her muscles. In the bath, she could take her time, cleansing her skin inch by inch, concentrating on nothing but the smell of soap and the buoyant feel of her body, free from the weight of the day's worries.

Nothing could completely purge her tension today, but her long soak had left her at least a modicum of peace. Jason had been right earlier. They needed a plan.

She'd been quick to judge him the unstable one, yet he was the one who had kept a level head through each disaster they'd found themselves in. He might have unresolved issues about his past and what had happened to his partner—his lover, she corrected herself with a twinge of pain. But he was still a good agent, a good man. And her only hope for saving Kelly. She could believe in him for that long. After that she honestly couldn't say.

She rubbed herself dry with a thick towel until the mauve terry left her skin warm and glowing. A pile of disgustingly dirty clothes stared up at her from the floor. She couldn't bring herself to put those things back on. Clutching the towel wrapped around her to her chest, she padded down the hall.

Finding the master bedroom, she pulled open the first drawer of a pine chest, hoping to find his supply of T-shirts. Her breath drew in sharply at what she found instead.

Where most men stored their socks and underwear, Jason had stuffed pictures. Lots of well-worn, much-handled pictures. Some in frames, some loose with dog-eared corners. Some black-and-white snapshots, yellowed from age, a few newer, color photos with studio signatures in the corner.

Lane recognized Nick in racing leathers at a local track, standing next to the motorcycle she had wrecked.

There were several professional portraits of a couple dressed in out-of-date styles, and then more recent photos of just the woman. Her smile gave her away as Jason's mother.

Lane laughed at a candid shot of a teenaged Jason with a girl, dressed to the nines and holding hands. From the nervous looks on their faces, it looked like prom night.

Something tightened in Lane, deep inside. She should feel guilty rummaging through Jason's life like this, but she couldn't stop. This was the man she needed to understand. The man behind the badge.

She picked through piles of pictures. Him with a group of men, all with the same haircuts, in front of FBI Headquarters, the Hoover Building in Washington, D.C. His class from the FBI training center at Quantico, she guessed.

Her heart contracted when she found the stack devoted to Karen. The two of them, climbing off a roller-coaster, looking windblown. Jason throwing her into a swimming pool. Her dunking him.

Digging deeper, she drew out a battered photo and studied it closely. A boy stood on a dock in front of an older man whose arm was draped over the boy's shoulders. The boy held up a fish so small it hardly qualified as a minnow, but the boy beamed up at the man who must be his father. It took a moment for it to register that the boy was Jason. A smile so wide it looked painful split his face in two.

The cord running taut within her snapped suddenly, and she almost choked on her own sob. Shuffling through the drawer, her eyes skimmed over the prints that included Jason. Old or new, they all had one thing in common: a smile that shone from the inside out, so full of life that it beamed off the glossy paper.

She had almost missed this side of him. She'd had her rare

glimpses: the day he'd stood laughing at her in the rain; when they'd made love in the cabin; as he patted Dora's dog on the head and fed it cupcakes. But instead of grabbing on to those moments, she'd glossed over them, only seeing the wounded side of him: his tortured confession that he'd been in love with his partner; the guilt he felt over her death.

She'd let herself believe that the bad times had destroyed his ability to live and to love. That he'd thrown his life away to guilt.

Looking at the stack of pictures, holding the one of him and his dad, she realized how wrong she had been. Jason Stateler hadn't thrown his life away. He'd tucked it away here, in this house, where he could come and visit.

Like a child with a special treasure, he pulled it out once in a while and relished it, let it make him strong and then put it away until he needed it again.

A sound came from the doorway. Glass clinking on glass. Lane was startled, caught in the act of running her finger over the boyhood image of Jason. Looking up, she found herself staring at the real thing, in full manhood.

His eyes had a heavy look. Hot and hungry.

A fist of anger socked Jason in the gut when he first saw her in his room, pawing through his pictures. He felt naked. Exposed to her inquisitive mind with no cover story.

He kept still, though, frozen by the emotions playing openly on her face. His anger congealed, became a painful stab of loneliness, then slowly dissolved into a throbbing ache in his groin. Having her here, where his dreams lived, only intensified the pain of knowing they had no future.

Her cheeks blushed as she stared up at him. The same blush that always made his groin pulse and his knees tremble. The blush he would always associate with her at the moment of climax.

"T-shirts and running shorts. Second drawer," he said, guessing why she was in his room. He gestured toward the dresser with the necks of both bottles twined in his fingers, then held them out so she could take a beer.

He should leave now. Give her some privacy to get dressed. Instead he took a long swig from his drink and wiped his mouth with the back of his hand.

She dropped her eyes to her bottle and frowned at the label. "This probably isn't a good idea on an empty stomach."

"Yeah, but it's all I've got, and it's cold."

Without taking her eyes off him, she wrapped her lips around the bottle and took a long swallow.

His body tightened as he watched her throat bob. Staying here was a really bad idea. He set the plate of peanut butter and crackers he'd brought up for her onto the dresser before he dropped it. "I found a couple of frozen dinners down there, but it'll take a while for them to thaw. I brought a snack to tide you over."

He meant to step back, out of the room, but instead he found himself closer to her.

When she lowered the bottle, he held a cracker to her mouth and held it firm while she bit off half. Her tongue dabbed at a smear of peanut butter left on the corner of her lips.

This was crazy. And leading to serious trouble. The ache in his groin became a palpable pulse, thrumming through his whole body.

He pressed closer and lifted her beer for her to wash down the dry treat. Her warm hand settled over his on the cool bottle while she closed her eyes and sucked greedily.

She was torturing him. Or maybe he was torturing himself. He wasn't sure. Either way, it was a slow and painful death.

She was the one who said she didn't want him. Why didn't she pull back? What did he have to do to scare her off again?

There was only one way to find out. He slid his hand along the back of her neck, tangled his fingers in her wet hair and pulled her hard against him, kissing her like he had that first time, in the warehouse. As if nothing else in the world existed.

And she responded to him.

She confused the hell out of him. He didn't know what had brought about this sudden change in her. Then again, he didn't much care. At the first touch of her lips, the need in his body had become short fused, urgent.

He slanted his mouth harder over hers. She tasted like peanut butter and heat lightning. His hands played up and down her sides, reaching from her rounded bottom up to the curve of her breasts. With each sweep of his hand his tongue thrust into her mouth.

Eventually his conscience was going to make him pay for this. He had told her he didn't want to use her the way he had used women all those years ago, when he'd picked them up in bars at night and dropped them at their cars in the morning without even asking their names.

He thought he'd been lost then. Now he knew that hadn't been lost at all. Out of control, maybe, but not lost.

This was lost.

Drowning in her eyes, two fathomless green oceans. Powerless against the pull of her current. Not trying to fight it. Not wanting to fight it.

His conscience would have to wait. Right now he could think only of touching her, tasting her.

She fell forward, rocking her hips into him. Their bodies clashed once, then found a rhythm that pleased them both. With a flick of his hand, the towel between them fell to the floor. Using up his last shred of control, Jason pulled back far enough to catch a breath. "Lane, if you're going to make me stop, please do it now."

She shook her head, cupping his face with her hands. "I don't want you to stop."

"What about Kelly?" He nuzzled his face into the soft spot at the base of her neck, unable to look at the hurt he knew her sister's name would bring to Lane's eyes.

"There's nothing we can do for Kelly until tomorrow. But we can do this, for each other, tonight."

"Just for tonight?" He hated himself for asking, knowing the answer would only hurt them both.

"I honestly don't know. I know I'd like to try, but..." She blinked up at him with tear-filled eyes. "All this time, I thought you were the one who hadn't dealt with your past, but it's not you who has a problem with trust, Jason. It's me. My father..."

"Shh," he quieted her, his hands smoothing the hair back from her face. "I know."

She turned liquid green eyes up to him. "I don't know about the future, Jason. But I know I need you now. Tonight."

Jason fought the feelings one last time before squeezing his eyes shut and conceding defeat once and for all. He'd thought he could live without this, this connection between two souls.

He'd been a fool.

Let it cost him his life or his sanity; it didn't matter. He couldn't stop loving her.

Wrapping his arms around her, he swept her off her feet. As he deposited her in the center of his oversize bed, his eyes feasted on her body. Grabbing a fistful of his T-shirt, she pulled him down with her.

His hands fed on her curves, the angle of her hip, the soft mound of her breast, while his mouth nibbled at the succulent flesh of her neck. "You're so beautiful, Lane. So perfect."

All the other secrets he wanted to tell her, about himself, about herself, melted into murmurs. Whispered half words that evaporated into quiet as he took the tender lobe of her ear between his teeth and milked it.

His gentle nursing inflamed her gluttonous desires. She didn't want gentle or slow or quiet. She wanted fierce love, dark and dangerous. She wanted rough passion, brutal desire unleashed. A heathen at a pagan feast, she wanted to slake her appetite in the bounty of his body.

She needed to consume and to be consumed.

He stripped out of his clothes quickly. Her heart hammered in her chest as she drank in the sight of his naked body, ripe with need, so close to her own. "I want you Jason, please. I need you now."

She opened herself to him, maneuvering herself under his hips while he raised himself over her. Never had she felt such total abandon, the primitive need for a mate. With a leg over his thighs, she pulled down and curved her back, reaching for him, trying to finish what was started between them.

He arched away from her.

Her eyes flew open at his resistance. His head hung so that his sweat-dampened forehead almost rested on hers.

"Damn. I didn't think," he said, his voice strained.

What the hell was he talking about? This was no time for thinking. She wriggled, trying to encourage him. Fear that he had changed his mind, that he didn't want her, gnawed her insides.

Groaning, he held her still with a hand on her shoulder. "I don't have a condom," he ground out.

She blew out her breath in relief. He hadn't changed his mind. Then his words sank in.

"You don't have anything here?" she asked tentatively.

"I've never brought a woman here."

She didn't know whether to be relieved or annoyed at his answer. The hunger in her soul made it irrelevant.

"Doesn't matter," she reassured him.

She tried again to force the joining of their bodies. His backside tightened against her pull.

"Like hell it doesn't." A fierce light shone from his eyes. "I can't protect you."

"It's not your protection I need, Jason. It never has been. It's your love."

His face contorted as if she'd struck him a physical blow. Slowly he closed the space between them.

"You know I love you," he breathed in her ear.

Her heart took flight, and she knew that, at least for now, he was hers. Wrapping her arms and legs around him, she smiled. "Yeah, I know."

His plunge took her by surprise, stretching her body to its limits, filling her heart and mind. Thrust by thrust she let him gorge himself on her. The pounding of their hearts mingled with the pounding of their bodies, carrying her higher and higher until she couldn't see his straining chest or hear his labored breathing. She could only feel. The feelings grew and grew until she cried out and bucked wildly against him. They found release together and he convulsed against her, nourishing her body with his seed.

Spent, he collapsed on her, rolling just enough to his side that she wasn't crushed. For several moments they lay still, content to be close. As her breath became less raspy and his less harsh, the chill of the air conditioner on her damp skin made her shiver.

She twisted and tugged the sheets down to crawl between them, but he pulled her back to him, planting a delicious kiss over her lips. His hand caressed her shoulder as they broke apart. "Are you cold?"

She murmured a yes, and he helped push the blankets down so she could get her legs underneath. When he rolled to his back to slide himself under with her, she wrapped her hand around the back of his neck and pulled herself close, ready to negotiate another kiss.

The next thing Lane knew she smelled coffee. Groggily she turned and rolled directly into the depression Jason made where he sat on the edge of the mattress. He caught her with one hand and held the coffee cup out of sloshing range with the other.

"Good morning," he said, an angelic smile gracing his face.

Sunlight streamed through the window, stinging her eyes. Lane bolted upright in pure panic.

"Morning? Oh, my God, Kelly—" She struggled to free herself from the twisted sheets that imprisoned her, so she could jump out of bed.

He stopped her with an arm around her waist. "Whoa, relax.

It's not. Morning, I mean. It was just an expression. You only slept a couple of hours. We have plenty of time."

Wide-eyed, Lane looked at the orange sun shining directly in the window. Belatedly she realized the window faced west, where the sun had begun to set. It was late afternoon; she hadn't wasted away the night. The breath whooshed out of her. "Sorry."

Handing her the coffee cup, he shook his head. "I didn't mean to scare you. I just meant it's time to get to work."

Lane slurped her coffee to keep it from burning her tongue. When she lowered the cup, she was looking directly into hazel eyes hotter than her steaming drink.

For a moment she couldn't fathom why he was looking at her like that. Until she realized she was sitting naked on the edge of the bed, the sheet slipped down to mid-thigh.

His hand raised and hovered between them a moment, then reached out and caressed her bared breast. His touch was as light as a whisper of a breeze. His knuckles brushed the underside, and then his palm molded her fullness.

With a start it all came back to her. Potent kisses. Intimate touches. In the depths of his dark, dilated pupils, the same memories burned for her to see.

She shrank back from the intensity of it. Suddenly shy, she dragged the sheet up over her nakedness. Her modesty was ridiculous, she knew, after what they had done. But knowing that couldn't stop the prickling skin that always accompanied the rush of color that must be rising on her face.

He let his hand fall away from her as she pulled back, but the feeling was imprinted there. All she would ever need to do would be to close her eyes, and the feeling would regenerate itself.

"I like it when you do that," he said.

"When I do what?"

One corner of his mouth curled upward. "Blush. It's...sweet."

She picked at the sheets. "It makes me feel like a schoolgirl."

"That's a bad thing?"

Drawing her knees up to her chest, she rocked back and forth once before resting her chin on them. He was a hard one to figure out. Who'd have thought he would go for the naive, blushing type?

Pulling her bottom lip between her teeth to suppress her grin, she glanced at him furtively. "Sweet, huh?"

He tasted her lips briefly with his tongue, then nodded solemnly. "As pure rock candy."

Sighing, he sat back. His face dropped into FBI mode. "The frozen dinners are in the oven. You have time for a shower first if you want." And then he left her alone.

Jason choked back another wave of desire when Lane strolled into the kitchen wearing a pair of his navy blue jogging shorts and an old FBI sweatshirt with the sleeves torn off. Every time he looked at her he wanted to pull her down and make crazy love with her for the precious little time they had left. They'd probably never get another chance.

But the time they had left wasn't theirs; it was Kelly's. He could tell from the tense set of Lane's shoulders that her worry for her sister was back, full force. He found some pride in knowing that for a few hours he had made it disappear.

As soon as they'd eaten and the dishes were in the sink, she pulled the papers he'd left in the center of the table over and studied them. He'd been sketching the layout of the distribution center and the surrounding buildings before she came down.

He refilled their coffee cups and sat beside her. Together they filled in the details from memory. Poring over the site map, they outlined possible strategies, plotted scenarios and reviewed everything they both knew about hostage situation tactics.

The problem was, if someone from the inside was involved, they would know all of those same tactics.

Hours later, still without a viable plan in place, Jason started pacing, rubbing his temples.

From under his hand he studied Lane. She tapped the sketch rhythmically with the eraser end of the pencil. Her eyes had progressed from stress lined to hollow and sunken. Her bleak expression made it clear she felt as hopeless about the situation as he did.

They had no idea how many suspects they were up against or where Kelly would be. No two people could cover that much area.

He squeezed his eyes shut, willing back his rising headache. "Are you any good with a rifle?"

The tapping stopped. "I've fired some—on the range." Her eyes narrowed. "Why?"

He put his palms flat on the table and leaned toward her. "I have a sharpshooter's weapon upstairs—scope and all. You can take a position in the building we used to watch the place before and cover the whole thing. I'll go in and draw them out."

"No way."

"It's the only way."

"No." Her voice was louder, but controlled. More threatening than yelling.

He raked his hand through his hair, grabbed on by the roots and pulled before sliding his fingers the rest of the way through. This headache was going to be a whopper when it hit full force.

He spun away from her. "I can lead them out. It's me they want."

"What makes you think that, when they broke into *my* house, kidnapped *my* sister?"

What could he say? Gut feeling? Instinct? He didn't know how, he just knew. Like a common word you suddenly couldn't remember, something lingered just out of reach of his conscious mind. Something that he should know. Something important.

She would write it off to paranoia.

"I don't want you in there. I—" *Can't protect you,* he'd almost said.

Her words echoed in his mind. *It's not your protection I need. It's your love.*

How could he give one without the other? That wasn't who he was. She was his responsibility, had been from the moment he'd walked up to her in that warehouse and kissed her like it was his last moment on earth.

Cursing, he swung around and grabbed his phone from the counter, punching buttons furiously. If she wouldn't take his protection, she was damn sure going to take someone's.

She put her hand over the keypad. "What are you doing?"

"Getting help."

They struggled for control of the phone. "You can't do that," she said.

With one powerful yank he got the telephone away from her. "I have to."

"No," she said, making a feeble swipe at his hands and missing. "You don't know who they've got on the inside. You could be playing right into their hands. You could get us *all* killed."

Damn her. His fingers hesitated over the buttons. "There are thousands of law enforcement officials of one type or another in the state of Georgia, Lane." He refused to acknowledge her accusing stare. "There's got to be someone we can trust."

When she moved forward, he thought she was making another attempt to get the phone, and he stiffened reactively, holding it out of her reach. Instead, she flung herself against his chest and held on tight.

"No," she said, the word muffled against the cotton of his shirt. "You're the only one I trust."

Just before dawn, Jason's headache hit like a freight train, as predicted. Its only redeeming quality was that it jarred him out of an ugly dream. Hell, why mince words. It had been a nightmare. Not the usual reenactment of the past, but a horrific prediction of the future.

Midnight had long since passed when they'd gone to bed. By mutual decision, they hadn't made love again. They'd lain in silence, taking comfort in each other's arms until fatigue won out over worry and sleep overcame them.

Jason found little peace, though, even in sleep, after giving in to Lane. They would both go into the building tomorrow. She wouldn't have it any other way.

"We're partners," she'd said. "We'll face this together."

Jason closed his arms around her and suppressed the low growl that rose in his throat as memories of his dream resurfaced. Lane looking up at him, all soft and muzzy and flushed from making love one minute, then in the next, bleeding in his arms, her chest rising slowly and painfully for the last time. Her eyes dulling as her final breath sighed from her parted lips.

And then stillness.

She whimpered in her sleep and pushed against his arms. He realized he was probably holding her too tightly, but he couldn't let go.

He nuzzled her hair, recognizing the familiar tangy scent of his soap and shampoo. She was in his bed, wearing his sweatshirt. After making love twice without birth control, she might already be carrying his child. She was his dream, his future.

She was his, and he wasn't going to lose her.

The gunmetal gray of dawn gradually edged out the blackness of night. Just a few more hours and it would be time to go. The pounding in his head threatened to split his skull.

Easing her out of his grasp, he headed to the bathroom for aspirin.

Sitting on the edge of the tub, resting his cheek against the cool tile of the shower wall, his mind replayed their discussion:

"She's my sister. I have to be there."

"You can't help her if you're dead."

"If I can't help her, I might as well be dead."

"You don't mean that. God, you sound like me. I'm not going to let you do this."

"Yes, you are. Because it's what you would do, in my place, and you know it."

He tried to think of what else he could have said to convince her. He should have tried harder. He never should have agreed to take her into that building tomorrow.

It was too much like before. Much too much. His stomach tightened and cramped.

It was exactly like before, in fact. Why hadn't he put it together sooner? The pattern locked together in his mind like pieces of a jigsaw puzzle. Lure your prey into the street by setting up some false meet. Not a bad strategy, get all the targets out in the open, then Bam! Death at a distance. The killer never even has to get his hands dirty.

Jason realized he hadn't seen it before because he'd been so focused on the case. What the hijackers wanted and what they would do next. These attacks weren't about the case at all. They were about *him.*

His stomach heaved and he gritted his teeth, trying not to vomit and at the same time wishing he could, just to get it over with, needing to purge himself.

It all made sense now. Lane had been right to suspect someone in his agency. But Jason suspected her attack was meant to be more than just a distraction. This killer wanted to hurt Jason, hurt him bad, like he had before. And whoever he was, he knew Jason's most vulnerable spot. He knew that hurting her would be a thousand times worse than hurting Jason himself.

Jason tried to force himself back into agent mode. Where was that mask of detachment he'd perfected over the years? It was gone for good, he was afraid. Crumbled into dust the moment he told Lane he loved her.

Groaning, he leaned closer to the toilet. His stomach ejected its contents into the john with painful contractions.

By the time he felt steady enough to stand, the first pink rays of the morning sun shone through the beveled-glass window above the tub. He ground his fists in his eyes, preparing himself for what had to be done.

He couldn't take her there, no matter what he'd promised. Not when this wasn't about her. It was about hurting him, and she was the most likely source of pain.

He'd find another way to help Kelly. By leaving Lane behind, betraying her trust, he knew he would be killing any feelings she had for him, but he'd gladly sacrifice her love for her life.

It would be for the best, anyway. *She was his future*—who was he kidding? He had no future with her. His dreams were a joke. How could he share a home with her, share a bed with her, raise a child with her?

She was a cop. She wore a gun to work every day with no more thought than most women gave to wearing a scarf. He couldn't live like that, knowing she was out there in the line of fire every day.

Quickly he searched the boxes and bottles in the medicine cabinet. The last time he'd been here, he'd been recovering from a knife wound in the ribs, the result of a clash with a drug dealer who hadn't been happy about having his meth lab busted.

His hands flew from one plastic bottle to the next: antibiotics, painkillers, vitamins, ah, there, sleeping pills.

Stepping carefully over the creaky floorboards, he crept downstairs to get a glass of water.

Chapter 15

Lane woke to the annoying clang of bells in her ear. She knew she should do something about them, but she couldn't figure out what. What were they? School bells? An alarm clock? Her head was fuzzy and her tongue felt too thick. A phone, it finally came to her. A phone was ringing, and she should answer it.

Her arm flopped across the empty bed as she reached for the nightstand. She had only started to put together the thought that if the bed was empty, then Jason was not with her, when she finally got a good hold on the receiver.

Nick's excited voice chittered out of the earpiece. ''Jason? Is that you?''

''No. Nick?''

''Lane, thank God. Are the two of you okay? Where have you been? And what's going on? You're all over the news.''

He was going too fast. She couldn't keep up. She rubbed her pounding temples. ''Nick—what? Slow down.''

''Slow down!'' She heard him take an exasperated breath on the other end of the line. ''Lane, are you all right? Where is Jason?''

"Um, I don't know. Where Jason is, I mean." The fog lifted slowly. "What did you mean, we're all over the news?"

"The TV, the radio, everything. Some jerk at the FBI made a statement this morning that you two were wanted in connection with a double murder on the east side. They said both of you were dirty—that you'd been working both sides in some truck-hijacking operation that went bad, and that you should be considered armed and dangerous. Some Atlanta PD captain immediately refuted it in a live interview, saying there was no evidence that you were involved and that until there was, they considered the two of you missing officers, not wanted felons."

Lane had questions. Her brain commanded her mouth to ask, but her mouth couldn't seem to remember how to shape words. She shook her head, which cleared her vision. Something ate at her thoughts, something she knew was wrong in the room, but she didn't know what.

"Where is Jason?" Nick asked again.

She shook her head, and suddenly she knew what was wrong with the room. It was too bright. The sun was up. She gasped. "Oh, my God."

"Lane, what's wrong?" Nick started to sound frantic.

"Jason—I don't—oh, I think he's gone by himself. What time is it?" A rush of adrenaline gave her some of her senses back.

She bolted out of bed, pulling her jeans on with one hand while she held the phone to her ear with the other and then struggling into her shirt.

"A little after eight. Why? He's gone where by himself?"

Lane fumbled with her weapon, almost dropping it as she lifted it from the nightstand. Why did it seem so much heavier than normal? She picked it up again. The barrel wobbled like a Saturday drunk.

"To the meet. I think he went without me." Looking for her shoes through tear-blurred eyes, she turned too quickly. Her head spun. She put her hand on the nightstand to steady herself and nearly knocked over a brown, plastic bottle. When she had her balance back, she held the bottle up and read the label. Not antibiotics, like he'd told her. "Nick, what is zolpidem tartrate?"

"A sleeping aid. Why?"

She closed her fist around the bottle. "Damn him."

She'd woken sometime around dawn to find Jason standing beside the bed, a glass in his hand.

"I got up to get a drink," he had said. "While I was in there I remembered I had some antibiotics in the medicine cabinet. I think you should take some, since we lost the ones Nick gave you."

The pills had been left in her car the day Nick gave them to her, before she'd had a chance to take even one.

"Your shoulder looked a little red earlier," he said in the darkness. "We shouldn't take any chances. You need to be at full strength tomorrow."

She'd been so tired, she'd hardly listened. She vaguely remembered swallowing the pills he'd put in her hand without looking at them, and washing them down with a drink of his water.

Her blood ran cold as she slipped her feet into her sneakers and quickly tied the laces. How dare he do this with her sister's life at stake?

Checking the load in her weapon, she answered Nick's continuing pleas. "The meet is at nine. I think he gave me something to make me sleep so he could go without me."

"He would do that, the fool."

"He's about to be a dead fool, and my sister with him." Without further explanation, or saying goodbye, she hung up the phone, tucked her pistol in the waist of her jeans and went after the fool.

In Morales's T-bird—Jason must have taken the Jeep she'd seen in the garage—she punched the accelerator and barreled onto the freeway, nearly kissing bumpers with an eighteen-wheeler cruising in the right-hand lane.

She forced herself to slow the car as she approached the

industrial area surrounding the distribution center. A couple of blocks ahead, the Jeep sat katy-whompus in the road, the driver's door hanging open. On the sidewalk across from it lay a man's crumpled form.

Lane stopped the car, got out and pulled her gun in one motion. Her heart lurched in relief when she got close enough to see the man's black hair and mustache. Alejandro.

Blood seeped from a wound on his shoulder and pooled on the blacktop beneath him. She checked for a pulse. He was alive, but he wouldn't be a threat anytime soon.

Lane scanned the area. Where was Jason? And Kelly?

A flash of denim and black leather up high caught her eye. She recognized him immediately. He stood on the second floor of the abandoned tenement they had used for their stakeout. His outline was clearly visible through the chewed-out section of wall that overlooked the street. She couldn't see anyone else, but he seemed to be talking to someone. His hands were out to his sides and slightly raised in a gesture of surrender.

Lane circled to the back of the building, the need for speed battling with the need for stealth. Bending through the same window she'd used before, she crept inside. Taking care to avoid the weak boards and praying the rest wouldn't squeak, she climbed the stairs.

As she raised her foot to the top step, she heard Jason's low, even voice. "Let her go. It's me you want."

Whoever he was talking to cackled in response.

His voice was tighter, more challenging, when he continued, "Come on. Stop hiding in the shadows. Come kill me face-to-face. That's what you want, isn't it?

With extreme caution, Lane leaned her head around the corner. Jason stood at the end of the room with no wall, an open drop to the street below at his side. On the other side of the room, in the shadow of the still-standing part of the wall, stood his boss, Jim Sturman. Sturman had Kelly in a choke hold in front of him and had a gun pressed to her head.

"If all I wanted to do was kill you," Sturman said, "I could have done it anytime."

"Then what do you want?" Like the first time she had seen Jason, he stood still as a statue, his face cold and impassive.

Sturman's face was the opposite, twisting and pinching as he spoke. He spat out his words like bad soup. "I want you to suffer like I did." He pounded a fist against his lame leg. "I want you to pay for doing this to me!"

Jason's eyelids flickered, almost unnoticeably, a momentary loss of his iron control. Guilt, Lane thought. Even for Sturman, he feels guilty.

"No. You did that yourself. I organized that raid, but you went in before I gave the go-ahead. You were so anxious to make sure you got credit for the bust that you put six other men's lives in jeopardy. We all could have been killed pulling you out of that crack house. The only mistake I ever made was to cover for you with the Bureau, because you were my *partner.* I should have told them the truth and let them boot you out instead of making you out to be a hero so that they promoted you to supervisor."

Sturman let out an unintelligible cry and shoved the gun harder into Kelly's temple. "It was your fault. I had it all, Stateler. Women. Action. Money. And then you, my perfect partner, ruined it."

"You were working both sides even then, weren't you, Jim? Selling our investigations. And since then…the leads that went nowhere, the blown covers, the informants that suddenly dried up. You were behind all of it. I was just too messed up to see it."

"You actually told me once that you thought you were unlucky. It was quite humorous, really."

Jason's hands clenched and unclenched rhythmically at his sides. "When did you graduate from selling information to illegal operations to actually running them? This whole truck hijacking thing was your gig, wasn't it? You were Alejandro's boss. You needed him as a middleman, since you couldn't deal with me directly.''

Sturman let go of Kelly's throat and grabbed her by the hair, yanking her head toward him. Lane stifled her gasp as pain twisted across Kelly's face. He had her arched backward. Kelly's back couldn't take that for long; it had to be excruciating for her.

''It was a sweet deal,'' Sturman said. ''A real cash cow, those electronics. Until you got the scent. You're always getting in my way—ruining things for me.''

''And that's what this is all about? Making me pay? What about Alejandro? You set him up, too. There never was any payoff, was there? You threw a bone in the street to lure him in and then shot him like a mongrel.

Sturman steadied himself, regaining his self-control, at least for the moment. He almost looked proud of himself. ''Once he'd taken out Grumman and Morales for me, his usefulness was over. Getting rid of him was part of the cleanup.'' He waved his free hand nonchalantly like murder was part of every good housekeeper's routine.

Jason stepped toward him, then stopped when Sturman wrapped that free hand around Kelly's neck to keep her head steady and moved the gun under her jaw.

''So, since you already had it all set up,'' Jason led him on, ''you decided to take care of me and Lane at the same time—a few more ducks for your hunt. On my way here, I heard that story you told the press. You set me and Lane up as rogue cops so you could blame Alejandro's murder on us, then you could kill us, too, and come out looking like a hero. But I blew your plan, didn't I? Coming up here instead of meeting him down in the street.''

''You made me change my plan, but the results will be the same. What tipped you off?'' Sturman's hand tightened on Kelly's throat and she whimpered, struggling for air.

Jason's fingers curled to a tight fist at his side as he watched. ''You did. It was such an obvious setup. Get us out in the street with Alejandro by making us think we're supposed to meet him here to make a deal for Kelly. It took a while, but last night I finally recognized the MO. It's the same way you set Lane up to be shot at a few days ago, and—''

Jason cut off a shudder with a deep breath. His nostrils flared. When he spoke again, his voice was solid and cold. ''It's the same method you used four years ago, when you killed Karen.''

Lane's heart leaped into her throat. Sturman killed Karen?

Sturman looked insane. Even from this distance Lane could see his hands tremble so hard she was afraid his gun might go off accidentally, killing Kelly just the same. ''I had a thing for her, you know. No, you never knew that, did you? Because she would never go out with me. I figured she was turned off by the leg. That's something else you took away from me—women don't like men who limp.''

''Or maybe they just don't like limp men,'' Jason said.

Lane barely caught her gasp before it became audible.

The vein on Sturman's forehead bulged. Lane wished it would explode with an aneurysm.

What exploded was the screech from his mouth. The cords in his neck strained as he aborted it. Latching his fingers into the hair at the back of Kelly's head, he yanked.

Jason flinched at Kelly's cry. His chest heaved. ''Come on, Jim. You want revenge on me, shoot. But let her go.''

This was a thin line Jason was walking, trying to incite Sturman to turn his rage to him and let go of Kelly in the process.

Lane's next breath wouldn't come. If it worked, if Sturman took that gun away from her sister's head for a half of a second, Lane could make the shot.

Please.

Sturman's breath evened. His face panned out flat again. ''Uh-uh. Where were we…oh, right, talking about Karen.'' He loosened his grip on Kelly's hair. His eyes gleamed with insane amusement. Clearly, he liked watching what this was doing to Jason. ''When I made supervisor I had hoped that

Karen might change her mind about me. So imagine my surprise when she comes in one day, all teary-eyed, saying she 'loves you' and 'wants to marry you' and how she's going to resign so the two of you can be together 'cause she doesn't want you to have to transfer—you loving your job so much and all.''

Sturman grinned malevolently. ''Imagine how I felt, finding out you had been doing her all along. Mr. Perfect Agent. Always gets his man. Or woman. Even if she's his partner.'' He laughed crazily. ''Doing your partner is not exactly correct FBI protocol, you know.''

Lane let her eyes slide to Jason. She couldn't imagine the force of will it took for him to stand there through this.

''So you killed her for that?'' He choked some on his words, the first sign of what Sturman's confession was doing to him.

''Nah. I wouldn't kill that sweet piece just because of that. You were too close to one of my operations. I had it all arranged to kill you. Sent you to that meet to do it. Only there was no meet. My men were supposed to finish you. Then when Karen showed up at my door with her resignation, I figured, why kill you when I can kill her? I knew you'd be too broken up to finish the case, and that way I got to see your pain. Not just a second's flash before you died, but the kind of agony that goes on and on. So I said congratulations and sent her right on out to give you the good news. It only took one phone call to get the boys to switch targets from you to her. Then I put her resignation in the shredder.''

Lane's heart cried for Jason. He finally had the truth about why Karen had come to him that day. She wanted to tell him she was ready to marry him, to give up her career for him and had given up her life instead. And Jason had lived four years without knowing why.

''I'm going to personally send you to hell for that, Sturman.'' He inched closer to Sturman, and Kelly's eyes widened even more as Sturman pulled her back.

Jason stopped, but Lane knew he had to be close to the edge

of his tolerance. How long before he broke and did something foolish? She had to get him, and Kelly, out of there.

Jason looked ready to make good on his threat. ''You were going to do it again. You were going to kill Lane just to get me off the case.'' Jason's stone face finally fractured into a picture of rage.

Sturman lifted his eyebrows in mock surprise. ''Oh, more than just to get you off the case, my friend. I saw the way you looked at her, that first night in the police station and I knew I had been given another chance. And this time, I was going to get to see you suffer, up close and personal.'' He laughed crazily. ''Why do you think I took the chance of coming to the meet this time. Yes, I was in the Lexus while my shooter targeted her from the roof. This time, I wanted to see your face while you watched her die.'' He snickered as he watched Jason's reaction to his words. ''I can see I was right about the two of you. What is it about you and partners, Stateler? Of course, I can't say I blame you. Tell me, is she as good as she looks?''

She thought Jason might rush him. That would surely get Kelly killed, but if Sturman kept taunting him like that, he might pass the point of caring. Giving in to her growing sense of urgency to bring this to an end, Lane slowly raised up, bringing her gun to firing level. Too late, she realized her mistake.

The low angle of the morning sun slanting through the open roof cast her shadow across the floor in front of Jason. Sturman jerked toward her, then laughed and relaxed. ''Well, well, speak of the devil.''

Lane raged at her own stupidity as much as Sturman's insanity. ''No. *You* are the devil.''

Sturman didn't look amused. ''Get up here. And drop that gun through the hole in the floor.''

Kelly choked back a sob as Lane complied.

Sturman's face coiled into a sick grin. He licked his lips and laughed at Jason's stricken expression. ''It looks like my plan is coming together after all. How does it feel, Jason, to watch two women you love die?''

Everything happened at once, and yet each frame of the scene clicked by one at a time, like the editing reel of a film.

Sturman pulled his gun away from Kelly and leveled it at Lane's head. Jason launched himself into the space between his boss and Lane. Kelly lurched to the side, falling out of the line of fire.

Two shots exploded in Lane's ears. Jason grunted. The force of the bullets propelled him backward, onto the floor. The rotten boards gave way underneath him. His upper body went through first. Snagging a moment, his left foot caught between two struts. Then it twisted unnaturally as it took the full weight of his body. One of the struts broke and he disappeared.

A solid thud resounded and a puff of dust drifted up through the gaping hole.

Smiling, Sturman stepped over Kelly toward Lane. As soon as the light of day hit his chest, he exploded. A rain of red droplets followed his slump to the floor.

But who fired the shot? Lane was beyond caring. Whoever it was, she thanked God they were there.

Jumping forward, she grabbed Sturman's gun, then pulled Kelly away from his dead body. Behind the protection of the wall, she hugged her sister and checked her for injuries at the same time.

Kelly's tear-stained face stared over Lane's shoulder at the gaping hole in the floor. ''Oh, my God...Jason!'' Kelly exclaimed, covering her mouth with her hand.

''Stay here,'' Lane ordered Kelly. Heedless of the unknown shooter outside, Lane bolted across the open area and down the stairs.

Jason lay on his back, splintered wood around him, one leg angled slightly to the side. Lane didn't bother with it. The injuries from the fall might be serious, but the bullets...

She felt for a pulse, gasping with relief when she found it, much too fast, but strong. Crouching beside him she searched for the entry wounds. There was no blood, but his chest didn't feel right. Panicked, she yanked his T-shirt up to his armpits. She didn't know whether to sing or cry, but it didn't matter because she didn't have the breath to do either.

Protruding from a bulletproof vest were the polished ends of two .38 caliber slugs.

She fell back, the tears she had been fighting finally spilling over. Once again, he'd kept his head, wearing a vest to the confrontation, while she'd lost hers, rushing headlong out of the house without a thought to protocol, or safety.

Jason sputtered and wheezed. His chest spasmed as he tried to get a breath. The cords in his neck strained tightly.

With fumbling fingers, Lane undid the fastenings on the shoulders of the vest and slid it off. A dark bruise was already spreading from his sternum outward. His rib cage rippled in another involuntary contraction, and she grabbed fistfuls of his shirt to steady him. When it passed, he seemed better.

His eyes opened. At first Lane thought they were the most beautiful sight in the world. Then she remembered what he had done.

"What the hell were you thinking?" The tears she had been holding at bay let loose in a downpour.

She'd been chased, shot and had her sister kidnapped. None of it hurt as badly as what he'd done to her. She'd put her faith, her trust, in him, and he'd let her down.

Her ragged breaths turned to sobs. "Damn you. I trusted you."

He stared up at her with half-open eyes. Horrified at the pain she saw there, she grew silent.

His eyes ran up and down her body, triggering the same response as if it had been his hands traveling that path. She shook the feeling off. "How could you do it, Jason?"

"How could I not?" he countered, still gasping for breath.

"That's not good enough. Tell me why."

He squirmed under her gaze, and then she saw his own anger flare and he stilled himself, meeting her challenge. "You heard him. He was waiting up here to kill you, just so he could watch me watch you die.''

Jason's voice started out weak and trailed off with his last words. She refused to give in to the urge to fall to her knees and hold him until he breathed easy.

He stared balefully up at her, struggling for the breath to continue. ''I couldn't let that happen. Not again.''

''I had a right to be here. She's my sister.''

His lids lowered to half-mast.

''Tell me this,'' she asked. ''If you hadn't been there when Karen died, would it have been any easier for you?''

''You know it wouldn't have.''

''At least you had a chance to try to save her. When you lost her, at least you knew you had done everything you could.''

Lane took a shuddery breath. ''What you did denied me that chance. If Kelly, or you, had died, I would never have known if I could have made a difference. And I couldn't have lived with that.''

Slowly he opened his eyes wide again, and the pain she saw in them transcended anything caused by his physical injuries. ''I'm sorry.''

She stood up and turned away from him, her heart a cold stone in her chest. ''Sorry always comes too late.''

As she faced the stairs, a half dozen black-clad SWAT team members burst into the building from all sides. Roland Bowling followed close behind them, shouting orders left and right. Dan North trailed close on the captain's heels, leading several officers up to the second floor, once they'd confirmed the first was secure.

Lane's jaw hung slack. ''Roland! What are you doing here? How did you know?''

The captain ignored Lane and strode to Jason's side. His cheeks puffed out and he expelled his breath in an exaggerated ''Whew,'' as he checked the rounds lodged in Jason's discarded vest. ''Damn, boy. I told you to lure him out where our sniper could sight him *before* he decided to shoot anybody.''

Jason grimaced. ''Sorry.'' He wheezed. ''Tried.''

Roland looked pointedly to Lane and then back to Jason. One big hand patted Jason gently on the shoulder. ''I'd say you did fine. You rest easy. Paramedics are on their way.''

Too much was happening for Lane to absorb. She looked at her captain in confusion. ''You mean you killed Sturman?''

''Of course, who did you think did it?'' Roland sent two more officers upstairs.

''I thought—I don't know.''

Roland shook his head and walked away, issuing a dozen orders in half as many seconds and directing traffic as more officers arrived on the scene.

One of the storm troopers emerged from the stairway, cradling Kelly in his arms. Lane turned her attention back to Jason, still trying to sort out what had happened. ''You called him?''

He hesitated, then nodded.

''But why? You didn't trust him.''

Jason's watery eyes burned with intensity. ''No, but you did, at least before I talked you out of it. And that was good enough for me.''

Chapter 16

Lane studied the picture in her hands, a black-and-white shot of her much-younger self with Kelly, her mom and her dad in a family hug, before she settled it carefully in the box with the rest of her personal belongings. There wasn't much else to do. All her files were sorted, clearly labeled and stacked for the next detective. She'd even cleaned the desktop, scrubbing until all the old coffee rings disappeared.

She hadn't even left yet, and it was like she'd never been there.

"So, you're really going through with this?" Her former partner surveyed the desk much the way Lane just had.

She squared her shoulders. "You know I am." Resigning from the police force to concentrate on her studies full-time had been a big decision, but one she knew was right for her.

"Things just won't be the same without you around here, you know. No more superpartner to solve all my cases for me."

"You can solve your own cases. You proved that."

Dan lowered his eyes. Honestly, she'd never known he was so shy. It took her being in trouble to bring out the real investigator in him. He'd been so worried about her that he'd worked night and day to trace the ownership of the distribution center address she'd given him all the way back to the office where Morales and Grumman were killed. He'd almost caught up with her there, too.

"I'll be back in a few years."

Roland joined the conversation, grimacing. "Yeah, as the department psychologist."

"Something wrong with that?" she baited him.

"No. The more we can figure out about what's going on in the minds of the wackos out there, the easier it will be to catch them." He picked up the picture she had just put in the box. "But that's not why you want the job, is it?"

"No," she answered truthfully.

Roland knew her better than that. He had insisted she take some time off after the scene with Sturman. He spent the time with her, helping her put her life back together, drinking stale coffee and listening.

Like the friend she'd always known him to be, the friend she never should have doubted, Roland had helped her realize what she should have known all along: who she really was and who she really wanted to be.

"There are a lot of cops out there, cops like my dad, even like Jim Sturman, who need someone to talk to," she said.

"And what about Stateler?" Roland asked, his voice quieter.

Lane's heart still dropped onto her solar plexus like a brick at the mere mention of his name. "Yeah, cops like him, too."

"That's not what I meant," Roland admonished her.

She knew that. "The case is over." She hadn't told Roland what had happened between her and Jason. She hadn't had to. He knew her too well to believe that all the two of them had shared was the case.

"I still can't believe he called you." She shook her head. She wouldn't have thought him capable of trusting like that.

"The boy kept his head," Roland said.

Lane smiled inwardly. It was hard to think of Jason as "the boy."

"It seems you're the one who went off half-cocked, busting into the middle of that scene without so much as putting on a vest," Roland continued. "Nearly gave me heart failure when I saw you crawl into that building."

Lane knew her captain was right. Jason had gotten help, taken precautions, worn a vest, done things by the book. She was the one who'd blown it. But if he had confided his plans to begin with... "I had a right to be there. My sister's life was at stake."

Roland clucked his tongue at her. "He did the right thing, trying to keep you away from that scene. You were in too deep, with Kelly involved. If it had been me, I would have had your fanny in the lockup if I'd had to, in order to keep you away from there."

Why was everyone taking Jason's side in this? Treating him like a hero after the way he'd tricked her, betrayed her? "At least you wouldn't have lied to me and drugged me."

"Don't underestimate what I'd do to keep you safe." He shrugged when she looked at him sharply. "It's a genetic thing. Men can't help it. Especially when it involves a woman they love."

Was he talking about himself, or Jason? Didn't he understand that Jason had done what he had to protect himself, not her? That he couldn't handle his fear of another partner, another woman, dying in his arms?

Jason had said he loved her. But just because he loved her didn't mean he was ready to hang on to that love for a lifetime, through all its trials, tribulations and heartaches, did it?

Roland wouldn't let it go. "He didn't just volunteer to go into that building and bait Sturman into the open where the SWAT guys could take him, he *insisted.* He said it was his responsibility. He put his life on the line for Kelly. And for you. Maybe you should give the man a chance, honey."

"What makes you think he wants a chance? I haven't seen

him or heard from him in weeks.'' The lightness she tried to force into her tone fell flat. She couldn't hide how much this conversation hurt.

Roland's near-eternal patience seemed to be wearing thin. ''Can you blame him, after the way you told him off?''

''No. I can't.''

''Then talk to him. Tell him you're sorry.''

Lane hefted the single box that was all she had to take with her for eight years of police work. This time she didn't even try to cover the misery in her voice. She fell facedown in her own philosophy. ''Sorry always comes too late.''

It was for the best. Jason Stateler, gallant but flawed undercover agent, was exactly the kind of man Lane could not risk being involved with. Loving him would only lead to disaster. Better a bruised heart now than a broken one later. So she'd told herself every night for the past two weeks. But that thought had been small comfort as she lay in bed alone and afraid.

Lane shut off the car engine in her driveway and rested her head on the back of the seat, eyes closed, listening to the chorus of crickets playing in the twilight.

As she pulled herself out of the car and walked toward the front porch, she inhaled a deep breath of cooling evening air. The scent of fresh-cut grass and the indefinable aroma from the mix of flowers in Kelly's garden welcomed her home, but not with the same sense of peace they used to. Instead of the haven it once was, home was now a place of restless discontent.

From the front walk Lane could see the light shining out the open window of her sister's office. Computer keys clacked in rhythm with the crickets. Lane imagined her sister deep in thought, plunking away at the keyboard. At times, Lane wished for a job like that. One which would take her off into worlds of flight and fancy with the closing of an office door and the whir of a hard drive.

Deciding to unload the car later, Lane put her keys in her purse. A dark pocket of shadow shifted on the front porch as she ambled up the walk. She tensed, automatically reaching for her gun and coming up empty. That part of her life was over. No more guns. But old habits were hard to break. And even after all this time the effects of the case had not worn off, never would. Lane would never feel the same security she once had.

Now who was paranoid?

Approaching the porch cautiously, she strained to see what had moved in the dark recesses. Maybe it was just the cat.

"S'just me." The familiar voice, a warm and breathy whisper, stopped her in her tracks. Despite all her vows not to let herself feel anything for him, she felt the familiar bloom in her chest.

Closer, she could make out his silhouette in the darkness as he struggled to stand up. He lurched forward, then back, cursing under his breath as he grabbed for the wall to keep from falling. Finally upright, he swayed slightly.

The alcohol Lane smelled on his breath turned her heart to stone. "Are you drunk?" She couldn't believe he would come here like this.

The flash of his white teeth stood out against the darkness. "Only a little."

"How did you get here?" She lost the white of his teeth. He must not be smiling now.

"Cab. What's wrong?" She heard the doubt in his voice. The confusion. Was he too drunk to figure out why she might be mad at him? He ought to know that this was all her fears come true.

Jason took a step toward her, away from the support of the wall, and stumbled.

Instinctively she caught him and supported him while he struggled to rebalance. She wanted to let him fall. She wanted to walk into the house and forget this had happened.

She wanted him to come back to her whole, not in pieces.

As he swayed in her arms, her knee bumped something hard and cold, metallic.

The porch light flicked on, and after blinking her eyes to

adjust, she found herself staring into the depths of Jason's hazel eyes. They were clear and bright.

She still smelled the beer, but it was lighter, masked by his cologne and his own unique male aroma. He was still in her arms, seemed in no hurry to leave. Looking down, she saw what her knee had bumped.

His pants leg was split up the side and a monstrous black neoprene and metal brace, held in place with velcro, showed through the seam.

From the doorway, Kelly's stifled giggle told Lane who was responsible for the porch light.

"Oops," Kelly said. "I thought I heard someth...that is...well... Oh, just, carry on." The door shut and the porch plunged back into darkness.

Lane struggled to calm her frayed nerves. Jason found his balance and limped back a step.

"I thought—" Lane started, then quit.

"I know. You thought I was falling down drunk."

She didn't have to see his scorching glare to feel the heat of it. It matched the anger in his voice. "But I'm not. I'm not your father, Lane."

She nodded, choked on the lump in her throat. He lifted her chin with his hand, and she felt patience, calmness, return to his touch.

"It was just a party, Lane. I couldn't very well skip the toast to my own promotion."

"Promotion?"

With a slight grin breaking out on his face, he nodded. "They offered me Sturman's job. I'm a supervisor now, overseeing case assignments and training for the agents in my department. I'm out of the field. Permanently."

"Is that what you want?"

"I'm not sure. But at least I don't have to live undercover anymore. I thought I'd try to find that life you told me I'd thrown away."

His gentle reminder of one more of her misjudgments only

made her feel worse. Had she ever done anything but hurt him? And yet he was here.

He was quiet a long time. Then he let go of her chin and hobbled over to the porch swing. ''Damn knee,'' he explained, ''I had arthroscopic surgery after that fall, but it still hurts.'' More silence. ''Come sit beside me?''

She did, and he draped his arm across the back of the swing, just inches from her shoulders, but not touching, and set the bench rocking with a push of his toe.

''How about you?'' he asked.

''What?''

''What are you looking for?

Her sigh mingled with the squeak of the old swing. ''You heard?''

''Mmm-hmm.''

''How?''

''Roland told me. I went by your precinct to file the last of the paperwork on the case.''

''Was that the only reason you dropped by? Just to turn in the reports?'' She met his eyes steadily, trying to see his truth in them and hoping he couldn't see the truth in her own gaze. She didn't want him to know how badly she'd missed him. Not yet. Not when she still didn't know whether or not they could ever find a future together.

''No. The paperwork wasn't the only reason. I wanted to see you. I needed to know how you were.''

It wasn't everything she'd hoped to hear, but it was a start.

''So what are you going to do now that you're off the force?'' he asked.

''I'm going to school full-time. I should be able to finish my degree a lot sooner that way.''

He nodded. ''I know that degree means a lot to you.'' He grimaced, hesitating. ''I had a few sessions with the Bureau shrink. It was one of the conditions of the new job. We talked about Sturman, and Karen, but I don't think it helped much.''

She didn't imagine it would. He was too private a person to share his pain with a stranger.

His fingers brushed the hair at her shoulder, lingering in the curls. "To tell the truth, he wasn't the one I wanted to be talking to."

They swung back and forth in silence until Lane thought she might scream. On each motion forward she wanted to fall into his arms and beg his forgiveness. Then with the backward glide her anger would reappear and she promised herself she'd send him away. Put him out of her life for good. In between she wanted to run in the house and put a pillow over her head until her two selves decided. Eventually she couldn't stand the pressure another minute.

She stopped the swing with her foot. "Why are you here, Jason?"

His chest heaved, and she could see him gathering his strength. When he raised his head, the determination in his eyes scared her. "I came to tell you that you were wrong."

She shook her head in confusion. "About you?"

"No. You were right about me. I'm a coward, and my mental stability is dubious at times. But at least I know my limits. And taking you to that meet was beyond them. What I came to tell you is that you were wrong about your father."

"Dad? What does he have to do with this?"

Jason leaned forward, ablaze with belief in what he was saying. "Everything. You said that every time he said he was sorry, it was too late. That the damage was already done. But you were wrong. It wasn't all the times that your old man said he was sorry that hurt you. It was the one time that he couldn't. Because he was dead."

How could he know this? How could he know her better than she knew herself? Tears sprang to her eyes, and she bit them back as he continued.

"You loved your father and you wanted him to love you. As long as he could say 'I'm sorry,' there was hope that things would be different next time. That he could change. That he *would* change, if he loved you enough. But he didn't—he died.''

The tears began to run down her face, and she looked away, not wanting him to see.

He gently guided her eyes back to his with fingertips on her jaw. He had to clear his throat to continue, and even then his voice was uneven. ''*I* love you enough, Lane.''

It took a force of will obvious even to Lane, distressed as she was, but he pulled back from her. His hand fell from her face back to the seat of the swing. ''So I came to tell you that I'm sorry, but that I can change, with your help. Because as long as we're both alive, it's never too late.''

Lane's whole world caved in. Before she realized how it got there, her ear lay against the beat of his heart. She clenched the lapels of his jacket in her fists. ''Oh, Jason. I thought that you wouldn't be able to live with what happened, that it would eat at you, bit by bit, until someday it would overwhelm you.''

Jason flinched at her words. ''You don't know how close you were to the truth. How many times I've raced the devil for my sanity.''

''But you won. The truth is I've been judging you by my father's standard since I met you. I was sure that you couldn't be as solid as you looked. I was just looking for weaknesses. I was so sure that you would have to cave in sooner or later. Because he let me down, I thought that you would, too. I shut myself off from everything you had to offer, because I didn't have enough courage to believe in you.''

A groan welled up from deep inside her. ''I've been such a fool. I know I hurt you. I want to make it right. I'm—''

He hushed her with a single finger on her lips. ''Shh. You don't have to say it.''

''Yes, I do.'' She tilted her head back and looked straight into his heart. ''I'm sorry. I'm sorry. I'm sorry.'' The words she had despised so long came out so easily and felt so good that she laughed. And the laughter quelled her tears.

Out of nowhere J.D. appeared, weaving himself in a figure

eight around her ankle and Jason's, binding them together in the pattern of infinity. Jason's lips pressed against her temple.

Her hands found the muscles rippling through his back like a strong river current.

His words came low and urgent like the rumble of white water. "Lane, if it weren't for what happened, for what I did, would you want to be with me?"

She sniffed one last time and looked up at him. "Are you asking me if I love you?"

He nodded.

She hesitated. Why was this so hard for her? Maybe because she knew once she stepped down this road there would be no going back. Only after she realized that she had taken those steps days ago did the truth become clear. She didn't want to go back. "What happens if I say yes?"

"Then I promise I'll make you forget everything else."

Her last tear caught in the corner of her smile. "In that case, the answer is yes." Jason's head dipped toward her. She met him halfway, and, like the first time they'd kissed, she forgot herself.

One thing about Jason, he always kept his promises.

This time she didn't fight it, but surrendered to the loss. There was no past, no present. Only him.

They moved in synchrony like two familiar dancers. Forward and back. Give and take. Partners. Forever.

When the kiss ended, Jason's nervous smile matched her own, rising and falling in the blink of an eye like he wasn't quite sure if he was awake or dreaming. His eyes looked down on her, full of wonder and amazement.

"Are you sure about this?" he asked. "We're not talking about a casual thing here. You're going to have to marry me to make this work."

She wrapped her arms around his neck. "Only if you're willing to have children with me."

He pulled back from her. "You're not...I mean, after we... Ah, hell. Are you pregnant?"

She laughed at his wide-eyed innocence. "No, not yet. But I'd like to work on that. Soon."

"The sooner, the better."

Pulling him close, she invited another kiss, which he obligingly provided.

A temperate breeze wafted over them. The heat wave over Georgia had finally broken, its oppressive mantle lifted away by the first feathery fingers of a new clime.

* * * * *

COMING NEXT MONTH

#919 THIS HEART FOR HIRE—Marie Ferrarella

Given the threats against him, Logan Buchanan knew he had no choice but to hire private investigator Jessica Deveaux, but seeing her again only reminded him of how much he'd once loved her. Now it was up to Logan to prove he'd changed, before someone took away his one last chance for happiness.

#920 THE FUGITIVE BRIDE—Margaret Watson

Cameron, Utah

FBI agent Jesse Coulton was having a hard time believing beautiful Shea McAllister was guilty of doing anything illegal on her Utah ranch. As he worked undercover to discover the truth, Jesse desperately hoped she was innocent—because the only place she belonged was in his arms!

#921 MIDNIGHT CINDERELLA—Eileen Wilks

Way Out West

After being accused of a crime he hadn't committed, Nathan Jones was determined to put his life back together. And when he met and fell for his sexy new employee, Hannah McBride, he knew he was on the right track. But then their newfound love was put to the test and it was up to Nate to prove that he was finally ready for happily-ever-after.

#922 THE DADDY TRAP—Kayla Daniels

Families Are Forever

When Kristen Monroe and her nephew Cody knocked on his door, Luke Hollister knew his life would never be the same. As she hid from Cody's abusive "father," Kristen shocked Luke with an incredible secret. And the longer they stayed, the more Luke fell in love—with the woman he desired and the son he'd always wanted....

#923 THE COP AND CALAMITY JANE—Elane Osborn

Bad luck seemed to follow Callie "Calamity Jane" Chance everywhere. But when she met sexy detective Marcus Scanlon, she knew her luck had changed. He was hot on the trail of suspected catnappers, and Callie was his only witness. Once the culprits were nabbed, would Callie accept Marcus's proposal—for a disaster-free future?

#924 BRIDGER'S LAST STAND—Linda Winstead Jones

Men in Blue

Detective Malcolm Bridger never thought he'd see Frannie Vaughn again after their one memorable night together. Then Frannie got mixed up in his current case. Suddenly Malcolm was falling for this forever kind of girl, and their near one-night stand was slowly becoming a one-*life* stand.